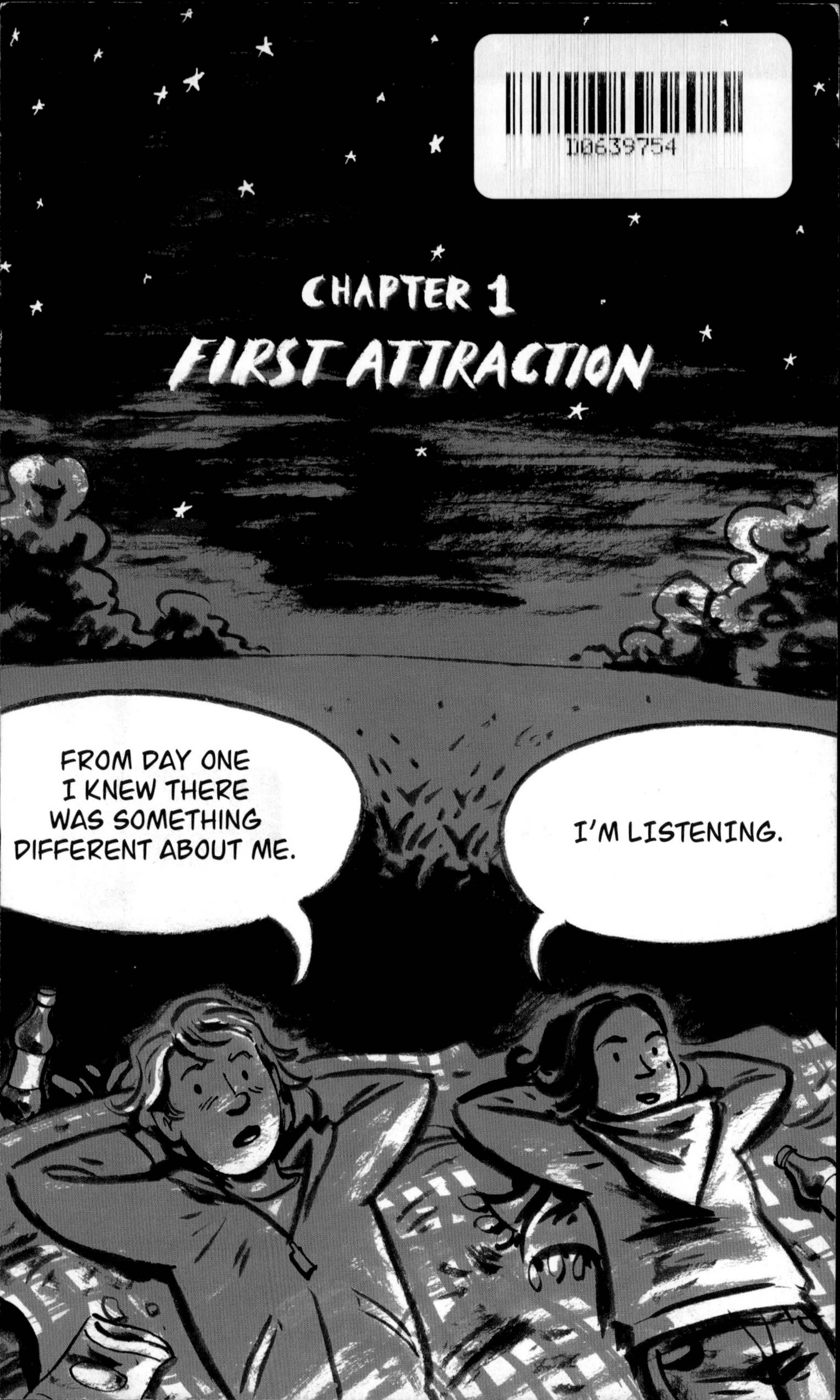
CHAPTER 1
FIRST ATTRACTION
FROM DAY ONE I KNEW THERE WAS SOMETHING DIFFERENT ABOUT ME.
I'M LISTENING.

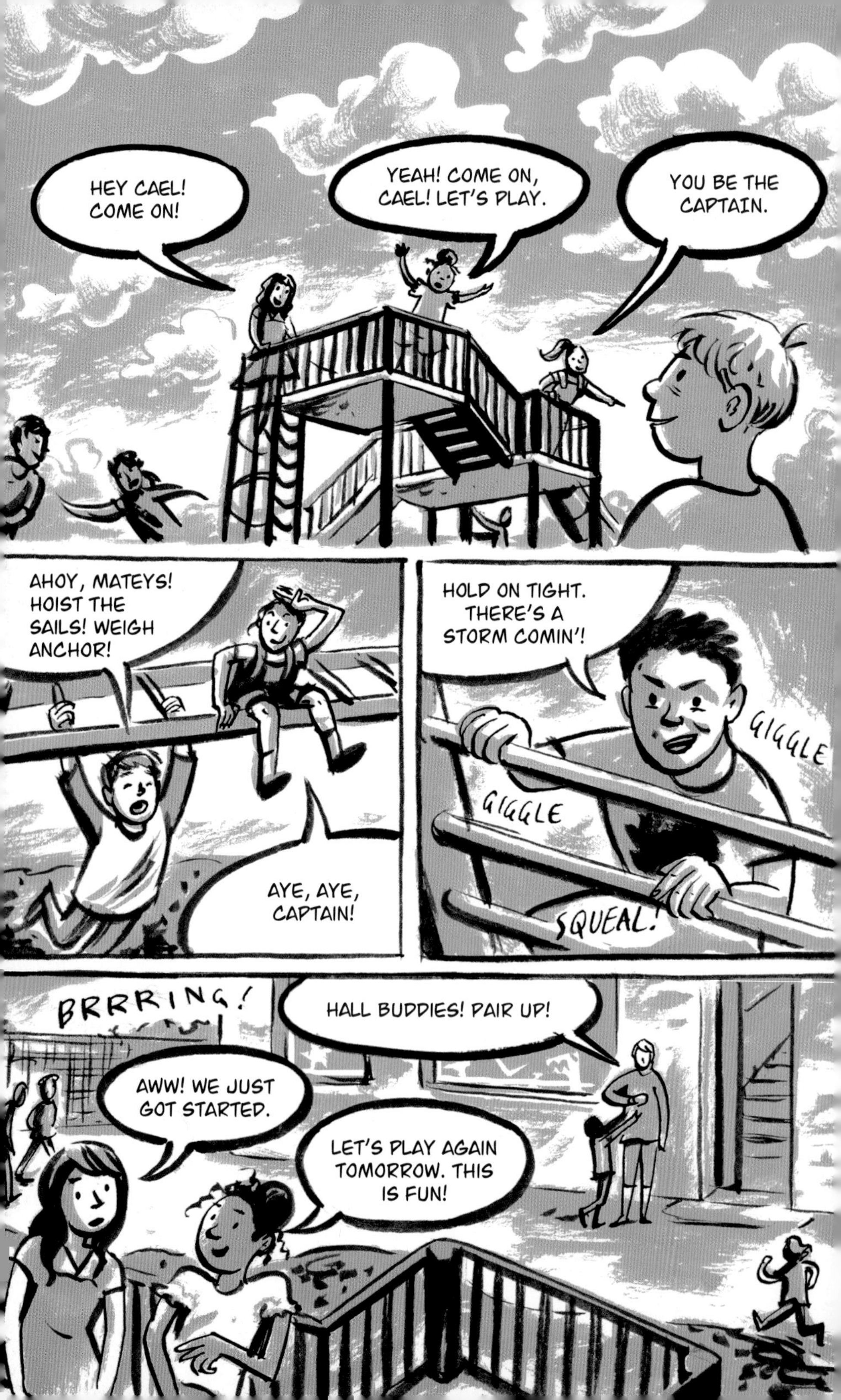
HEY CAEL! COME ON!
YEAH! COME ON, CAEL! LET'S PLAY.
YOU BE THE CAPTAIN.
AHOY, MATEYS! HOIST THE SAILS! WEIGH ANCHOR!
AYE, AYE, CAPTAIN!
HOLD ON TIGHT. THERE'S A STORM COMIN'!
GIGGLE
GIGGLE
SQUEAL!
BRRRING!
HALL BUDDIES! PAIR UP!
AWW! WE JUST GOT STARTED.
LET'S PLAY AGAIN TOMORROW. THIS IS FUN!

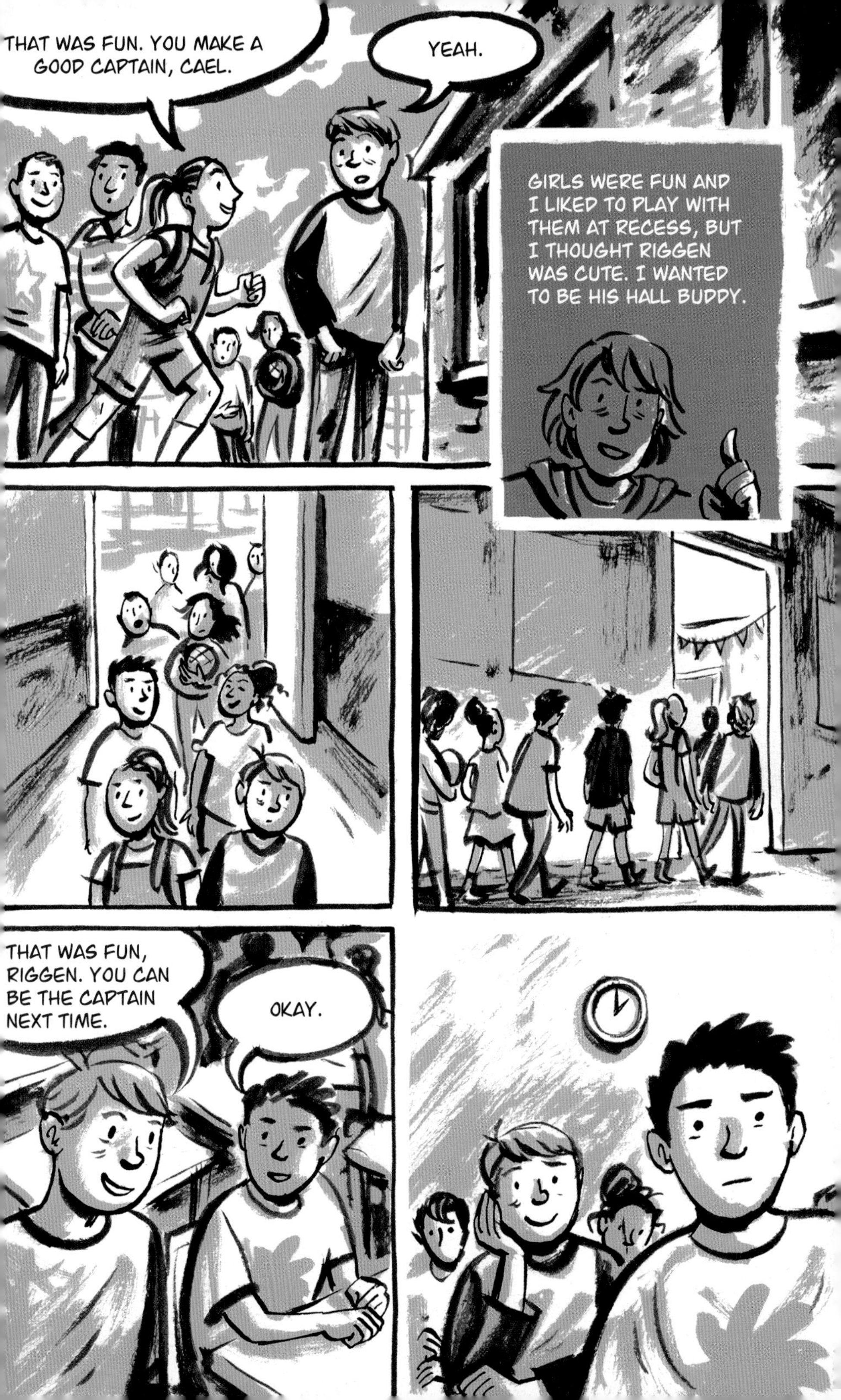

THAT WAS FUN. YOU MAKE A GOOD CAPTAIN, CAEL.
YEAH.
GIRLS WERE FUN AND I LIKED TO PLAY WITH THEM AT RECESS, BUT I THOUGHT RIGGEN WAS CUTE. I WANTED TO BE HIS HALL BUDDY.
THAT WAS FUN, RIGGEN. YOU CAN BE THE CAPTAIN NEXT TIME.
OKAY.

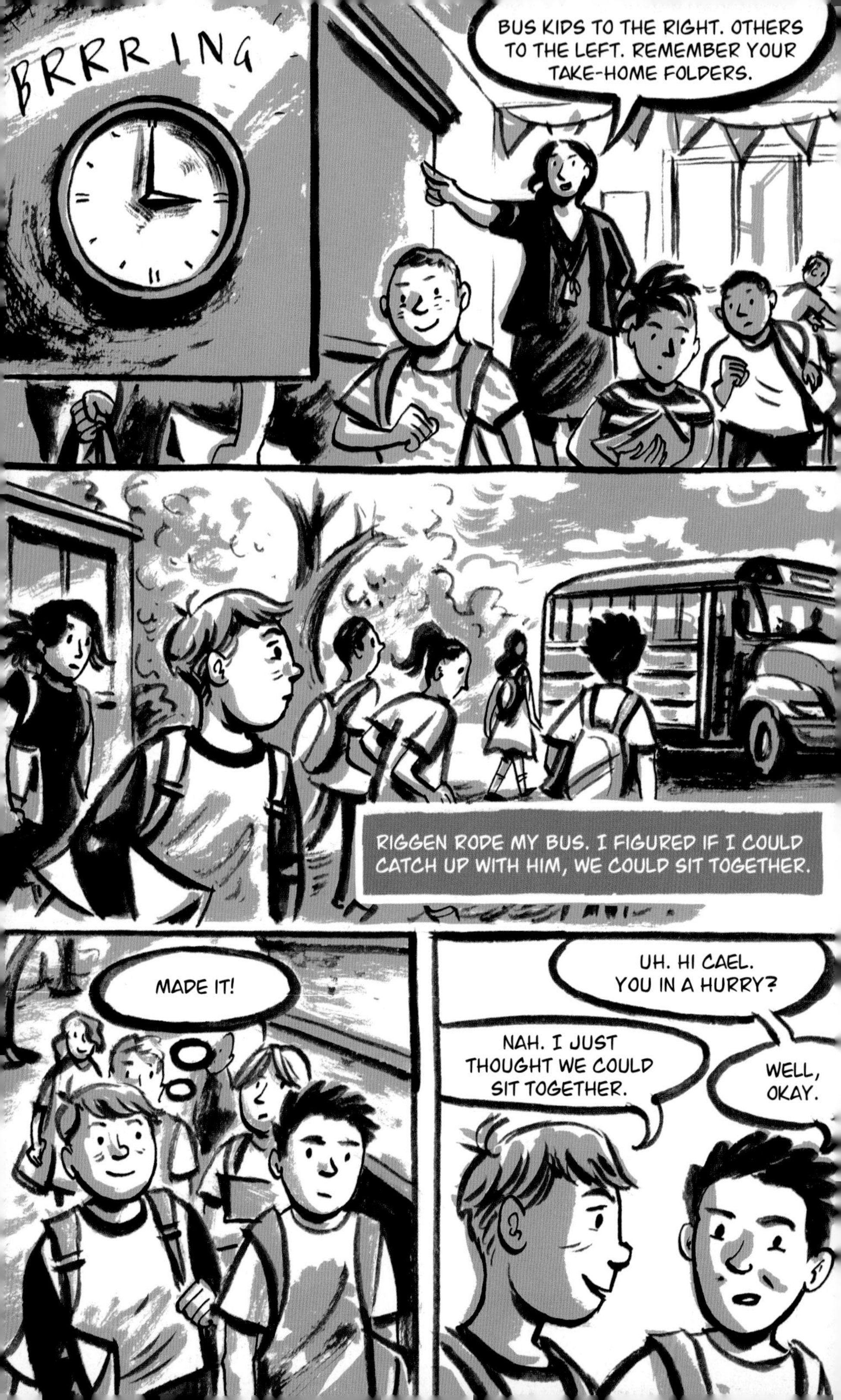
BRRRING
BUS KIDS TO THE RIGHT. OTHERS TO THE LEFT. REMEMBER YOUR TAKE-HOME FOLDERS.
RIGGEN RODE MY BUS. I FIGURED IF I COULD CATCH UP WITH HIM, WE COULD SIT TOGETHER.
MADE IT!
UH. HI CAEL. YOU IN A HURRY?
NAH. I JUST THOUGHT WE COULD SIT TOGETHER.
WELL, OKAY.

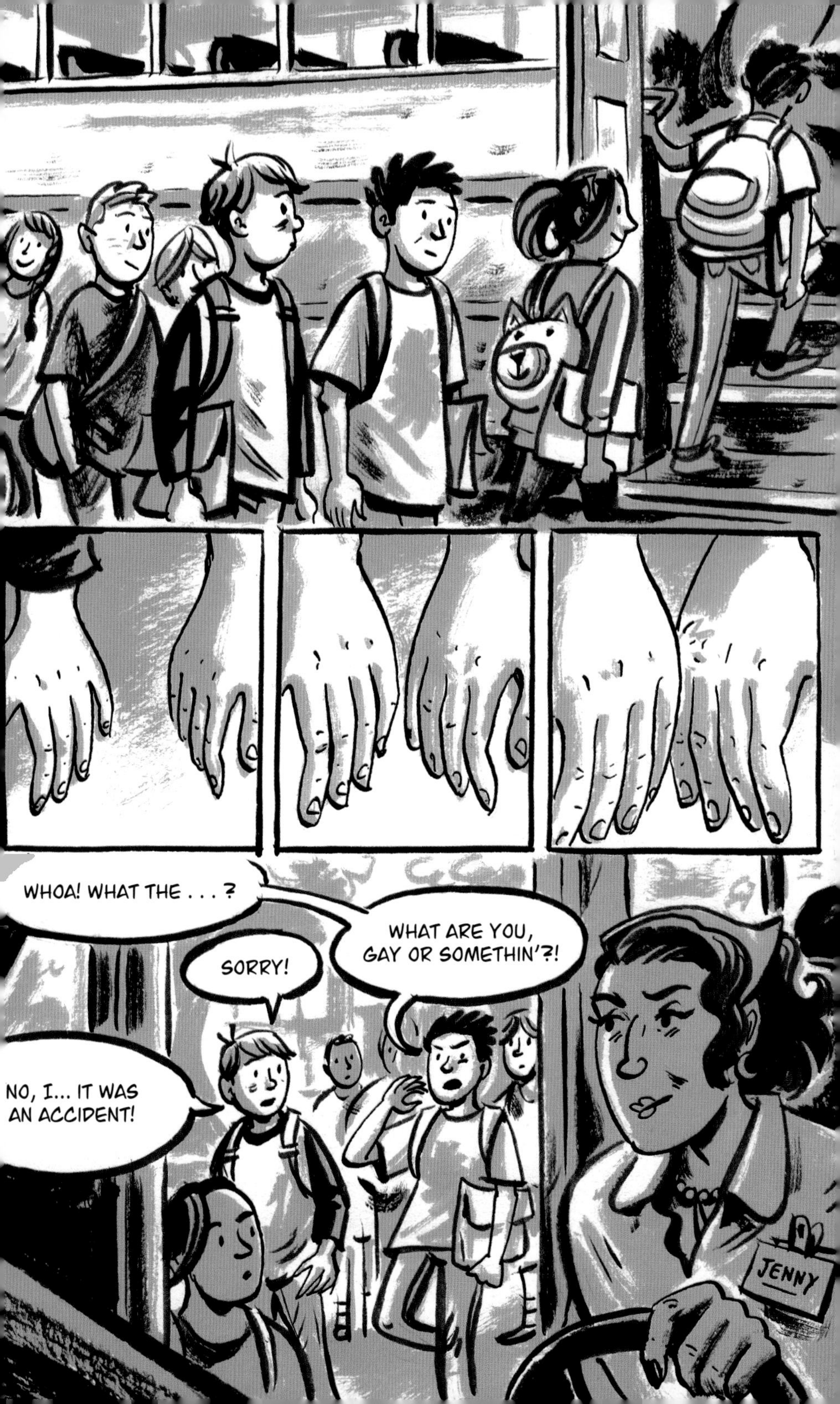

WHOA! WHAT THE . . . ?
WHAT ARE YOU, GAY OR SOMETHIN'?!
SORRY!
NO, I... IT WAS AN ACCIDENT!
JENNY

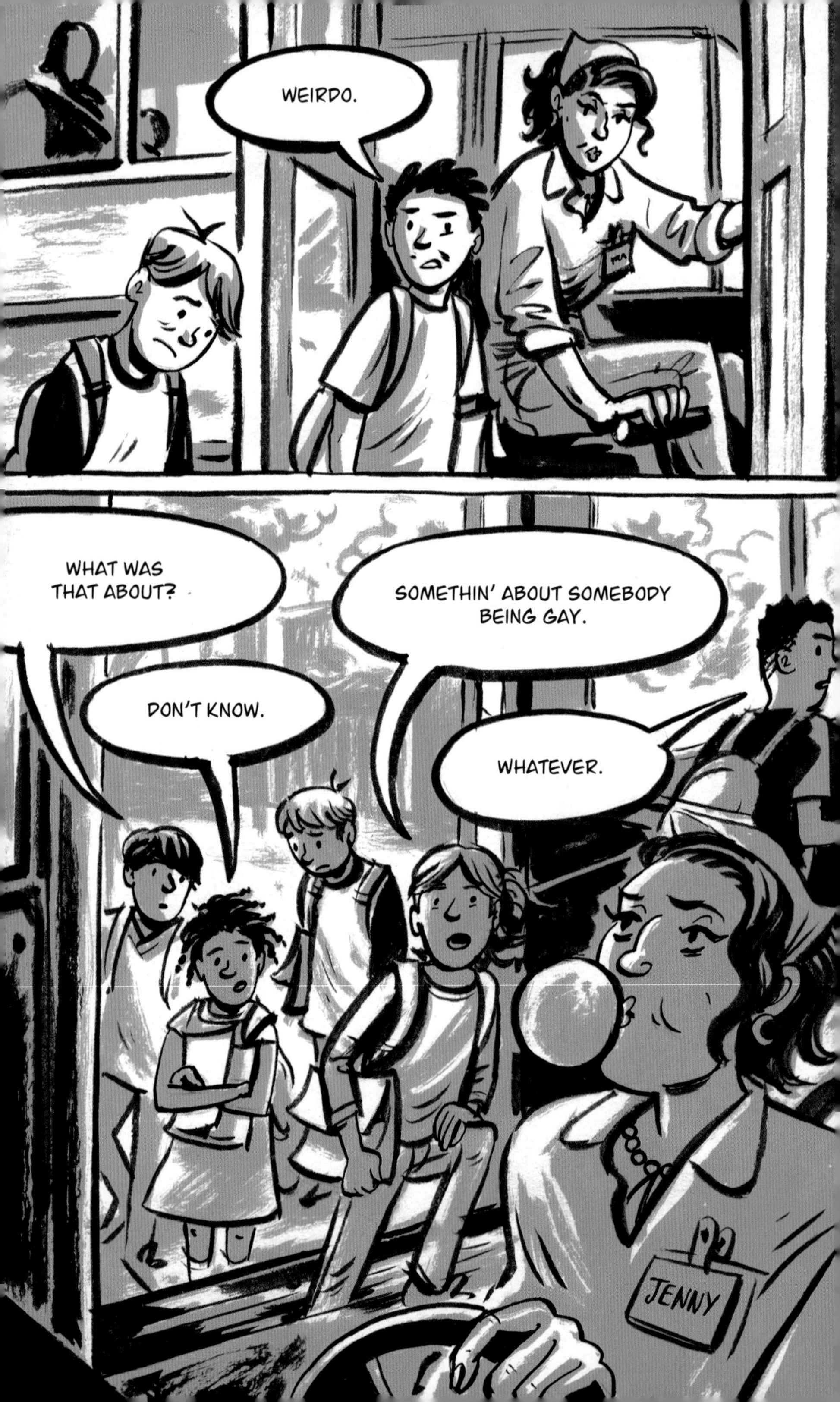
WEIRDO.
WHAT WAS THAT ABOUT?
SOMETHIN' ABOUT SOMEBODY BEING GAY.
DON'T KNOW.
WHATEVER.
JENNY

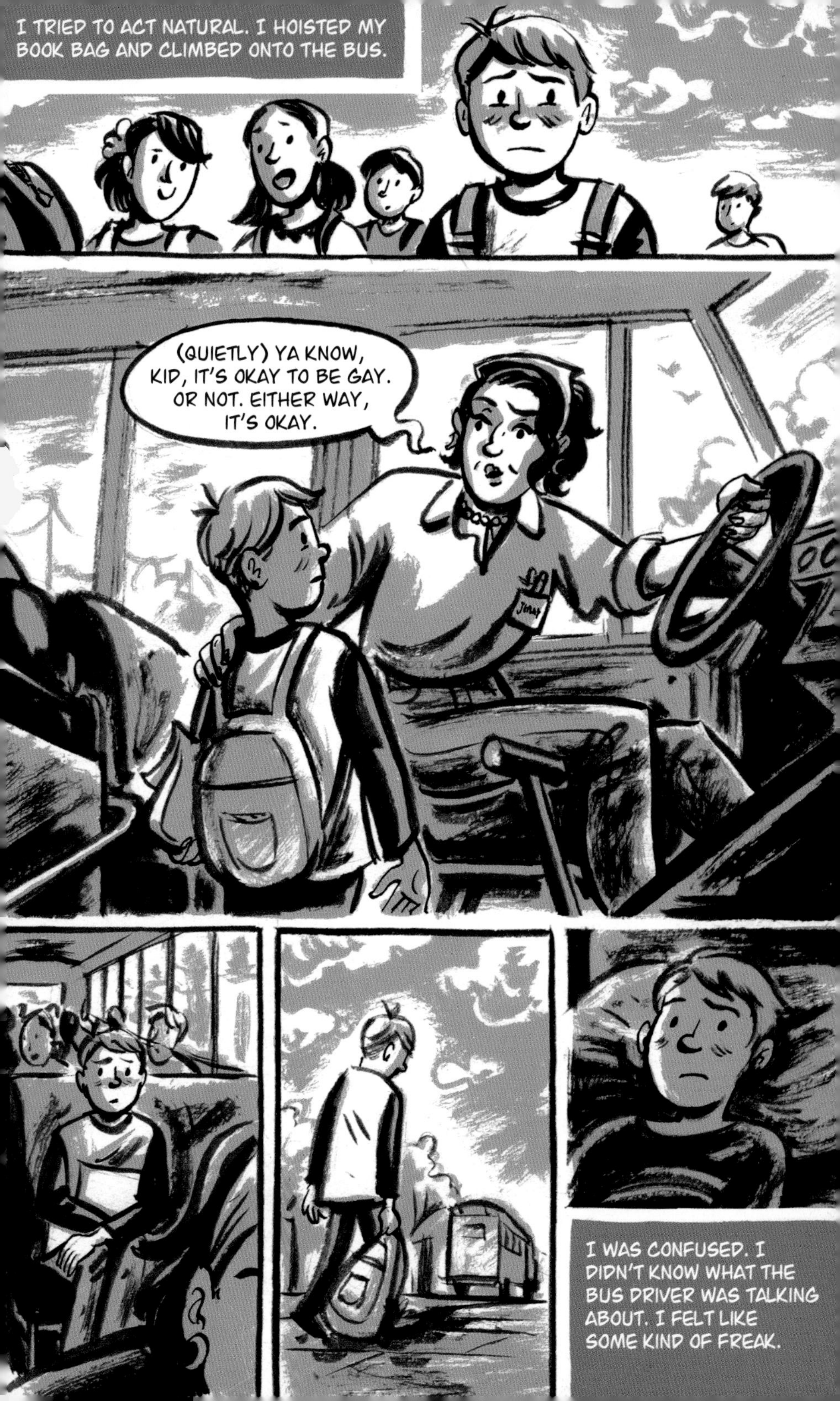
I TRIED TO ACT NATURAL. I HOISTED MY BOOK BAG AND CLIMBED ONTO THE BUS.
(QUIETLY) YA KNOW, KID, IT'S OKAY TO BE GAY. OR NOT. EITHER WAY, IT'S OKAY.
I WAS CONFUSED. I DIDN'T KNOW WHAT THE BUS DRIVER WAS TALKING ABOUT. I FELT LIKE SOME KIND OF FREAK.

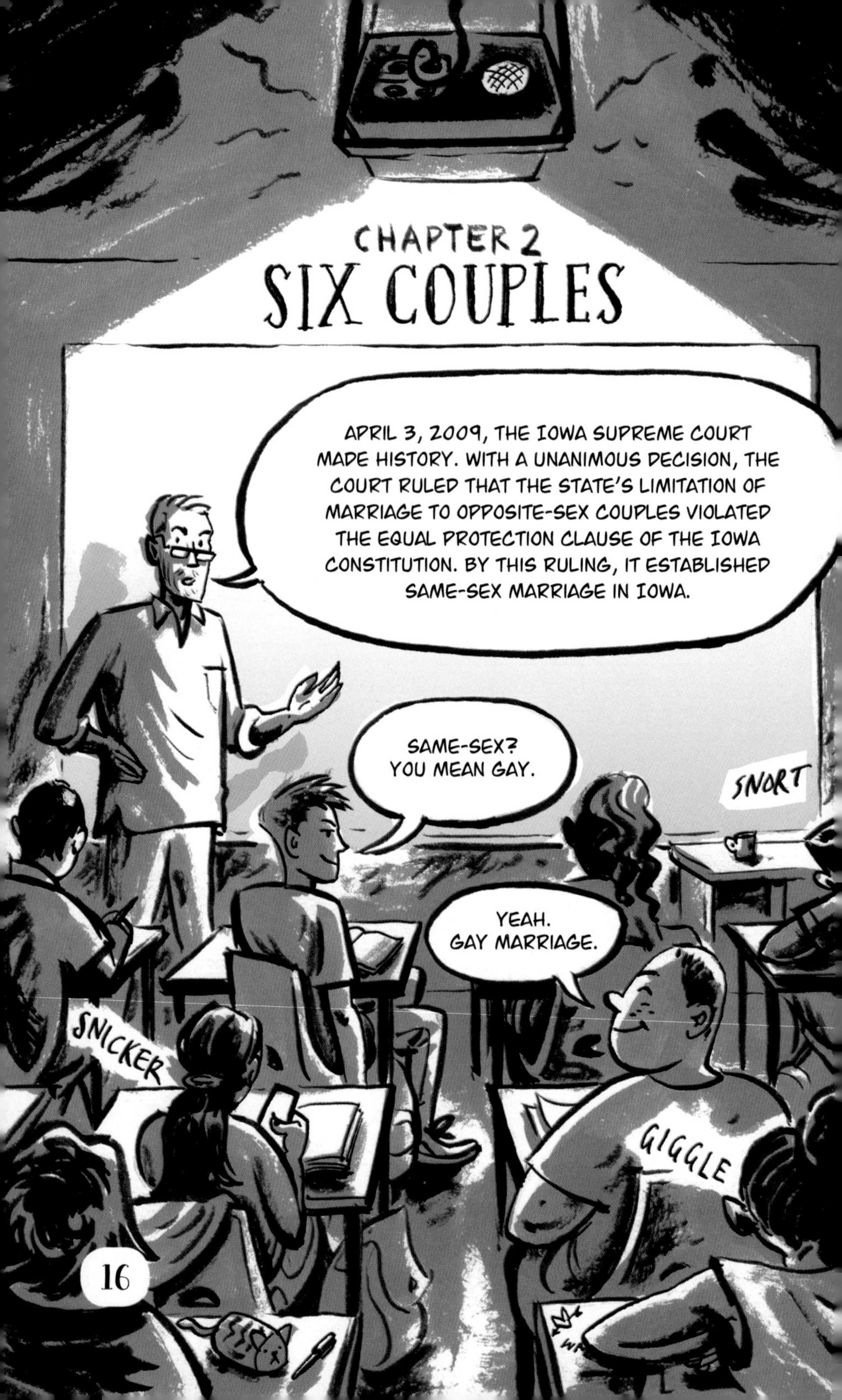
CHAPTER 2
SIX COUPLES
APRIL 3, 2009, THE IOWA SUPREME COURT MADE HISTORY. WITH A UNANIMOUS DECISION, THE COURT RULED THAT THE STATE'S LIMITATION OF MARRIAGE TO OPPOSITE-SEX COUPLES VIOLATED THE EQUAL PROTECTION CLAUSE OF THE IOWA CONSTITUTION. BY THIS RULING, IT ESTABLISHED SAME-SEX MARRIAGE IN IOWA.
SAME-SEX? YOU MEAN GAY.
SNORT
YEAH. GAY MARRIAGE.
SNICKER
GIGGLE

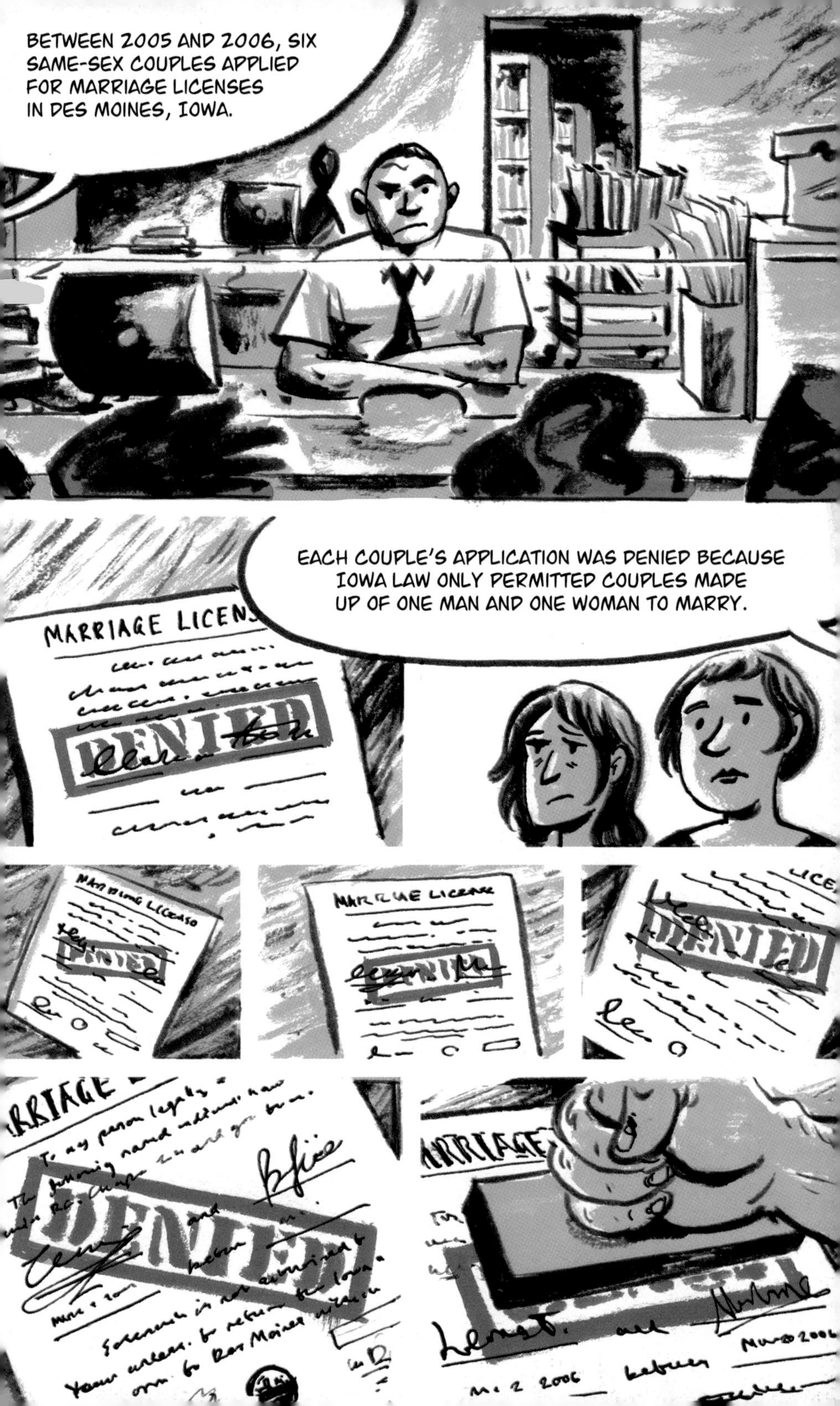
BETWEEN 2005 AND 2006, SIX SAME-SEX COUPLES APPLIED FOR MARRIAGE LICENSES IN DES MOINES, IOWA.
EACH COUPLE'S APPLICATION WAS DENIED BECAUSE IOWA LAW ONLY PERMITTED COUPLES MADE UP OF ONE MAN AND ONE WOMAN TO MARRY.
MARRIAGE LICENS
DENIED
DENIED
DENIED
DENIED

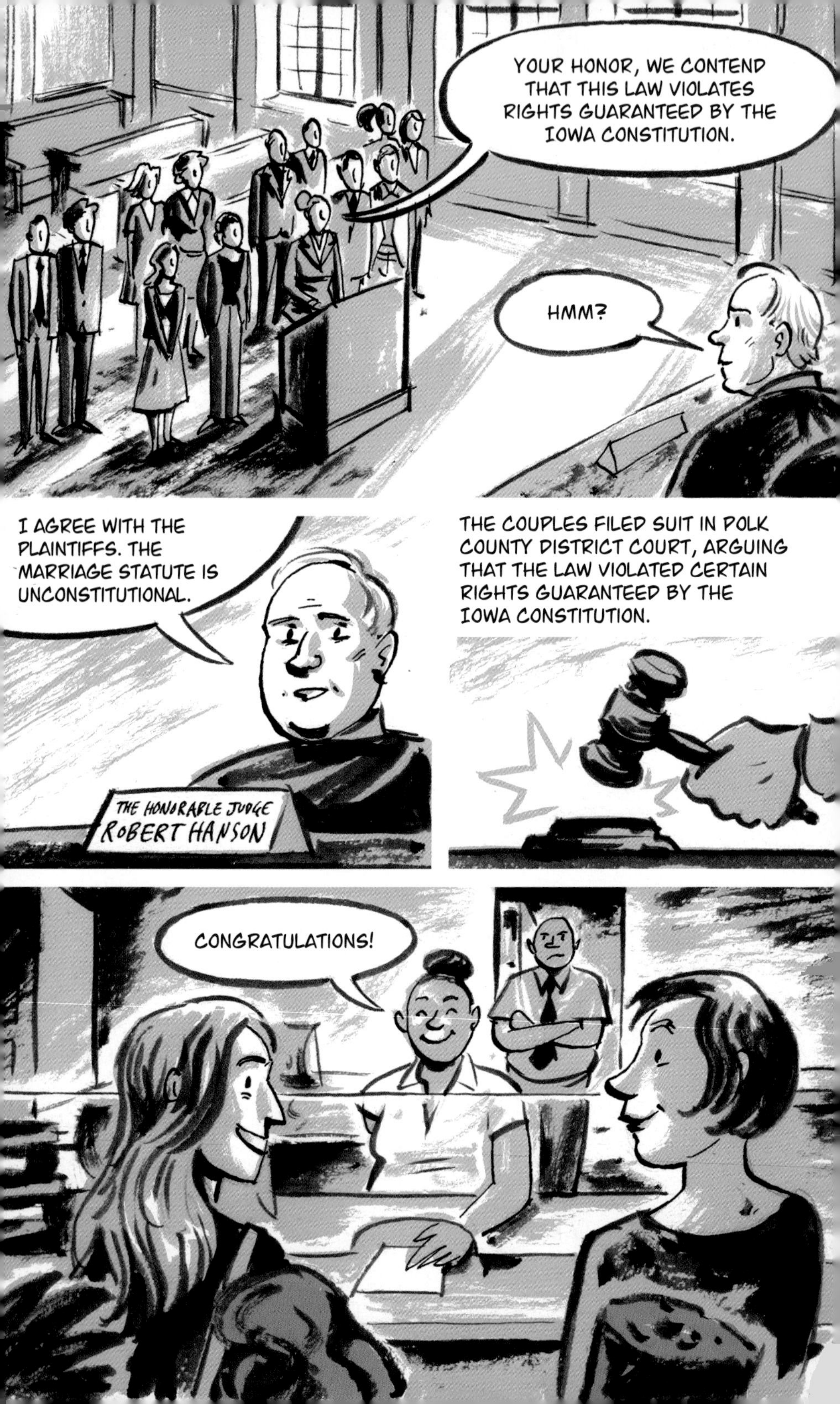

YOUR HONOR, WE CONTEND THAT THIS LAW VIOLATES RIGHTS GUARANTEED BY THE IOWA CONSTITUTION.
HMM?
I AGREE WITH THE PLAINTIFFS. THE MARRIAGE STATUTE IS UNCONSTITUTIONAL.
THE HONORABLE JUDGE ROBERT HANSON
THE COUPLES FILED SUIT IN POLK COUNTY DISTRICT COURT, ARGUING THAT THE LAW VIOLATED CERTAIN RIGHTS GUARANTEED BY THE IOWA CONSTITUTION.
CONGRATULATIONS!

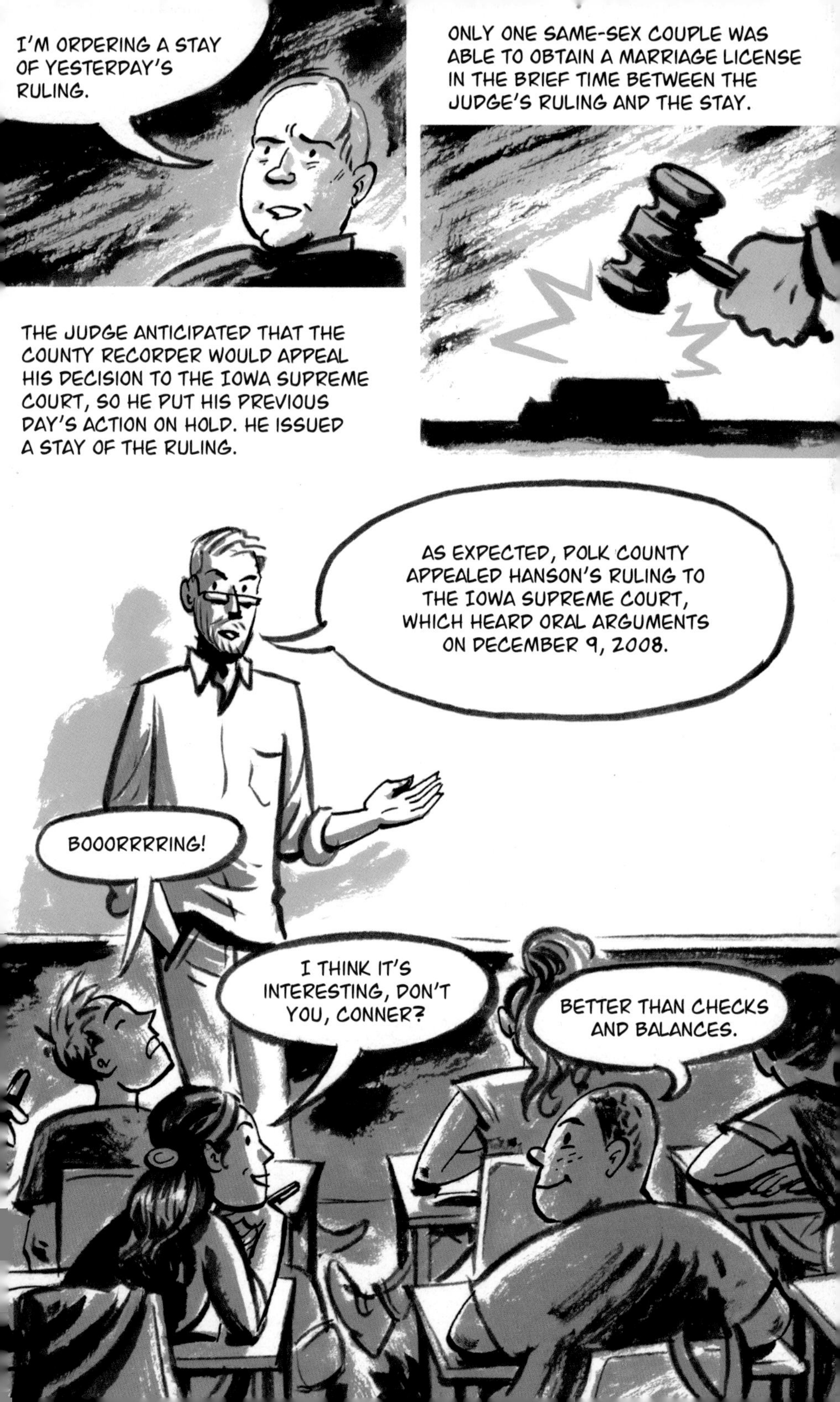
I'M ORDERING A STAY OF YESTERDAY'S RULING.
ONLY ONE SAME-SEX COUPLE WAS ABLE TO OBTAIN A MARRIAGE LICENSE IN THE BRIEF TIME BETWEEN THE JUDGE'S RULING AND THE STAY.
THE JUDGE ANTICIPATED THAT THE COUNTY RECORDER WOULD APPEAL HIS DECISION TO THE IOWA SUPREME COURT, SO HE PUT HIS PREVIOUS DAY'S ACTION ON HOLD. HE ISSUED A STAY OF THE RULING.
AS EXPECTED, POLK COUNTY APPEALED HANSON'S RULING TO THE IOWA SUPREME COURT, WHICH HEARD ORAL ARGUMENTS ON DECEMBER 9, 2008.
BOOORRRRING!
I THINK IT'S INTERESTING, DON'T YOU, CONNER?
BETTER THAN CHECKS AND BALANCES.

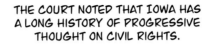

THE COURT NOTED THAT IOWA HAS A LONG HISTORY OF PROGRESSIVE THOUGHT ON CIVIL RIGHTS.

17 YEARS BEFORE THE DRED SCOTT CASE WAS DENIED BY THE U.S. SUPREME COURT, THE IOWA SUPREME COURT REFUSED TO TREAT A HUMAN BEING AS PROPERTY.

DRED SCOTT, c.1857

OUR LAWS MUST EXTEND EQUAL PROTECTION TO PERSONS OF ALL RACES AND CONDITIONS.

SEGREGATION IN PUBLIC SCHOOLS ENDED BY COURT

86 YEARS BEFORE 'SEPARATE BUT EQUAL' WAS STRUCK DOWN BY THE U.S. SUPREME COURT IN BROWN VS BOARD OF EDUCATION, THE IOWA SUPREME COURT RULED SUCH PRACTICES UNCONSTITUTIONAL IN IOWA.

UNCONSTITUTIONAL.

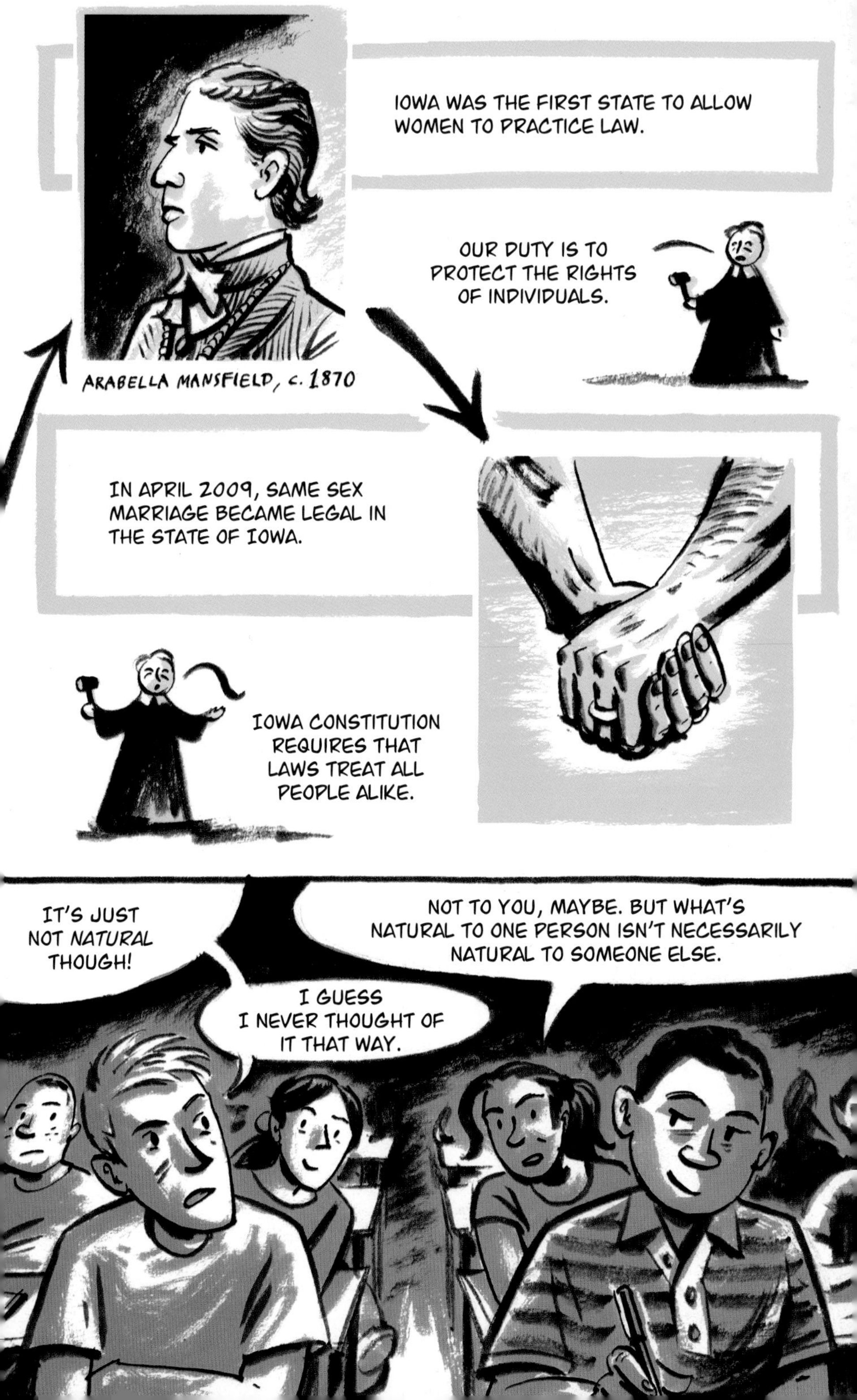

IOWA WAS THE FIRST STATE TO ALLOW WOMEN TO PRACTICE LAW.
ARABELLA MANSFIELD, c. 1870
OUR DUTY IS TO PROTECT THE RIGHTS OF INDIVIDUALS.
IN APRIL 2009, SAME SEX MARRIAGE BECAME LEGAL IN THE STATE OF IOWA.
IOWA CONSTITUTION REQUIRES THAT LAWS TREAT ALL PEOPLE ALIKE.
IT'S JUST NOT *NATURAL* THOUGH!
NOT TO YOU, MAYBE. BUT WHAT'S NATURAL TO ONE PERSON ISN'T NECESSARILY NATURAL TO SOMEONE ELSE.
I GUESS I NEVER THOUGHT OF IT THAT WAY.

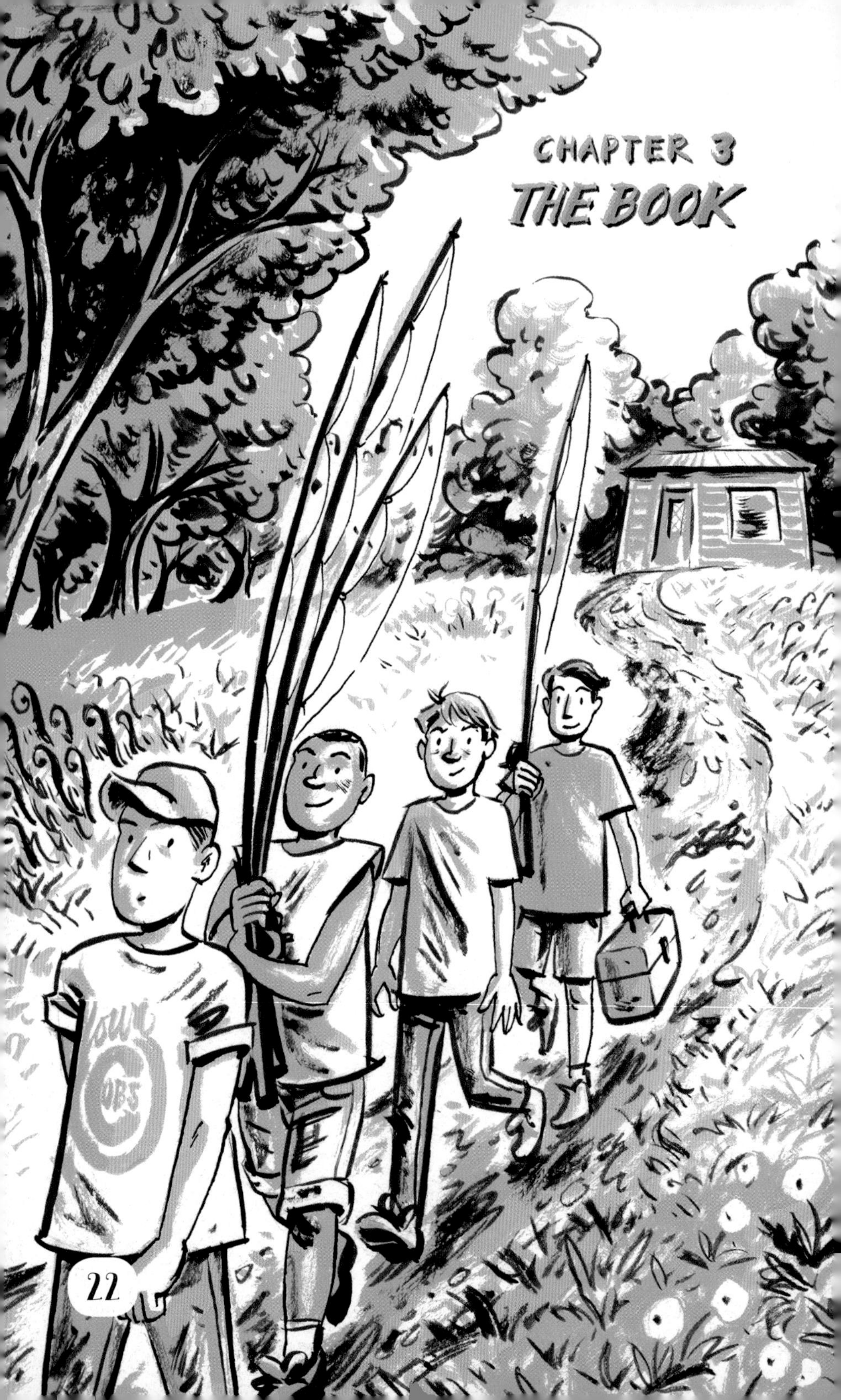
CHAPTER 3
THE BOOK

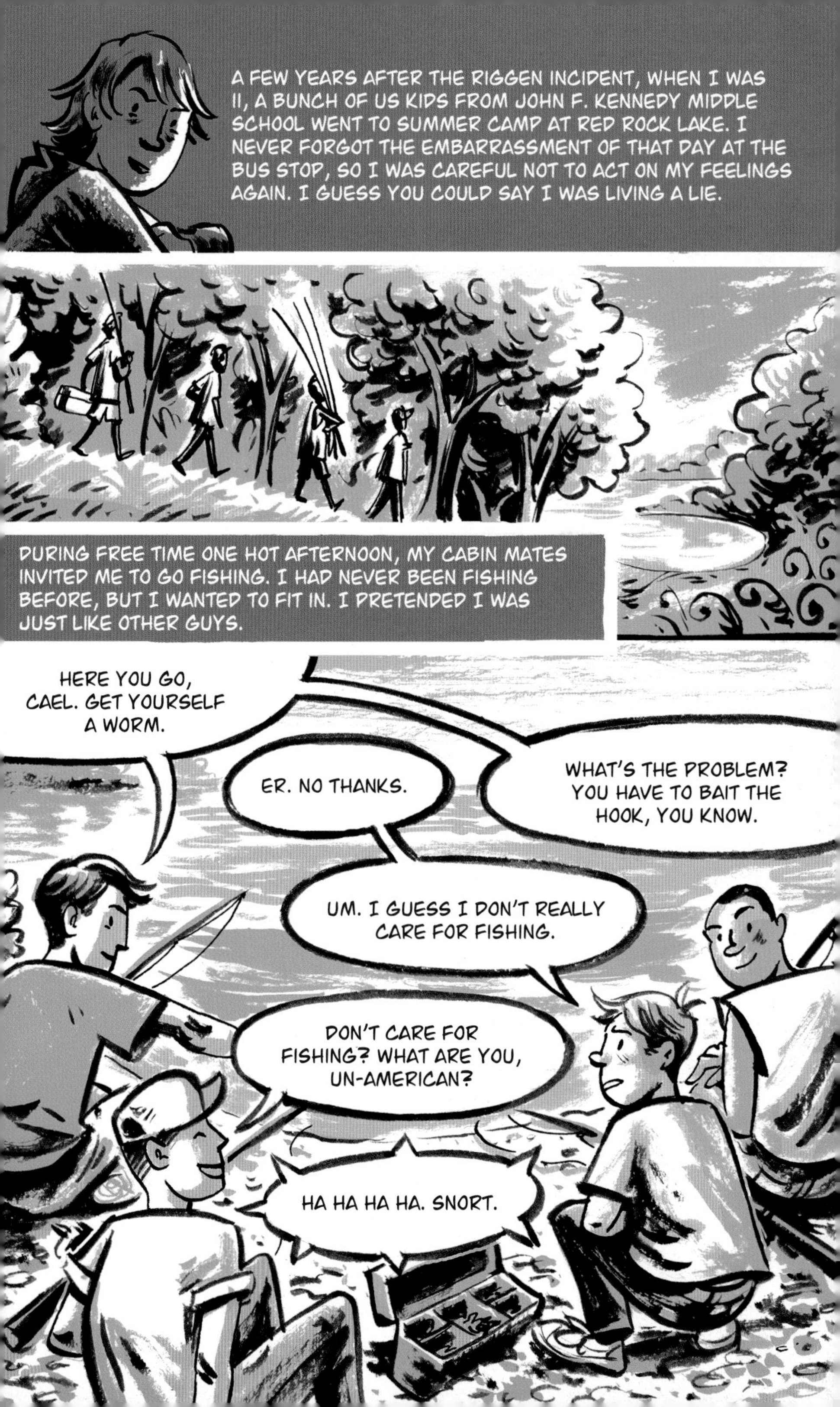
A FEW YEARS AFTER THE RIGGEN INCIDENT, WHEN I WAS 11, A BUNCH OF US KIDS FROM JOHN F. KENNEDY MIDDLE SCHOOL WENT TO SUMMER CAMP AT RED ROCK LAKE. I NEVER FORGOT THE EMBARRASSMENT OF THAT DAY AT THE BUS STOP, SO I WAS CAREFUL NOT TO ACT ON MY FEELINGS AGAIN. I GUESS YOU COULD SAY I WAS LIVING A LIE.
DURING FREE TIME ONE HOT AFTERNOON, MY CABIN MATES INVITED ME TO GO FISHING. I HAD NEVER BEEN FISHING BEFORE, BUT I WANTED TO FIT IN. I PRETENDED I WAS JUST LIKE OTHER GUYS.
HERE YOU GO, CAEL. GET YOURSELF A WORM.
ER. NO THANKS.
WHAT'S THE PROBLEM? YOU HAVE TO BAIT THE HOOK, YOU KNOW.
UM. I GUESS I DON'T REALLY CARE FOR FISHING.
DON'T CARE FOR FISHING? WHAT ARE YOU, UN-AMERICAN?
HA HA HA HA. SNORT.

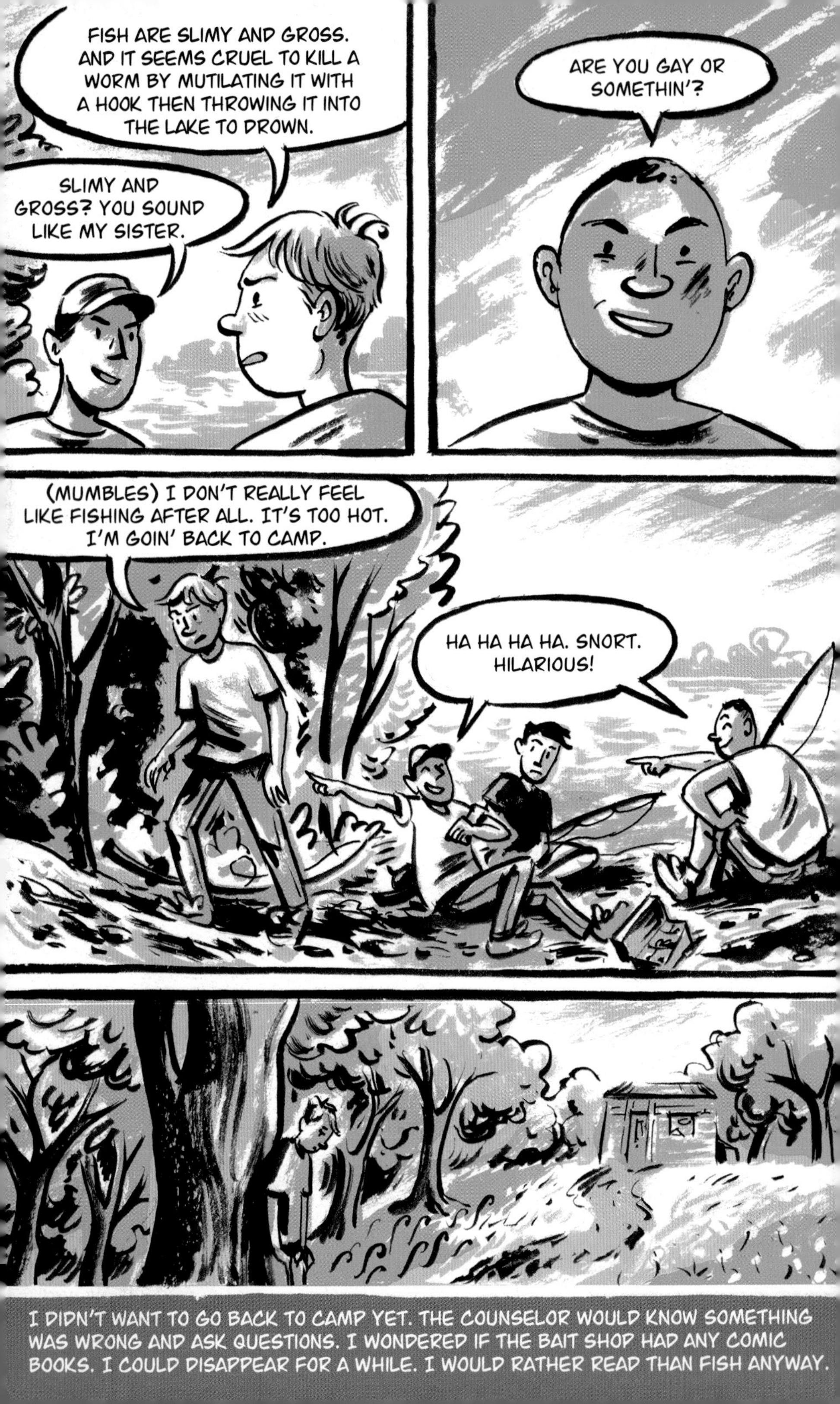
FISH ARE SLIMY AND GROSS. AND IT SEEMS CRUEL TO KILL A WORM BY MUTILATING IT WITH A HOOK THEN THROWING IT INTO THE LAKE TO DROWN.
SLIMY AND GROSS? YOU SOUND LIKE MY SISTER.
ARE YOU GAY OR SOMETHIN'?
(MUMBLES) I DON'T REALLY FEEL LIKE FISHING AFTER ALL. IT'S TOO HOT. I'M GOIN' BACK TO CAMP.
HA HA HA HA. SNORT. HILARIOUS!
I DIDN'T WANT TO GO BACK TO CAMP YET. THE COUNSELOR WOULD KNOW SOMETHING WAS WRONG AND ASK QUESTIONS. I WONDERED IF THE BAIT SHOP HAD ANY COMIC BOOKS. I COULD DISAPPEAR FOR A WHILE. I WOULD RATHER READ THAN FISH ANYWAY.

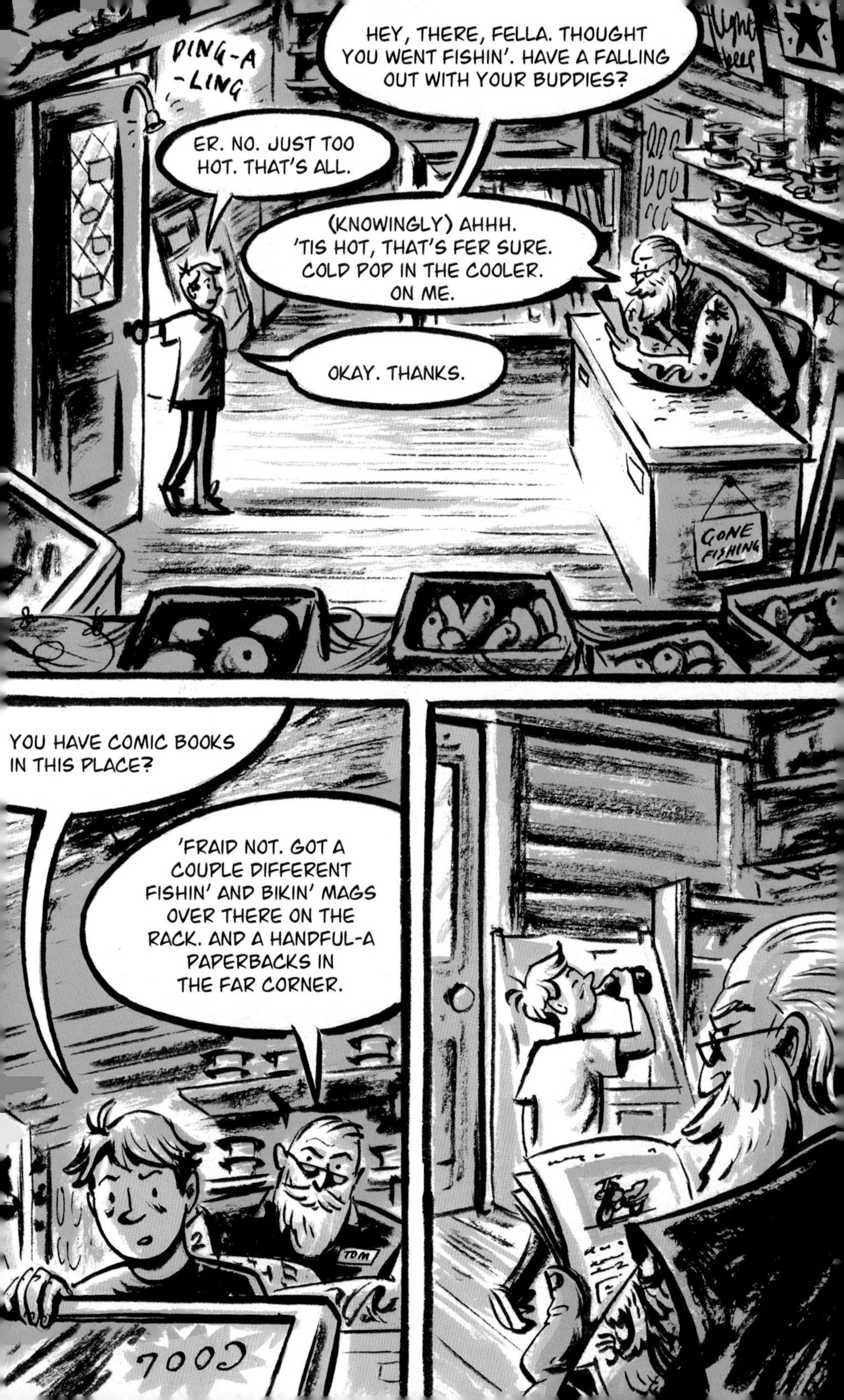
DING-A-LING
HEY, THERE, FELLA. THOUGHT YOU WENT FISHIN'. HAVE A FALLING OUT WITH YOUR BUDDIES?
ER. NO. JUST TOO HOT. THAT'S ALL.
(KNOWINGLY) AHHH. 'TIS HOT, THAT'S FER SURE. COLD POP IN THE COOLER. ON ME.
OKAY. THANKS.
GONE FISHING
YOU HAVE COMIC BOOKS IN THIS PLACE?
'FRAID NOT. GOT A COUPLE DIFFERENT FISHIN' AND BIKIN' MAGS OVER THERE ON THE RACK. AND A HANDFUL-A PAPERBACKS IN THE FAR CORNER.

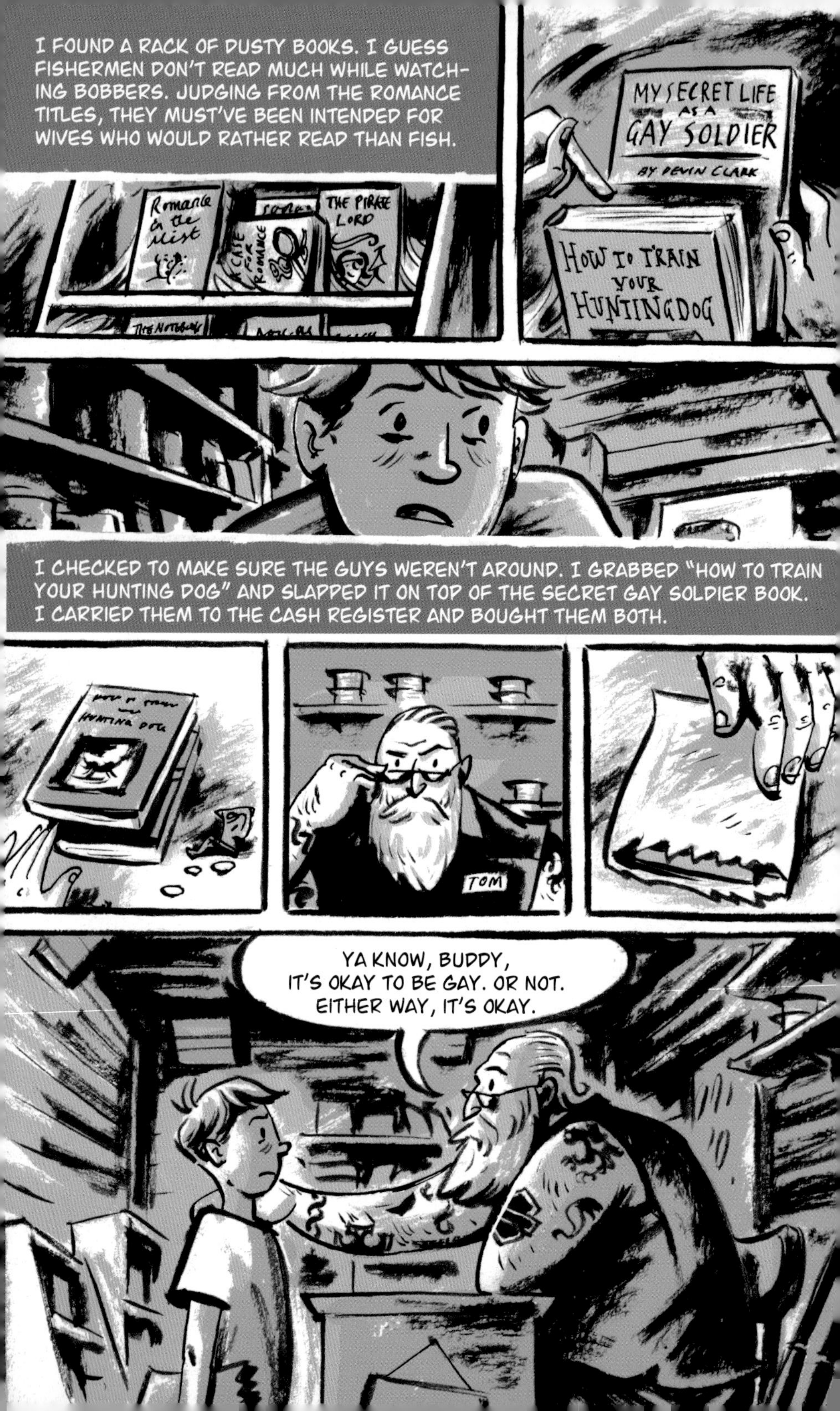
I FOUND A RACK OF DUSTY BOOKS. I GUESS FISHERMEN DON'T READ MUCH WHILE WATCHING BOBBERS. JUDGING FROM THE ROMANCE TITLES, THEY MUST'VE BEEN INTENDED FOR WIVES WHO WOULD RATHER READ THAN FISH.
Romance in the Mist
A CASE FOR ROMANCE
THE PIRATE LORD
MY SECRET LIFE AS A GAY SOLDIER
BY DEVIN CLARK
HOW TO TRAIN YOUR HUNTING DOG
I CHECKED TO MAKE SURE THE GUYS WEREN'T AROUND. I GRABBED "HOW TO TRAIN YOUR HUNTING DOG" AND SLAPPED IT ON TOP OF THE SECRET GAY SOLDIER BOOK. I CARRIED THEM TO THE CASH REGISTER AND BOUGHT THEM BOTH.
TOM
YA KNOW, BUDDY, IT'S OKAY TO BE GAY. OR NOT. EITHER WAY, IT'S OKAY.

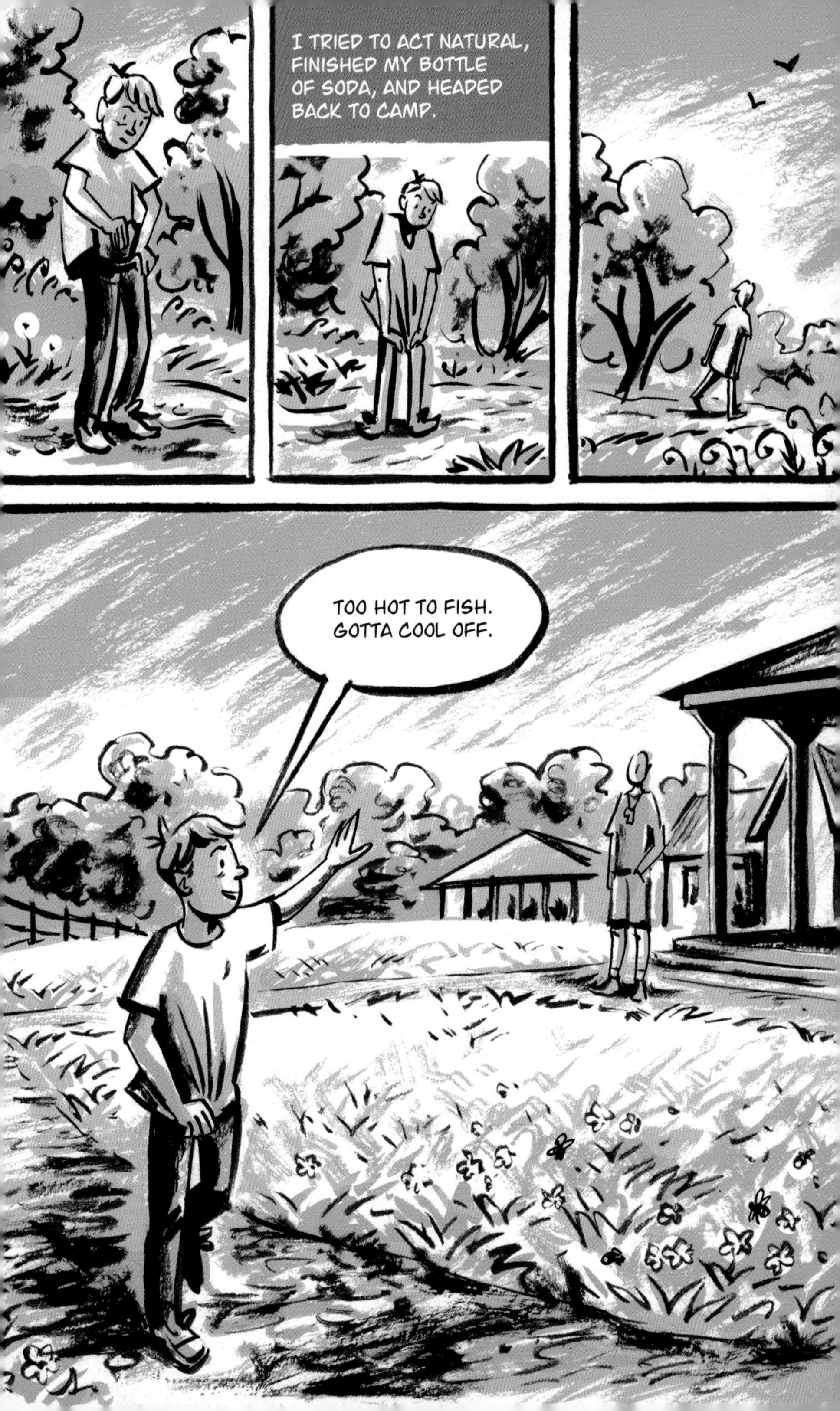
I TRIED TO ACT NATURAL, FINISHED MY BOTTLE OF SODA, AND HEADED BACK TO CAMP.
TOO HOT TO FISH. GOTTA COOL OFF.

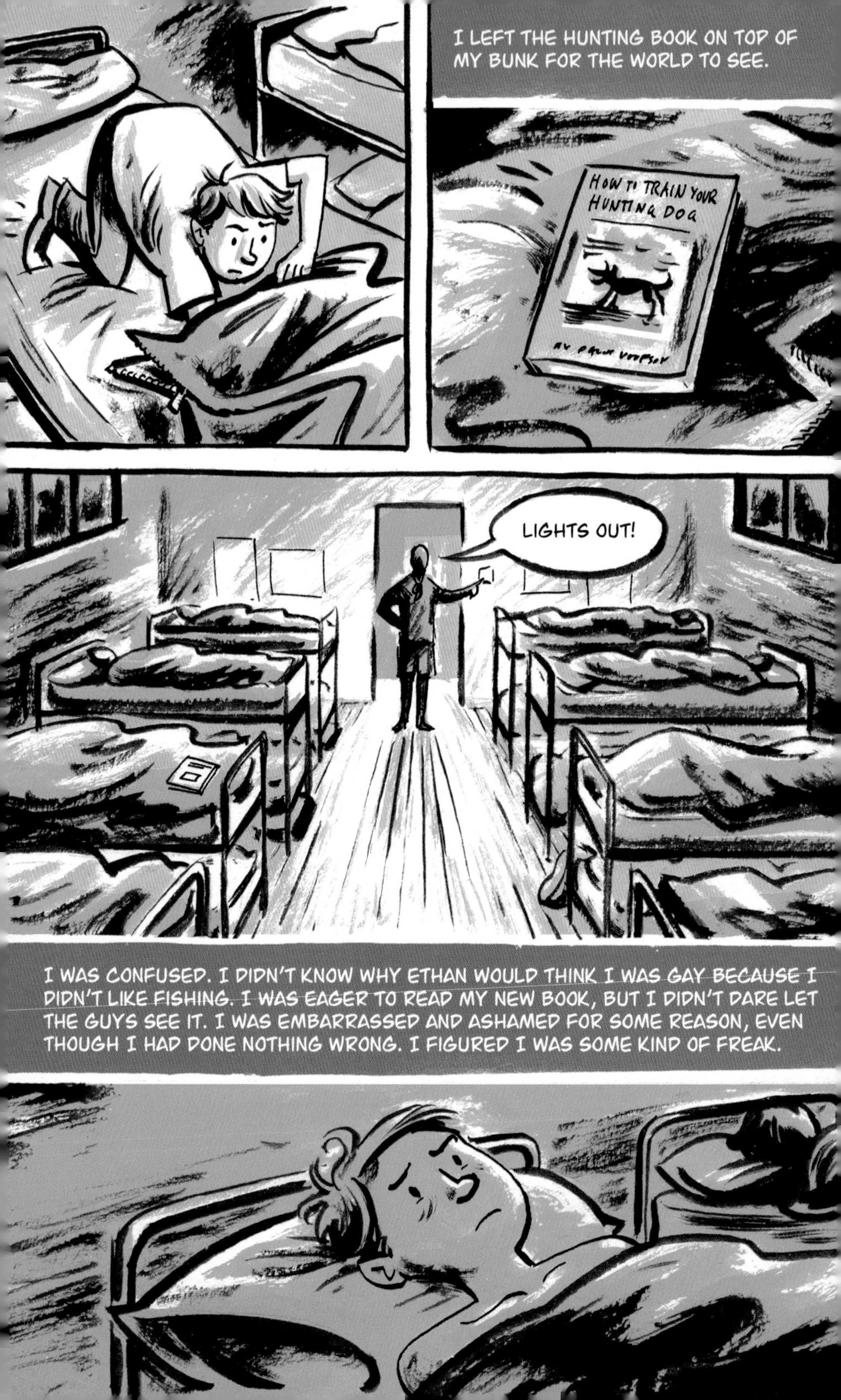
I LEFT THE HUNTING BOOK ON TOP OF MY BUNK FOR THE WORLD TO SEE.
HOW TO TRAIN YOUR HUNTING DOG
LIGHTS OUT!
I WAS CONFUSED. I DIDN'T KNOW WHY ETHAN WOULD THINK I WAS GAY BECAUSE I DIDN'T LIKE FISHING. I WAS EAGER TO READ MY NEW BOOK, BUT I DIDN'T DARE LET THE GUYS SEE IT. I WAS EMBARRASSED AND ASHAMED FOR SOME REASON, EVEN THOUGH I HAD DONE NOTHING WRONG. I FIGURED I WAS SOME KIND OF FREAK.

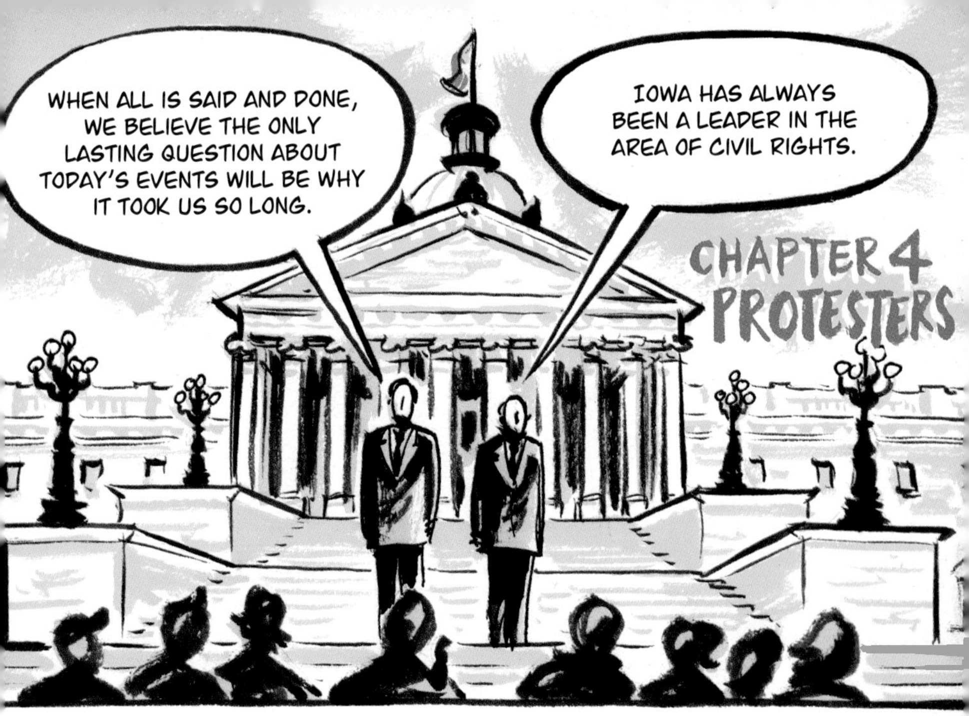
WHEN ALL IS SAID AND DONE, WE BELIEVE THE ONLY LASTING QUESTION ABOUT TODAY'S EVENTS WILL BE WHY IT TOOK US SO LONG.
IOWA HAS ALWAYS BEEN A LEADER IN THE AREA OF CIVIL RIGHTS.
CHAPTER 4
PROTESTERS

TREATING EVERYONE FAIRLY IS A MATTER OF COMMON SENSE AND DECENCY.

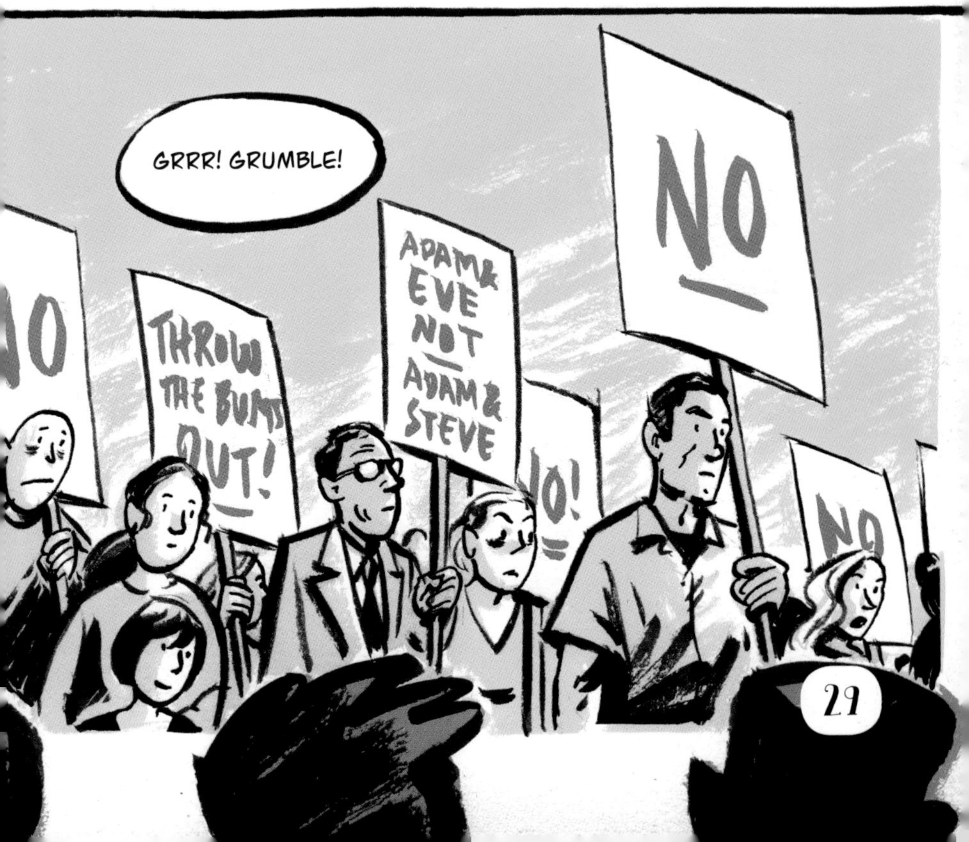
GRRR! GRUMBLE!
NO
THROW THE BUMS OUT!
ADAM & EVE NOT ADAM & STEVE

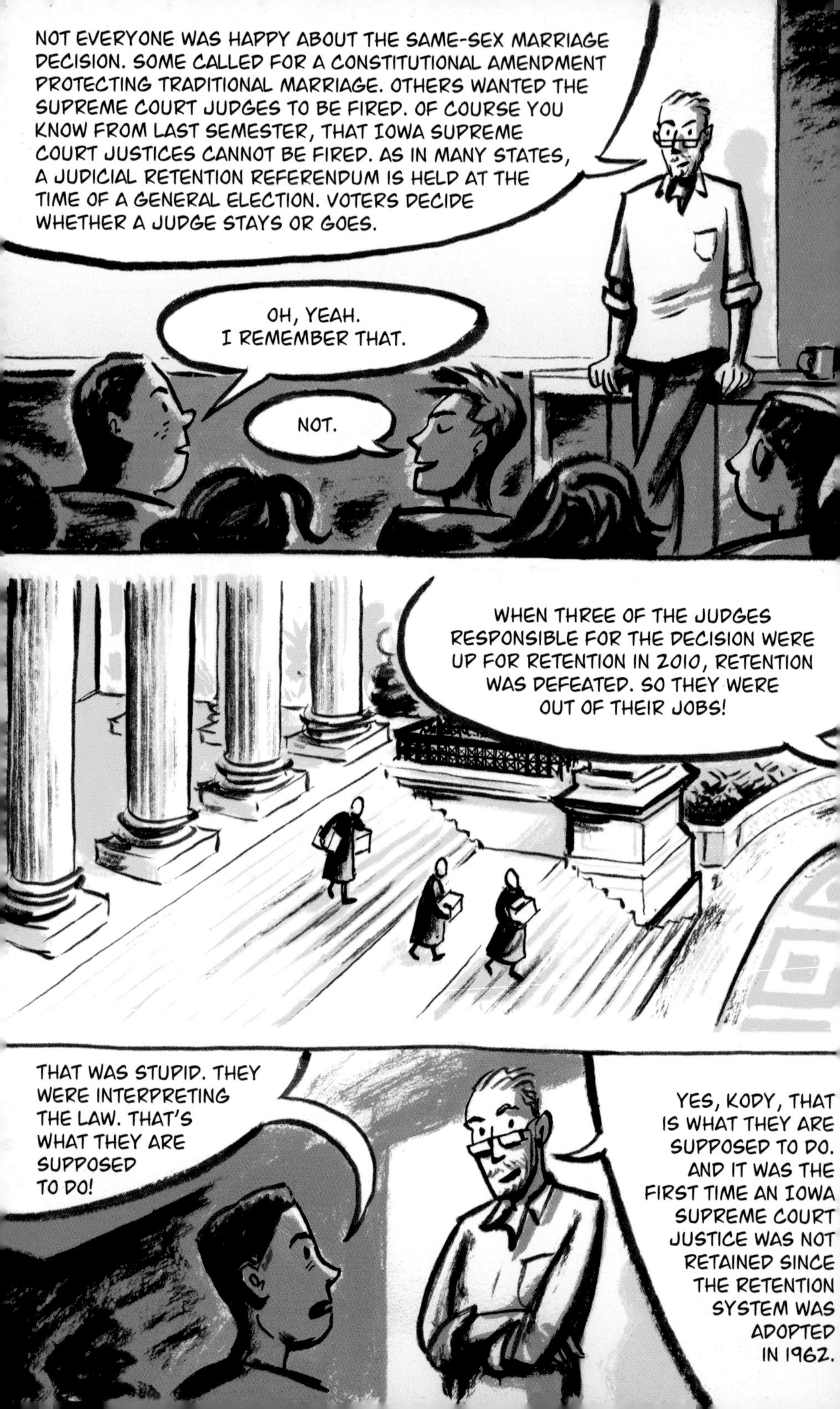
NOT EVERYONE WAS HAPPY ABOUT THE SAME-SEX MARRIAGE DECISION. SOME CALLED FOR A CONSTITUTIONAL AMENDMENT PROTECTING TRADITIONAL MARRIAGE. OTHERS WANTED THE SUPREME COURT JUDGES TO BE FIRED. OF COURSE YOU KNOW FROM LAST SEMESTER, THAT IOWA SUPREME COURT JUSTICES CANNOT BE FIRED. AS IN MANY STATES, A JUDICIAL RETENTION REFERENDUM IS HELD AT THE TIME OF A GENERAL ELECTION. VOTERS DECIDE WHETHER A JUDGE STAYS OR GOES.
OH, YEAH. I REMEMBER THAT.
NOT.
WHEN THREE OF THE JUDGES RESPONSIBLE FOR THE DECISION WERE UP FOR RETENTION IN 2010, RETENTION WAS DEFEATED. SO THEY WERE OUT OF THEIR JOBS!
THAT WAS STUPID. THEY WERE INTERPRETING THE LAW. THAT'S WHAT THEY ARE SUPPOSED TO DO!
YES, KODY, THAT IS WHAT THEY ARE SUPPOSED TO DO. AND IT WAS THE FIRST TIME AN IOWA SUPREME COURT JUSTICE WAS NOT RETAINED SINCE THE RETENTION SYSTEM WAS ADOPTED IN 1962.

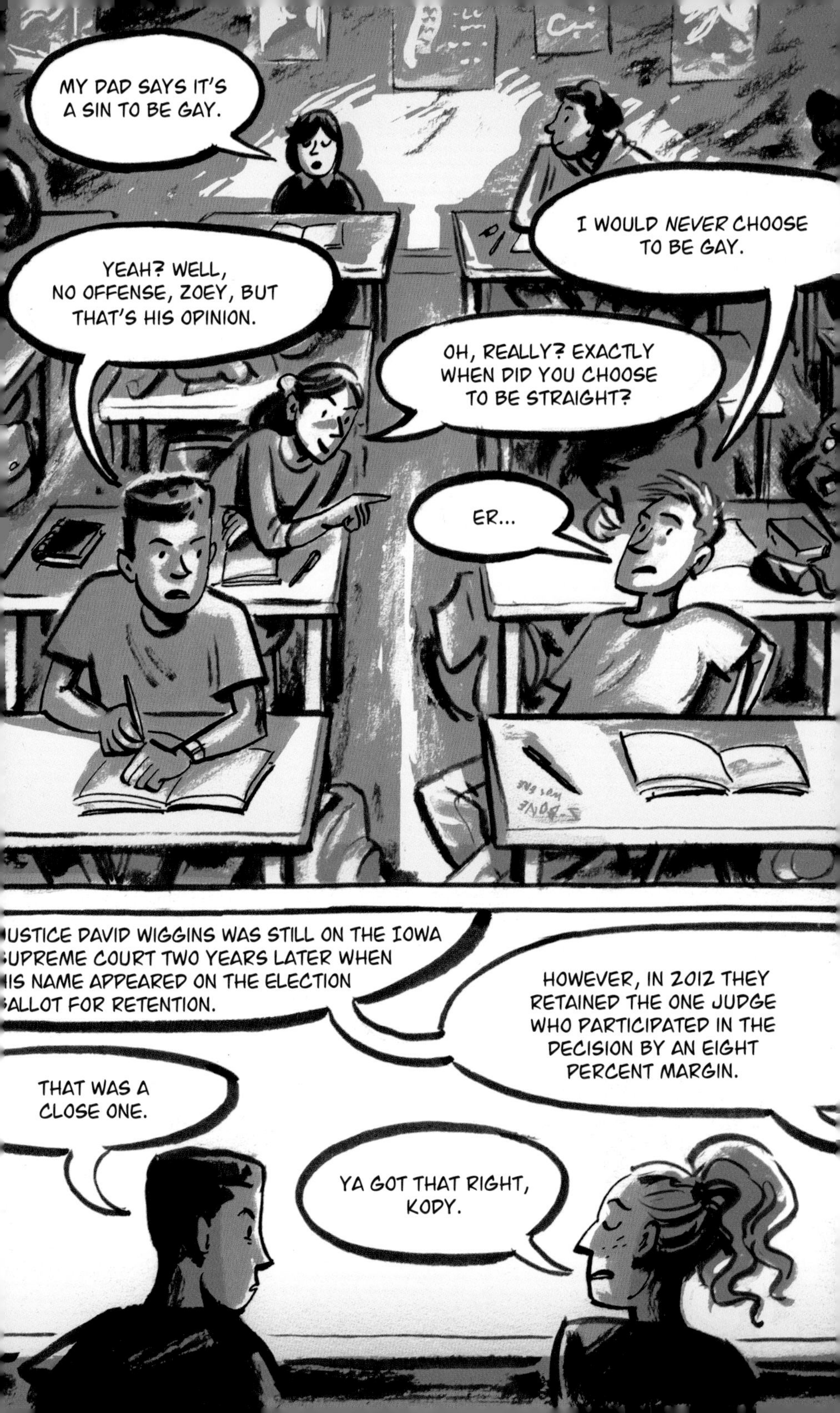
MY DAD SAYS IT'S A SIN TO BE GAY.
YEAH? WELL, NO OFFENSE, ZOEY, BUT THAT'S HIS OPINION.
I WOULD NEVER CHOOSE TO BE GAY.
OH, REALLY? EXACTLY WHEN DID YOU CHOOSE TO BE STRAIGHT?
ER...
USTICE DAVID WIGGINS WAS STILL ON THE IOWA UPREME COURT TWO YEARS LATER WHEN IIS NAME APPEARED ON THE ELECTION ALLOT FOR RETENTION.
HOWEVER, IN 2012 THEY RETAINED THE ONE JUDGE WHO PARTICIPATED IN THE DECISION BY AN EIGHT PERCENT MARGIN.
THAT WAS A CLOSE ONE.
YA GOT THAT RIGHT, KODY.

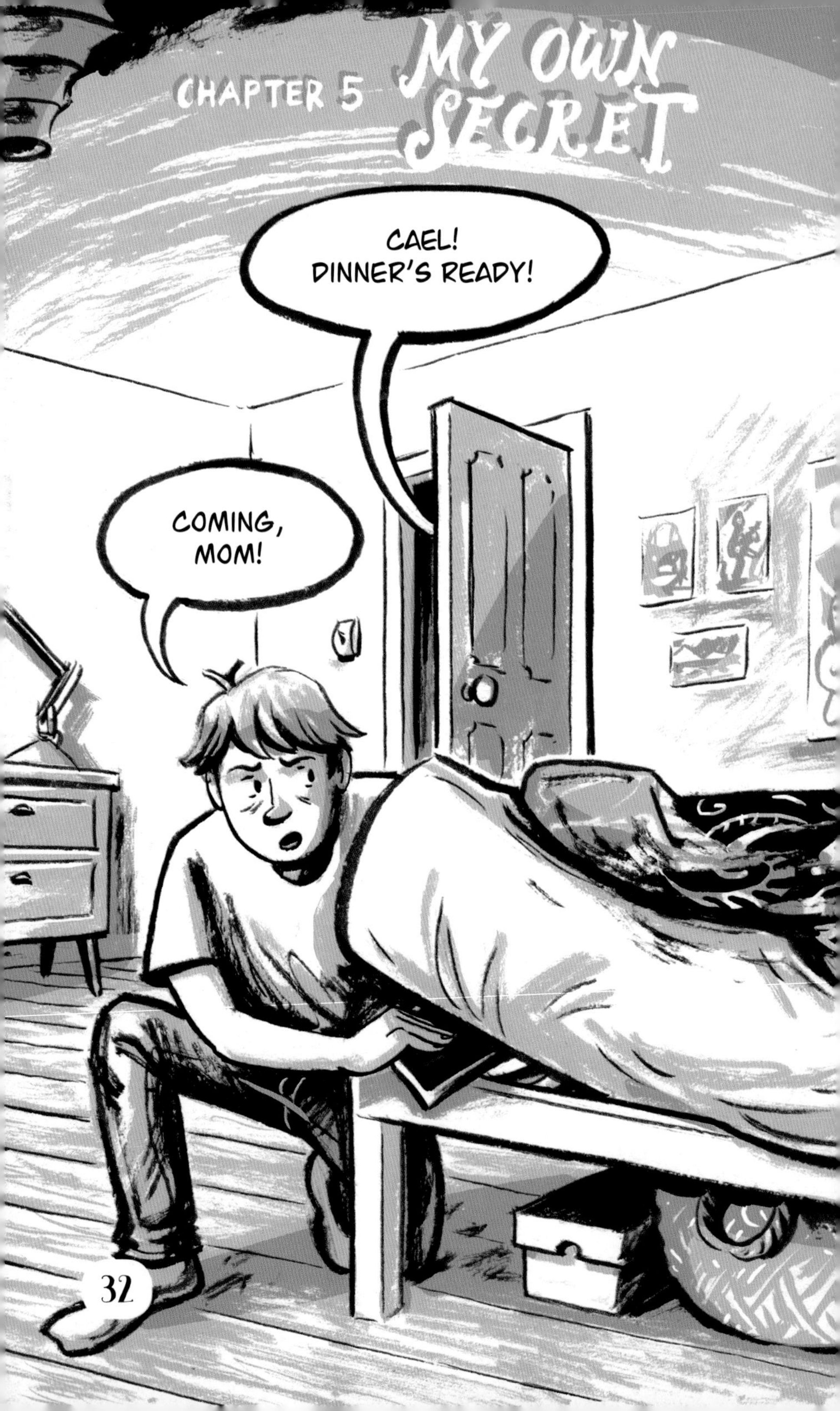
CHAPTER 5
MY OWN SECRET
CAEL! DINNER'S READY!
COMING, MOM!

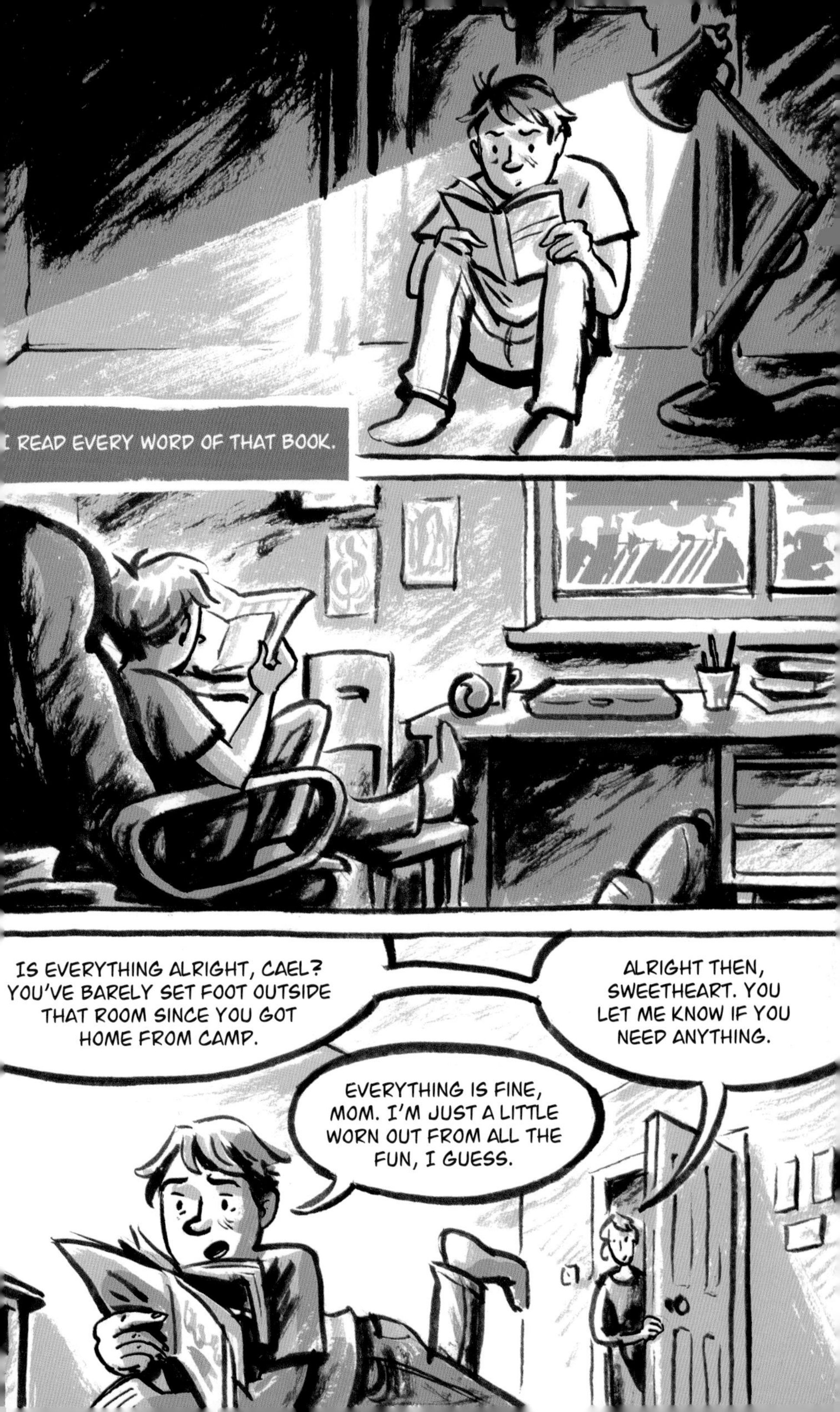
I READ EVERY WORD OF THAT BOOK.
IS EVERYTHING ALRIGHT, CAEL? YOU'VE BARELY SET FOOT OUTSIDE THAT ROOM SINCE YOU GOT HOME FROM CAMP.
EVERYTHING IS FINE, MOM. I'M JUST A LITTLE WORN OUT FROM ALL THE FUN, I GUESS.
ALRIGHT THEN, SWEETHEART. YOU LET ME KNOW IF YOU NEED ANYTHING.

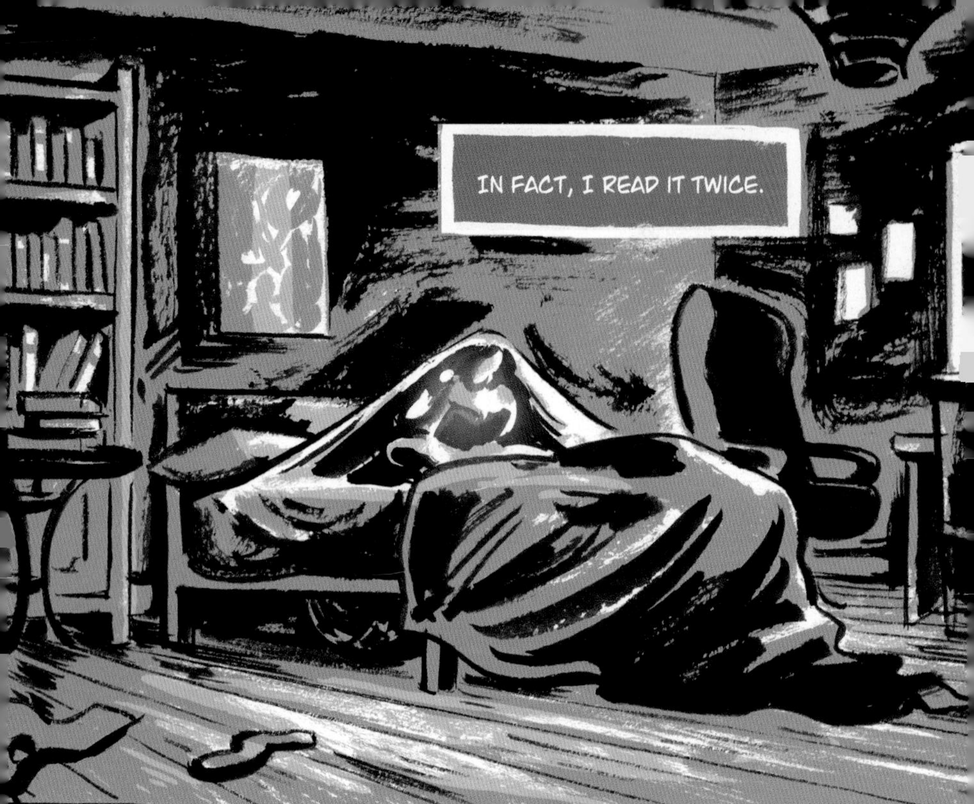
IN FACT, I READ IT TWICE.

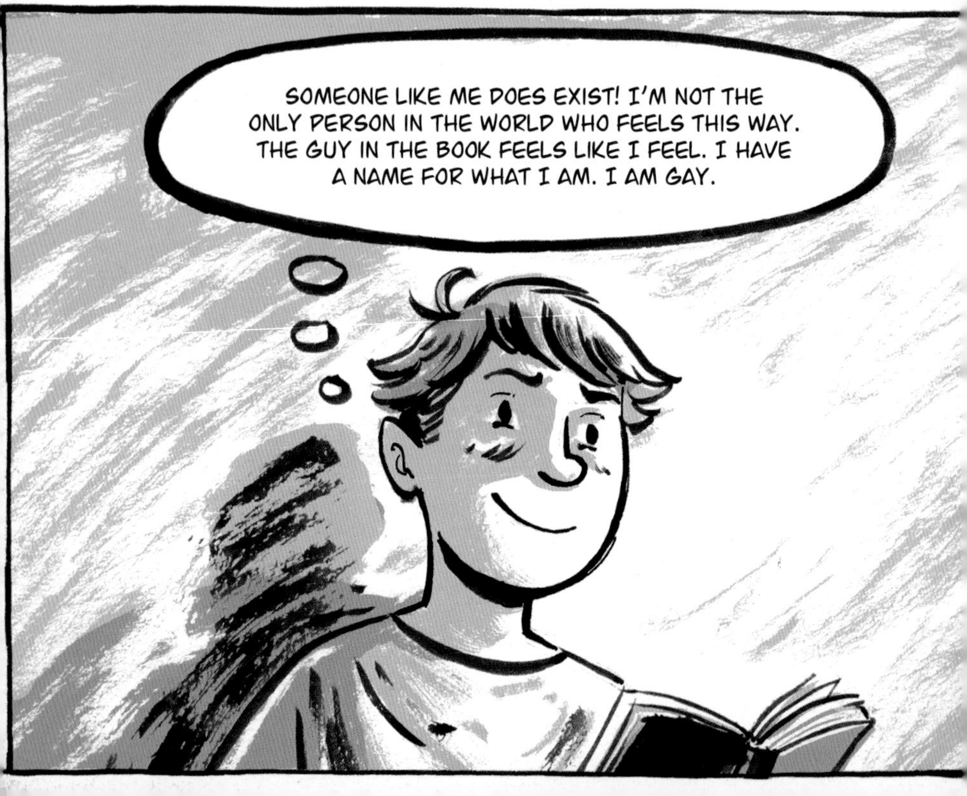
SOMEONE LIKE ME DOES EXIST! I'M NOT THE ONLY PERSON IN THE WORLD WHO FEELS THIS WAY. THE GUY IN THE BOOK FEELS LIKE I FEEL. I HAVE A NAME FOR WHAT I AM. I AM GAY.

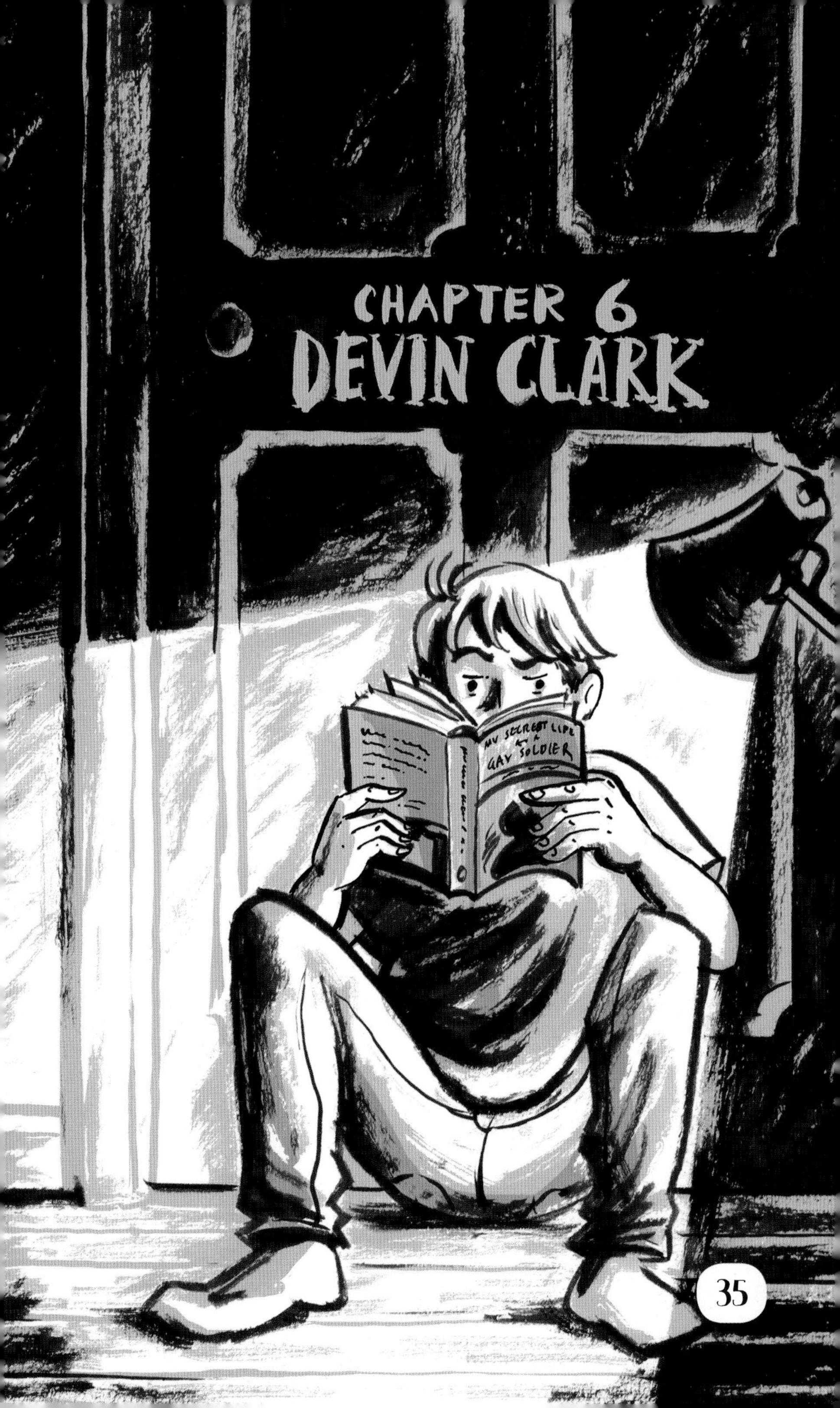
CHAPTER 6
DEVIN CLARK
MY SECRET LIFE AS A
GAY SOLDIER

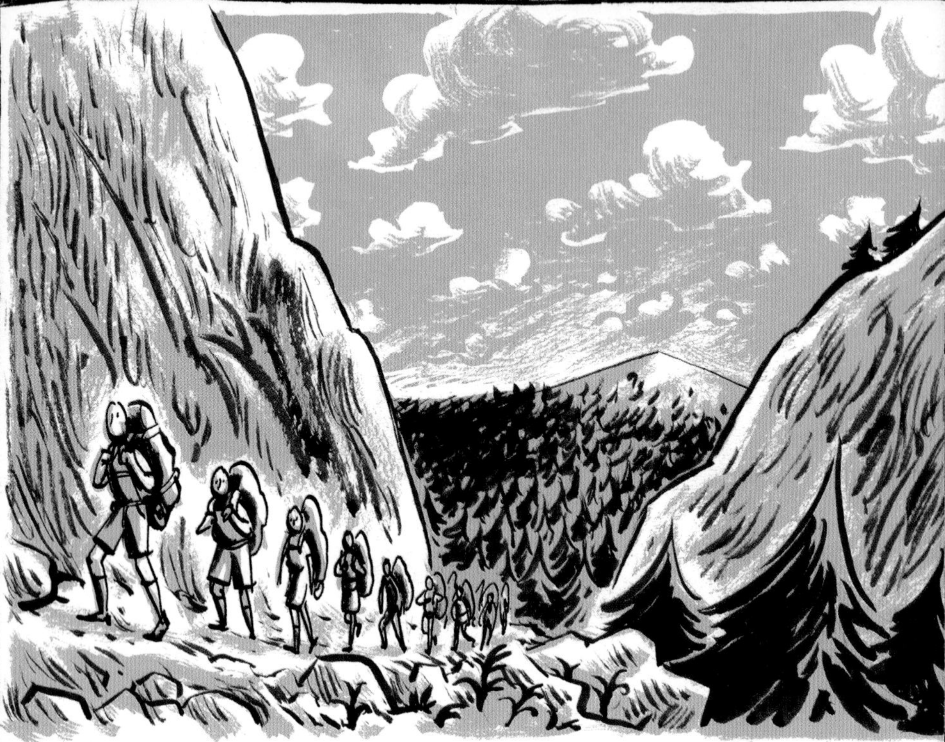

TWELVE-YEAR-OLD DEVIN CLARK WAS BACKPACKING WITH HIS SCOUT TROOP WHEN
AN UNEXPECTED THUNDERSTORM CAUGHT THE GROUP OFF-GUARD.

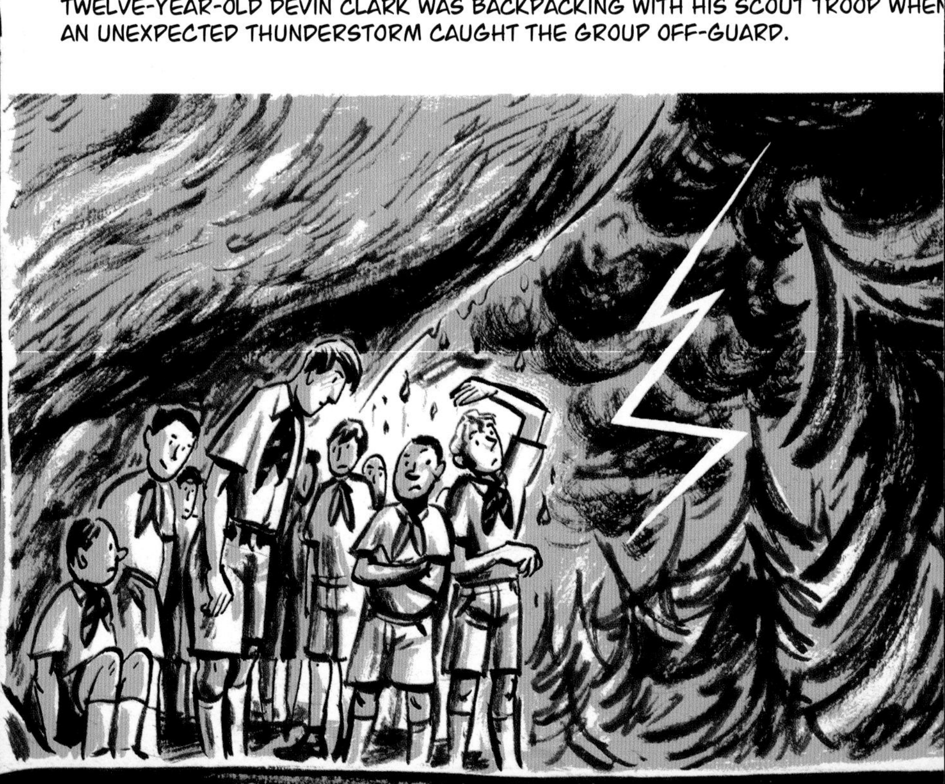

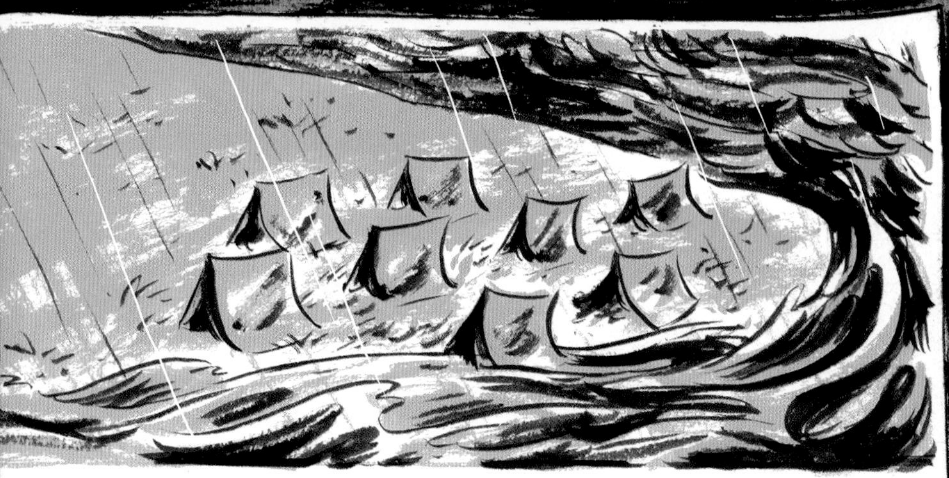

FLASH FLOODING CAUSED THE USUALLY TRICKLING CREEK NEAR WHICH THE GROUP HAD PITCHED CAMP TO SWELL SUDDENLY AND BECOME A RAGING TORRENT. FORTUNATELY NO ONE WAS INJURED, BUT ONE PUP TENT WAS SWEPT AWAY IN THE RUSHING STREAM.

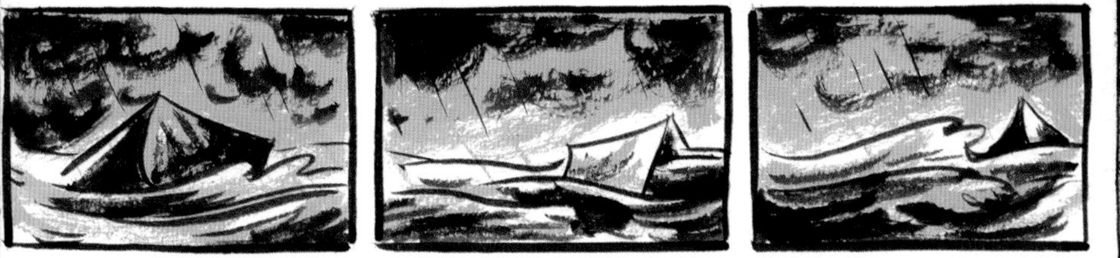

THE WATER SUBSIDED AS QUICKLY AS IT HAD RISEN AND THEIR LEADER GAVE THE ORDER TO PULL UP STAKES AND RELOCATE TO HIGHER GROUND, ONE TENT SHORT.

THAT LEFT TWO SCOUTS WITH NO SHELTER. DEVIN AND HIS TENT MATE WERE TOLD TO SHARE THEIR SPACE WITH ONE KID AND THE OTHER BUNKED ELSEWHERE.

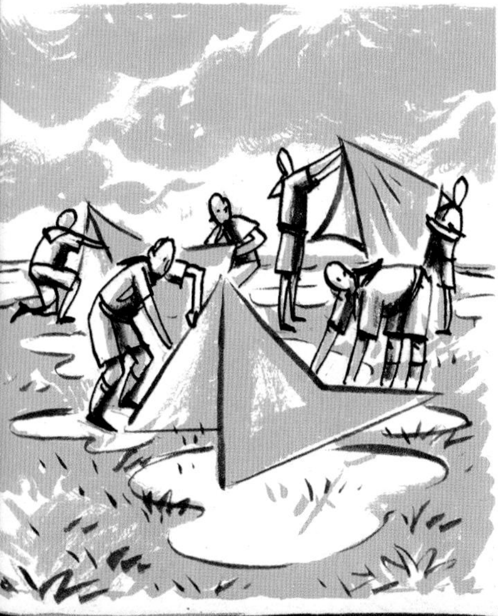

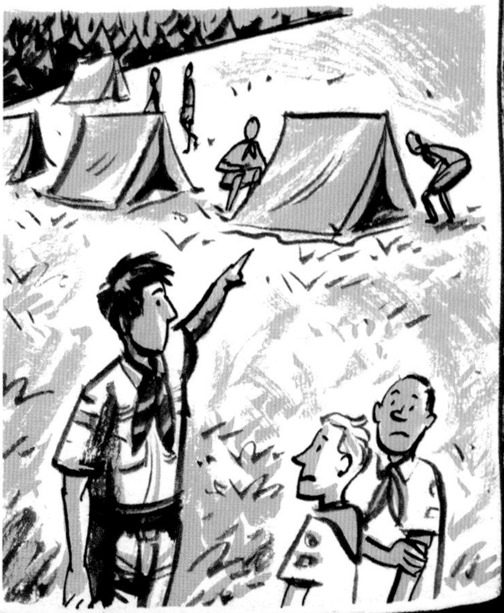

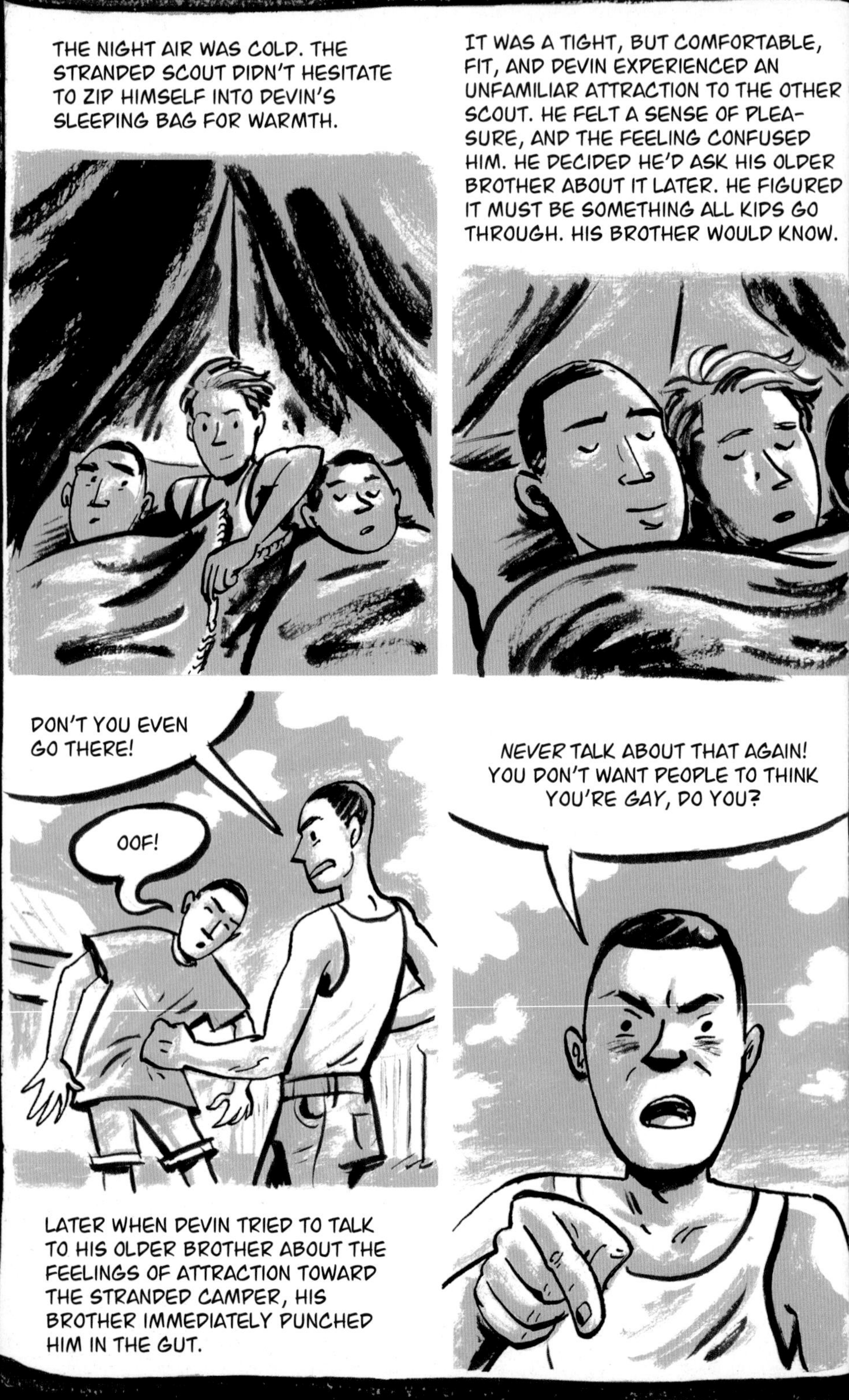
THE NIGHT AIR WAS COLD. THE STRANDED SCOUT DIDN'T HESITATE TO ZIP HIMSELF INTO DEVIN'S SLEEPING BAG FOR WARMTH.
IT WAS A TIGHT, BUT COMFORTABLE, FIT, AND DEVIN EXPERIENCED AN UNFAMILIAR ATTRACTION TO THE OTHER SCOUT. HE FELT A SENSE OF PLEASURE, AND THE FEELING CONFUSED HIM. HE DECIDED HE'D ASK HIS OLDER BROTHER ABOUT IT LATER. HE FIGURED IT MUST BE SOMETHING ALL KIDS GO THROUGH. HIS BROTHER WOULD KNOW.
DON'T YOU EVEN GO THERE!
OOF!
LATER WHEN DEVIN TRIED TO TALK TO HIS OLDER BROTHER ABOUT THE FEELINGS OF ATTRACTION TOWARD THE STRANDED CAMPER, HIS BROTHER IMMEDIATELY PUNCHED HIM IN THE GUT.
NEVER TALK ABOUT THAT AGAIN! YOU DON'T WANT PEOPLE TO THINK YOU'RE GAY, DO YOU?

CHAPTER 7
ORAL REPORTS

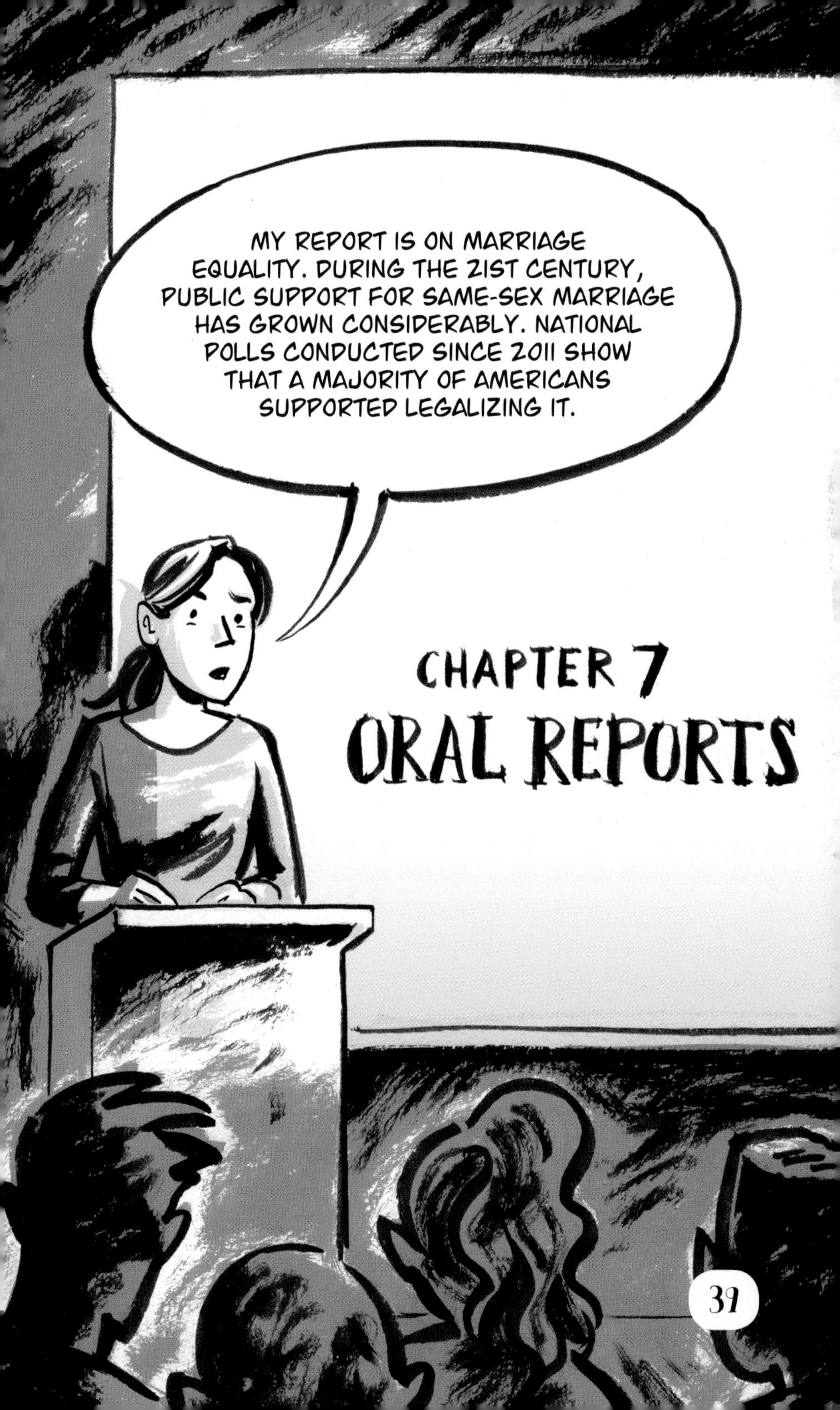

IN A CASE SIMILAR TO THE ONE IN IOWA THAT MR. TOPHER TOLD US ABOUT, MASSACHUSETTS BECAME THE FIRST U.S. STATE AND THE SIXTH JURISDICTION IN THE WORLD TO LEGALIZE SAME-SEX MARRIAGE IN 2004.
MORE THAN 10,000 SAME-SEX COUPLES MARRIED IN MASSACHUSETTS IN THE FIRST FOUR YEARS WITH ALMOST 6,100 IN THE FIRST SIX MONTHS.
THIS CONTINUED AT A RATE OF ABOUT 1,000 PER YEAR.

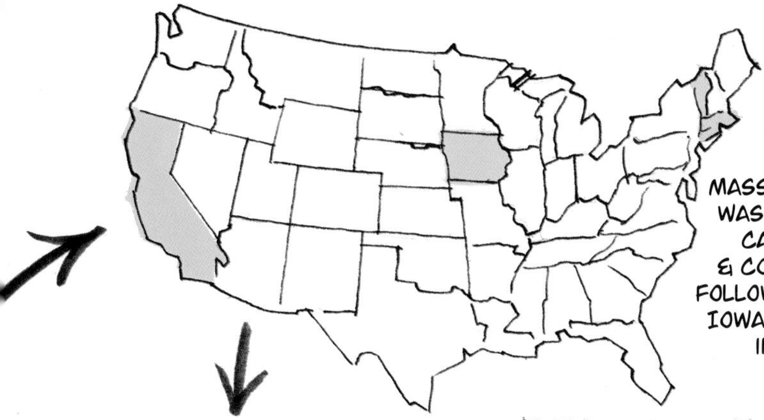

MASSACHUSETTS WAS THE FIRST. CALIFORNIA & CONNECTICUT FOLLOWED IN 2008. IOWA & VERMONT IN 2009.

IN 2012, PRESIDENT BARACK OBAMA BECAME THE FIRST U.S. PRESIDENT EVER TO PUBLICLY DECLARE SUPPORT FOR THE LEGALIZATION OF SAME-SEX MARRIAGE.

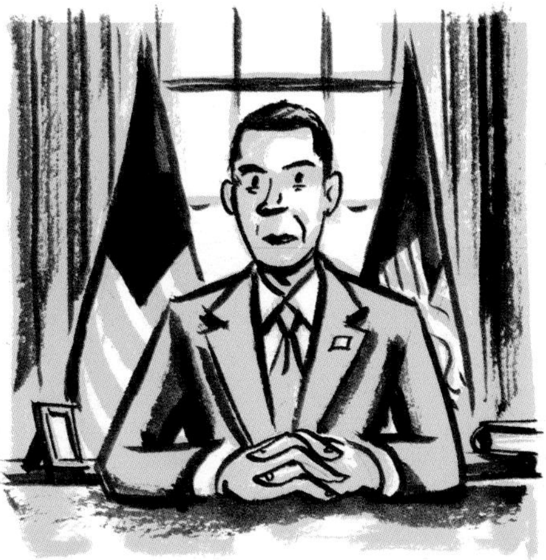

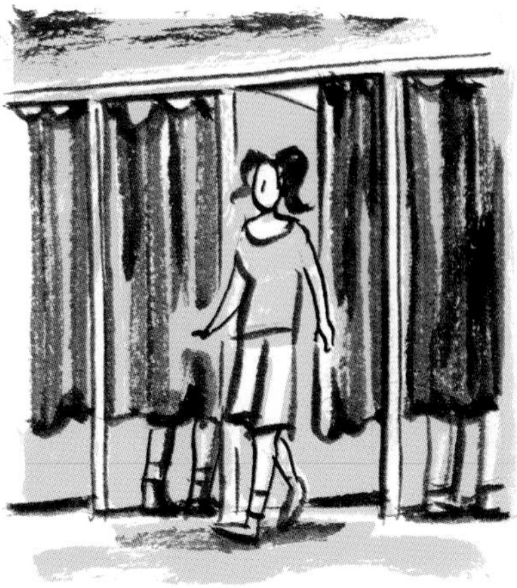

ON NOVEMBER 6, 2012, MAINE, MARYLAND, AND WASHINGTON BECAME THE FIRST STATES TO LEGALIZE SAME-SEX MARRIAGE THROUGH POPULAR VOTE.

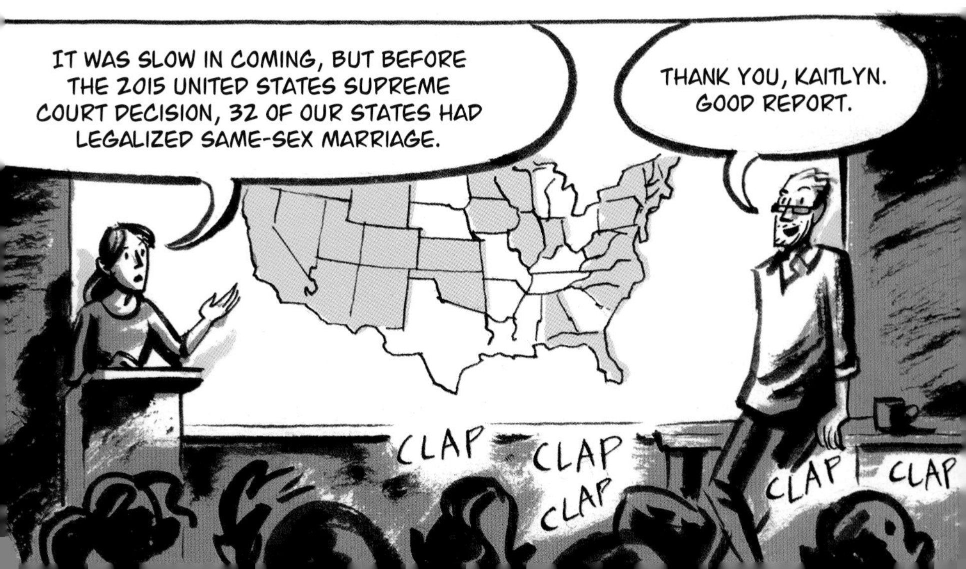
IT WAS SLOW IN COMING, BUT BEFORE THE 2015 UNITED STATES SUPREME COURT DECISION, 32 OF OUR STATES HAD LEGALIZED SAME-SEX MARRIAGE.
THANK YOU, KAITLYN. GOOD REPORT.
CLAP
CLAP
CLAP
CLAP
CLAP

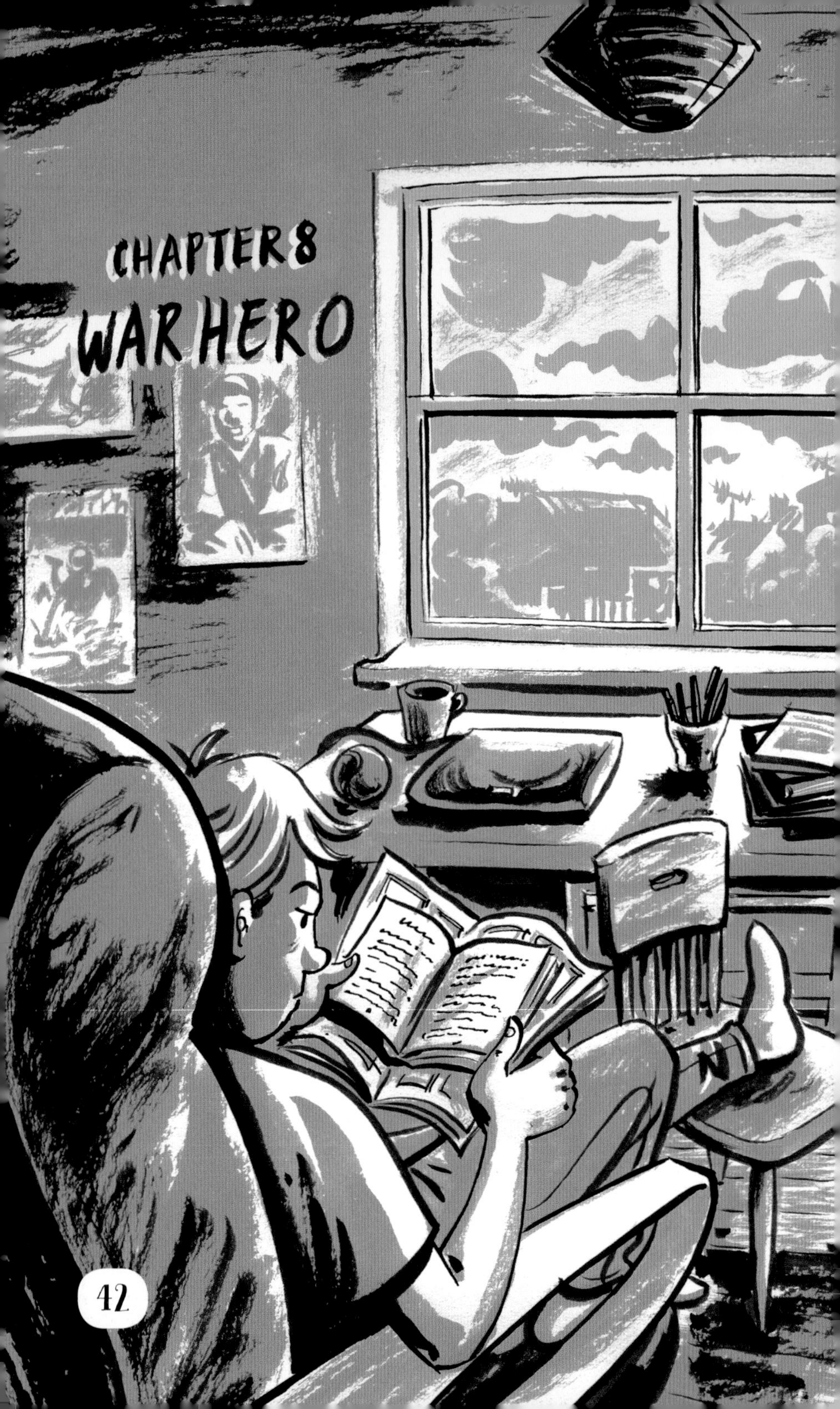
CHAPTER 8
WAR HERO

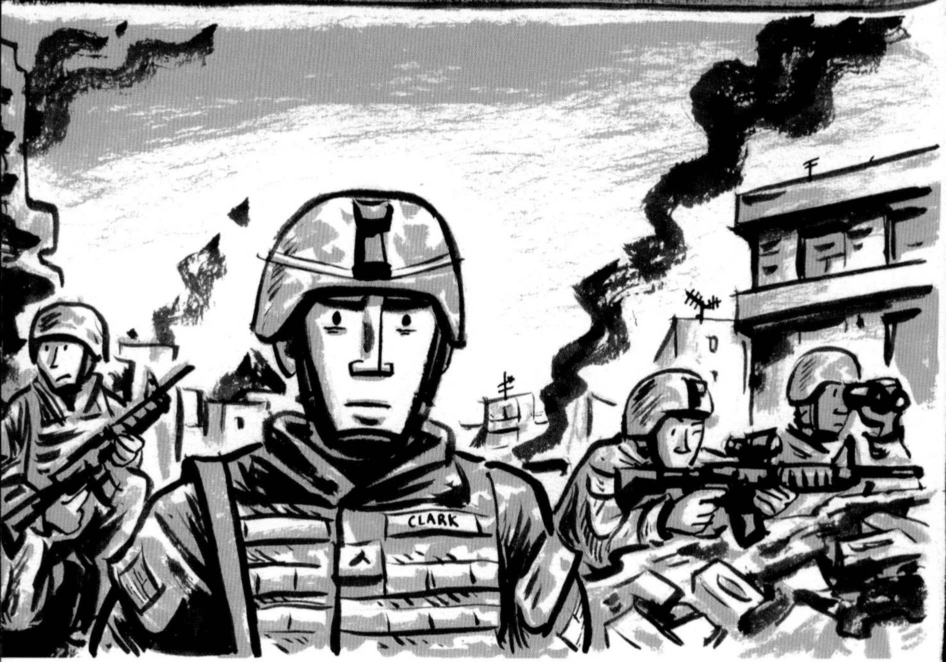
CLARK

DEVIN HEEDED HIS BROTHER'S WARNING AND NEVER MENTIONED HIS FEELINGS OF AFFECTION FOR ANOTHER MALE TO ANYONE IN HIS FAMILY EVER AGAIN.

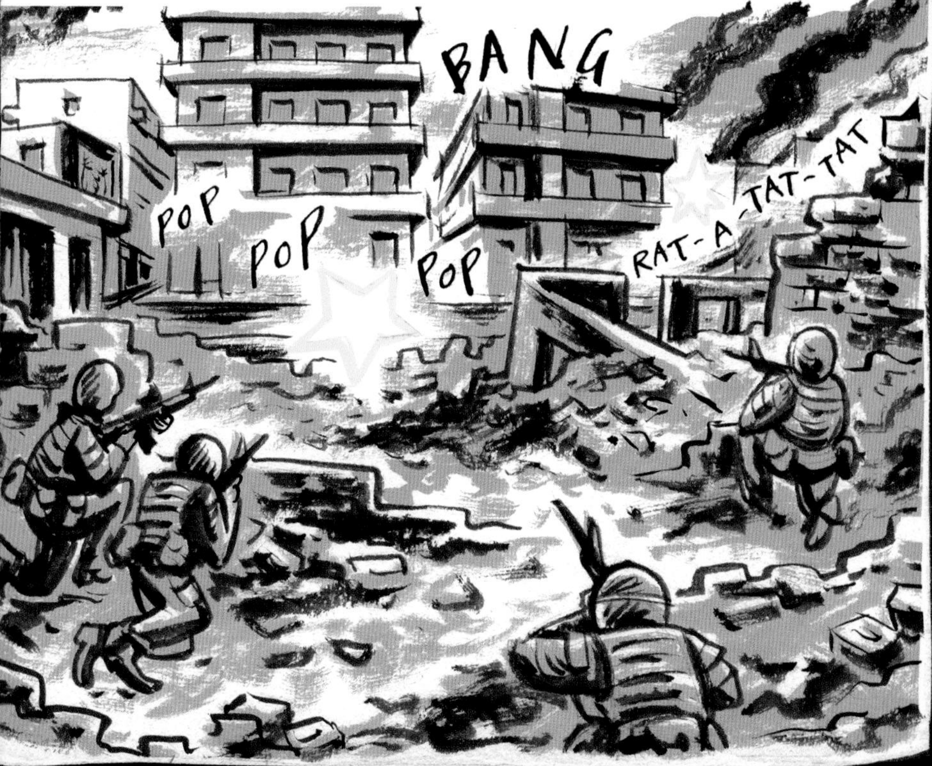
BANG
POP
POP
POP
RAT-A-TAT-TAT

WHEN A GRENADE LANDED AT THEIR FEET,
DEVIN REACTED WITHOUT HESITATION.

CLINK

FOR HIS BRAVERY IN THE LINE OF DUTY, DEVIN WA
AWARDED THE DISTINGUISHED SERVICE MEDAL.
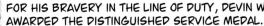

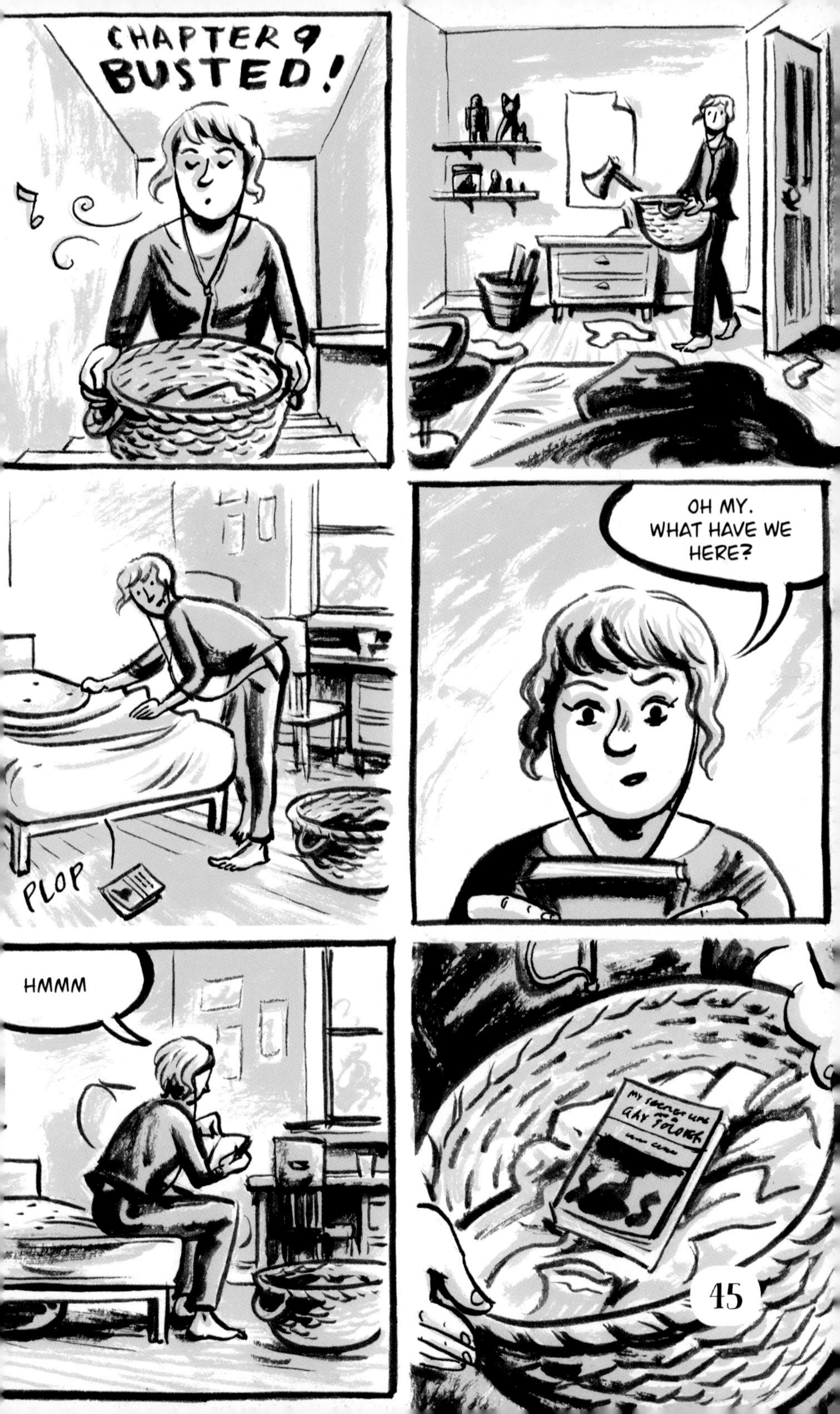
CHAPTER 9
BUSTED!
PLOP
OH MY.
WHAT HAVE WE
HERE?
HMMM

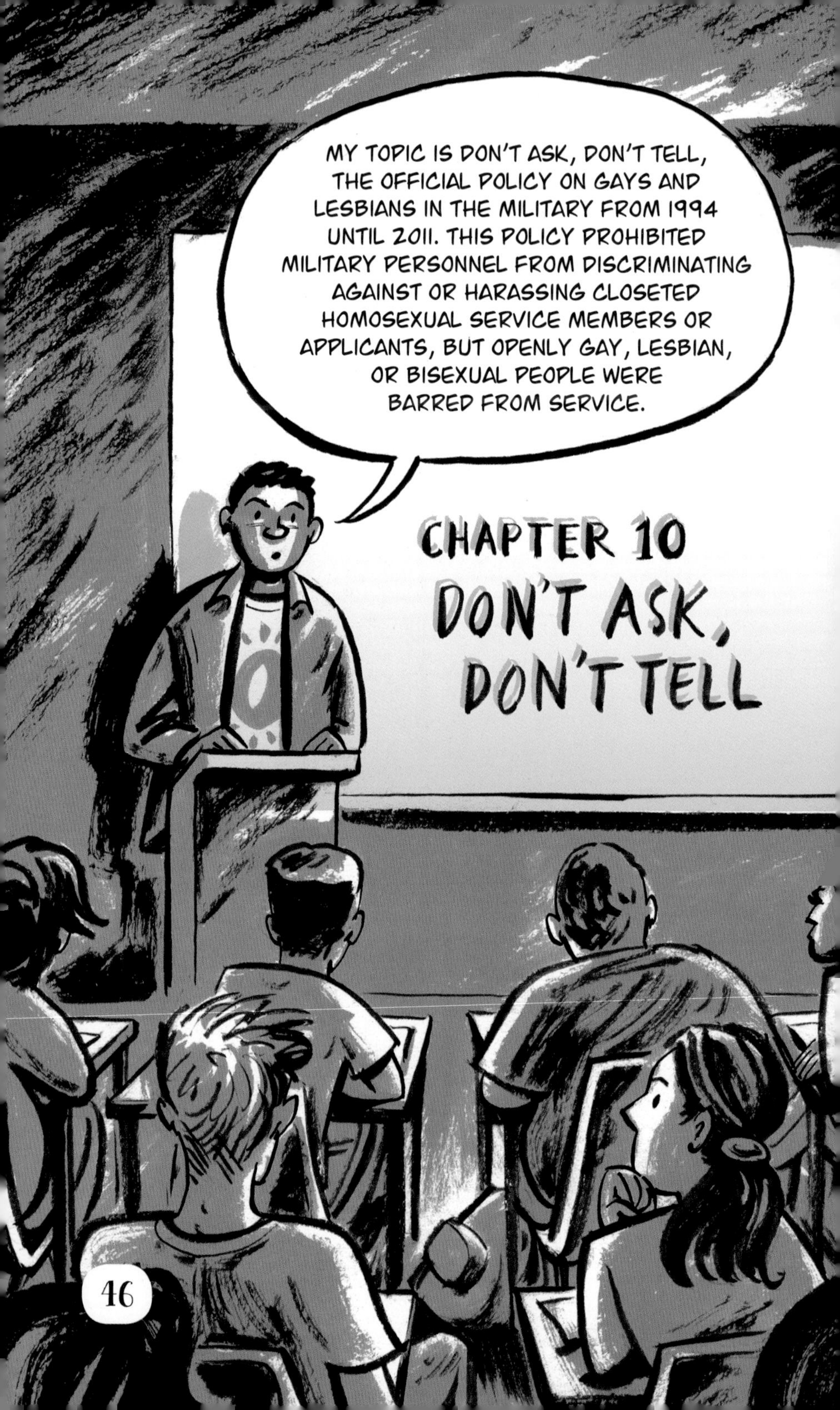
MY TOPIC IS DON'T ASK, DON'T TELL, THE OFFICIAL POLICY ON GAYS AND LESBIANS IN THE MILITARY FROM 1994 UNTIL 2011. THIS POLICY PROHIBITED MILITARY PERSONNEL FROM DISCRIMINATING AGAINST OR HARASSING CLOSETED HOMOSEXUAL SERVICE MEMBERS OR APPLICANTS, BUT OPENLY GAY, LESBIAN, OR BISEXUAL PEOPLE WERE BARRED FROM SERVICE.
CHAPTER 10
DON'T ASK, DON'T TELL

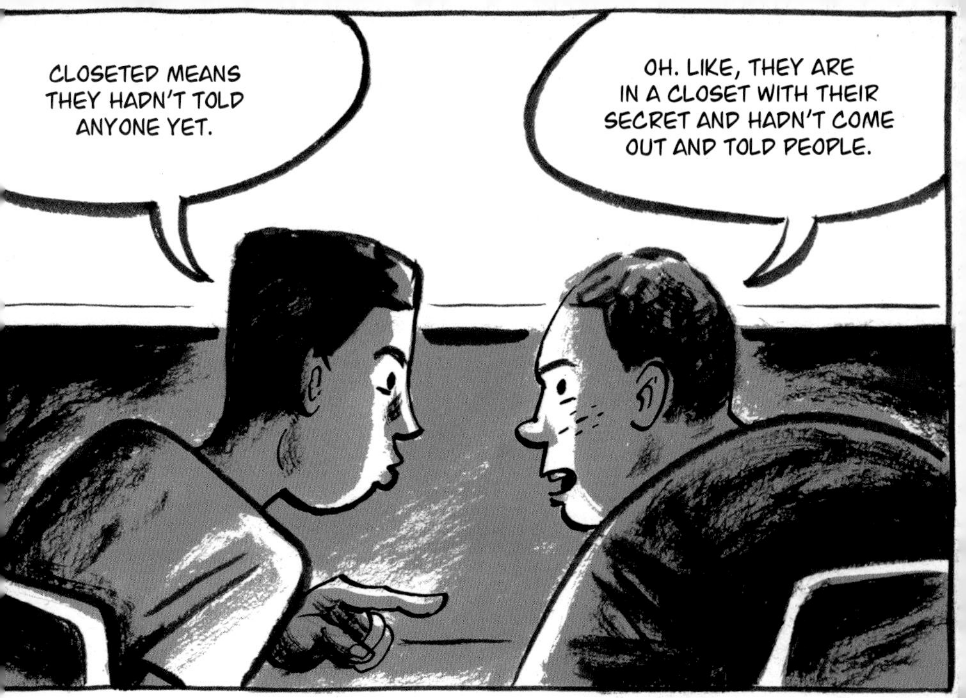
CLOSETED MEANS THEY HADN'T TOLD ANYONE YET.
OH. LIKE, THEY ARE IN A CLOSET WITH THEIR SECRET AND HADN'T COME OUT AND TOLD PEOPLE.

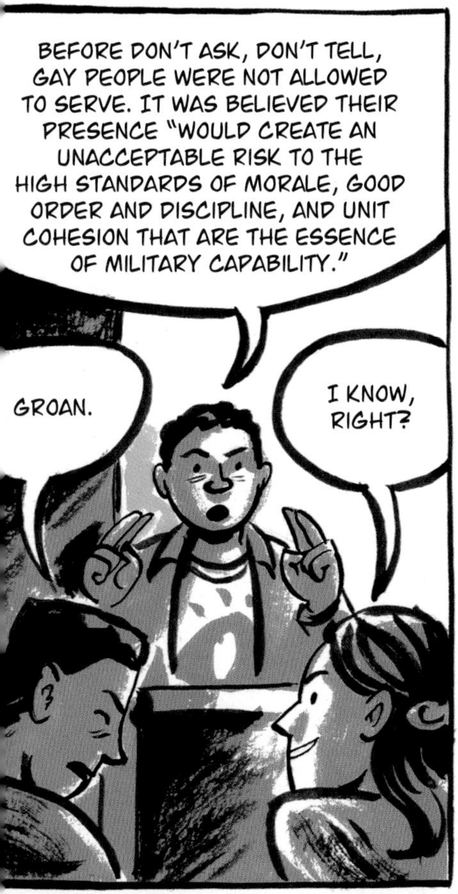
BEFORE DON'T ASK, DON'T TELL, GAY PEOPLE WERE NOT ALLOWED TO SERVE. IT WAS BELIEVED THEIR PRESENCE "WOULD CREATE AN UNACCEPTABLE RISK TO THE HIGH STANDARDS OF MORALE, GOOD ORDER AND DISCIPLINE, AND UNIT COHESION THAT ARE THE ESSENCE OF MILITARY CAPABILITY."
GROAN.
I KNOW, RIGHT?

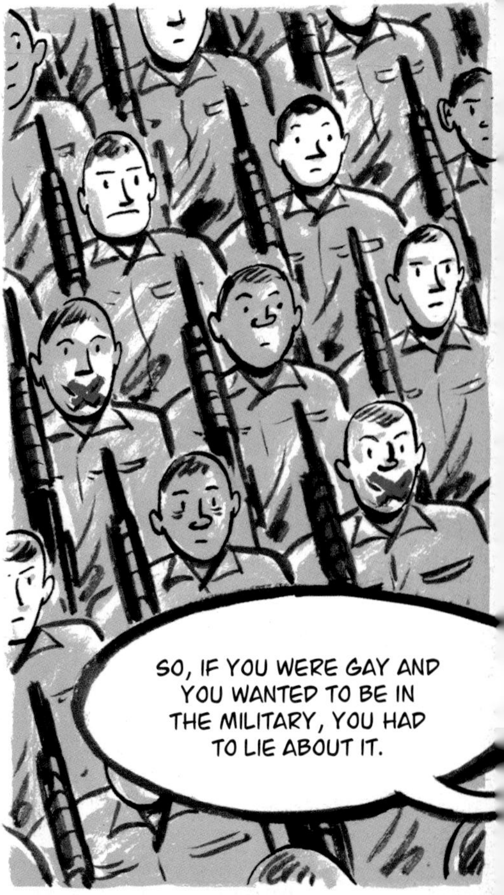
SO, IF YOU WERE GAY AND YOU WANTED TO BE IN THE MILITARY, YOU HAD TO LIE ABOUT IT.

LEGISLATION TO REPEAL DON'T ASK, DON'T TELL WAS ENACTED, AND THE POLICY ENDED SEPTEMBER 20, 2011.
WHAT WAS THE IMPACT OF THE REPEAL, PAYTON?
GAYS CAN SERVE OPENLY NOW, MR. TOPHER. PENTAGON OFFICIALS SAY THAT RECRUITING, RETENTION, AND MORALE WERE NOT AFFECTED, AND NONE OF THE TERRIBLE PREDICTIONS OCCURRED, LIKE A MASS EXODUS OF SOLDIERS OR SOMETHING. MILITARY LEADERS SAY THAT ANY FORM OF DISCRIMINATION, HATE CRIMES, HAZING, BULLYING, AND SEXUAL ASSAULTS WILL NOT BE TOLERATED.
WELL, THAT'S A GOOD THING!
AS IT SHOULD BE!
CLAP
CLAP
CLAP
CLAP
CLAP

CHAPTER 11
THE TALK

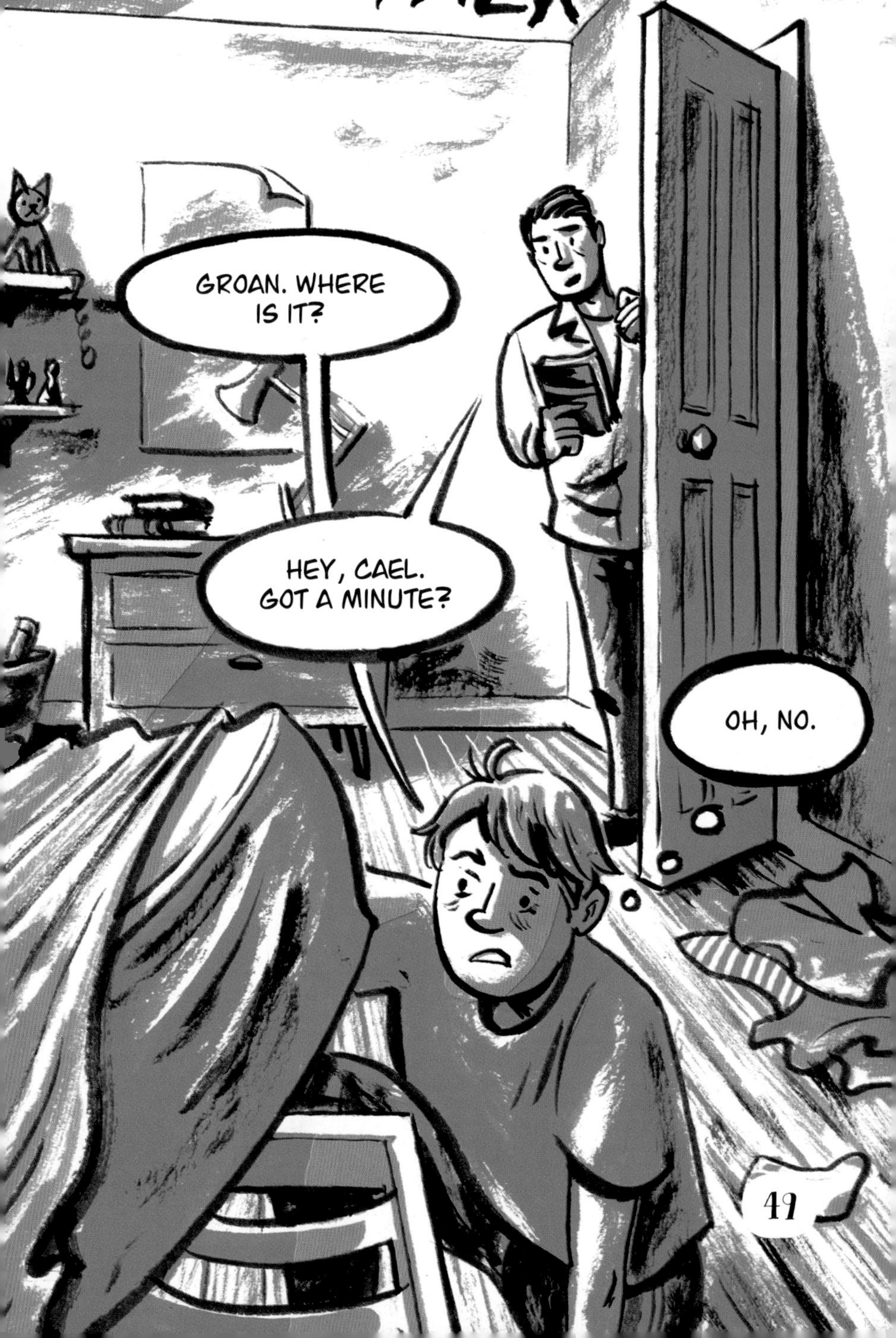
GROAN. WHERE IS IT?
HEY, CAEL. GOT A MINUTE?
OH, NO.

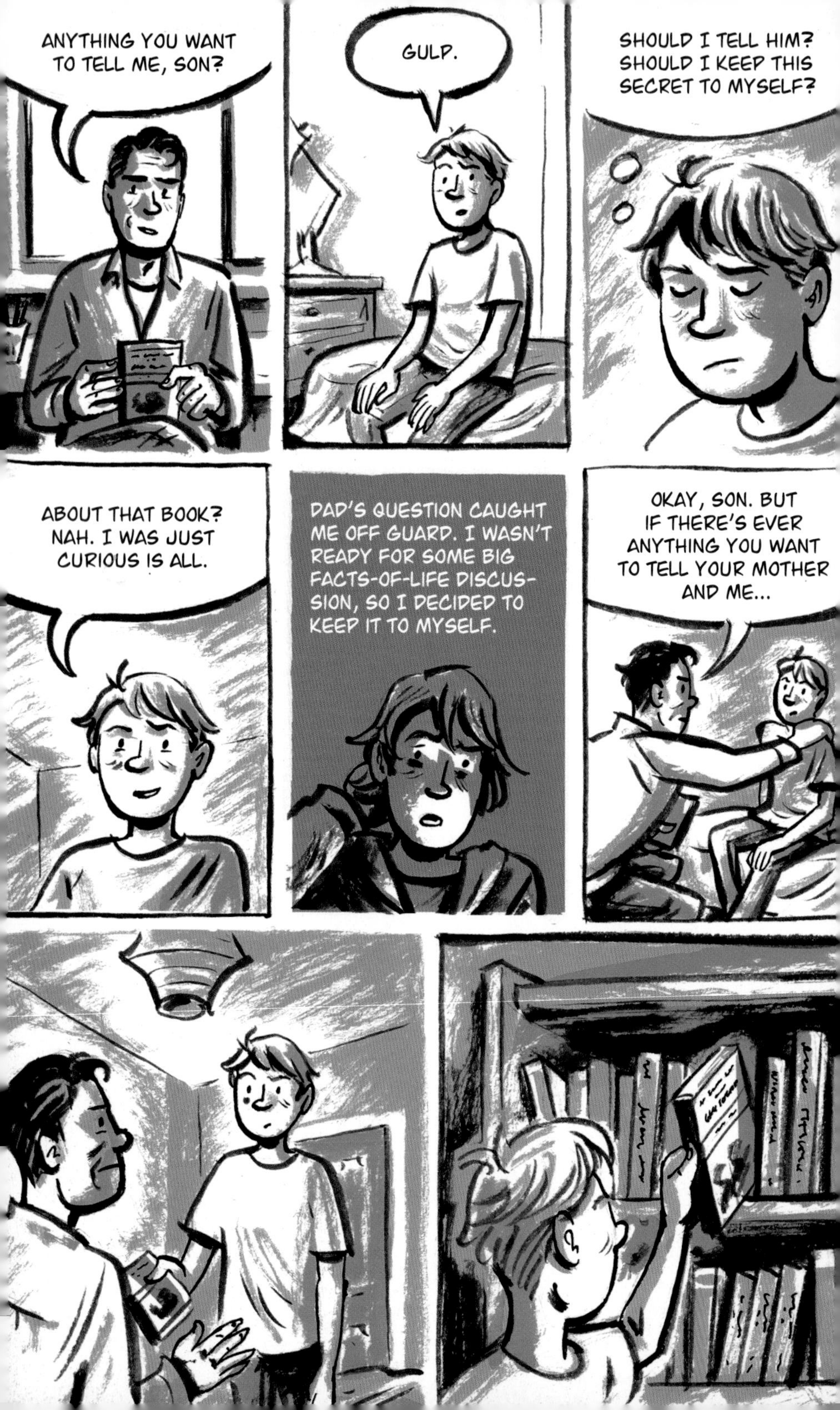
ANYTHING YOU WANT TO TELL ME, SON?
GULP.
SHOULD I TELL HIM? SHOULD I KEEP THIS SECRET TO MYSELF?
ABOUT THAT BOOK? NAH. I WAS JUST CURIOUS IS ALL.
DAD'S QUESTION CAUGHT ME OFF GUARD. I WASN'T READY FOR SOME BIG FACTS-OF-LIFE DISCUSSION, SO I DECIDED TO KEEP IT TO MYSELF.
OKAY, SON. BUT IF THERE'S EVER ANYTHING YOU WANT TO TELL YOUR MOTHER AND ME...

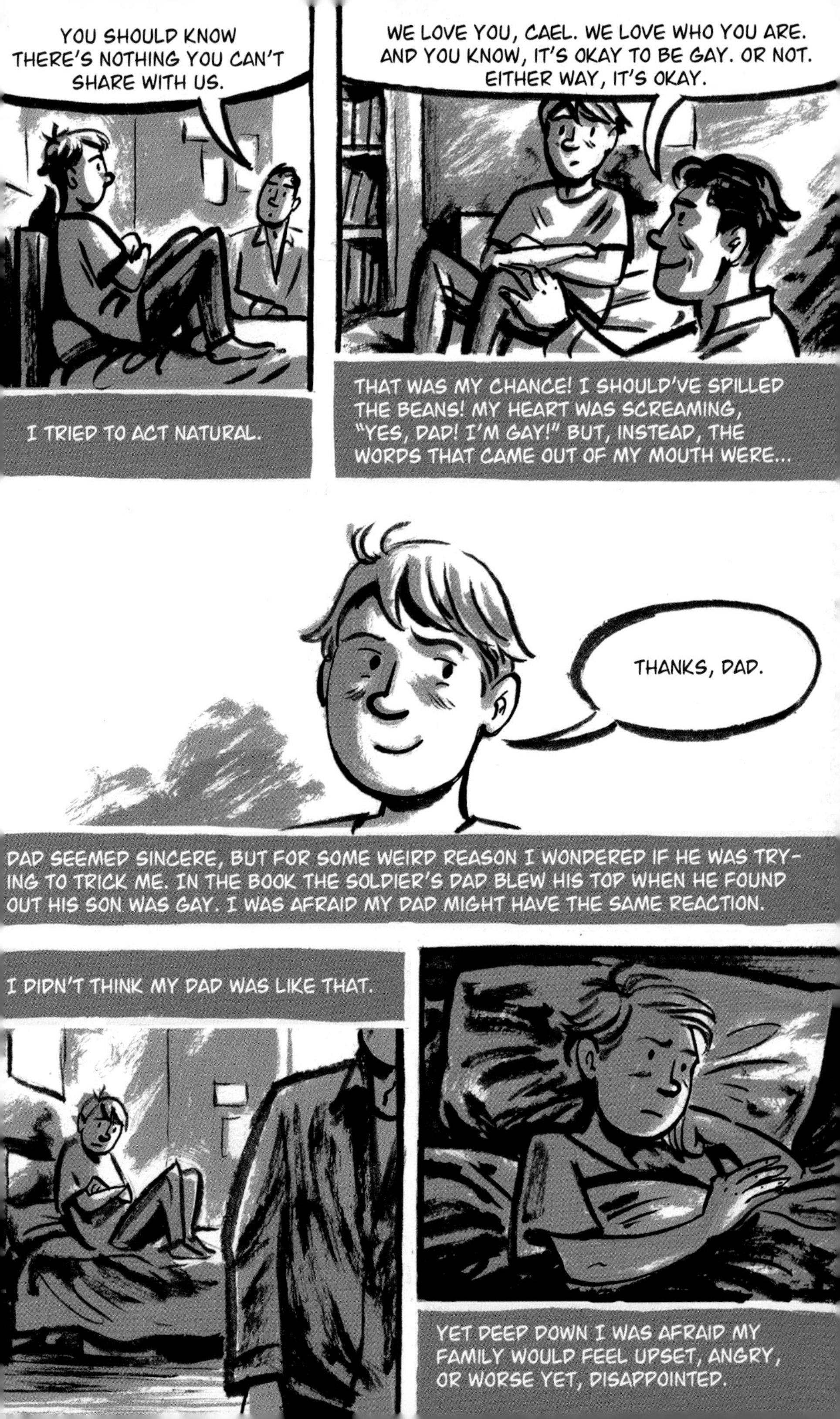
YOU SHOULD KNOW THERE'S NOTHING YOU CAN'T SHARE WITH US.
I TRIED TO ACT NATURAL.
WE LOVE YOU, CAEL. WE LOVE WHO YOU ARE. AND YOU KNOW, IT'S OKAY TO BE GAY. OR NOT. EITHER WAY, IT'S OKAY.
THAT WAS MY CHANCE! I SHOULD'VE SPILLED THE BEANS! MY HEART WAS SCREAMING, "YES, DAD! I'M GAY!" BUT, INSTEAD, THE WORDS THAT CAME OUT OF MY MOUTH WERE...
THANKS, DAD.
DAD SEEMED SINCERE, BUT FOR SOME WEIRD REASON I WONDERED IF HE WAS TRYING TO TRICK ME. IN THE BOOK THE SOLDIER'S DAD BLEW HIS TOP WHEN HE FOUND OUT HIS SON WAS GAY. I WAS AFRAID MY DAD MIGHT HAVE THE SAME REACTION.
I DIDN'T THINK MY DAD WAS LIKE THAT.
YET DEEP DOWN I WAS AFRAID MY FAMILY WOULD FEEL UPSET, ANGRY, OR WORSE YET, DISAPPOINTED.

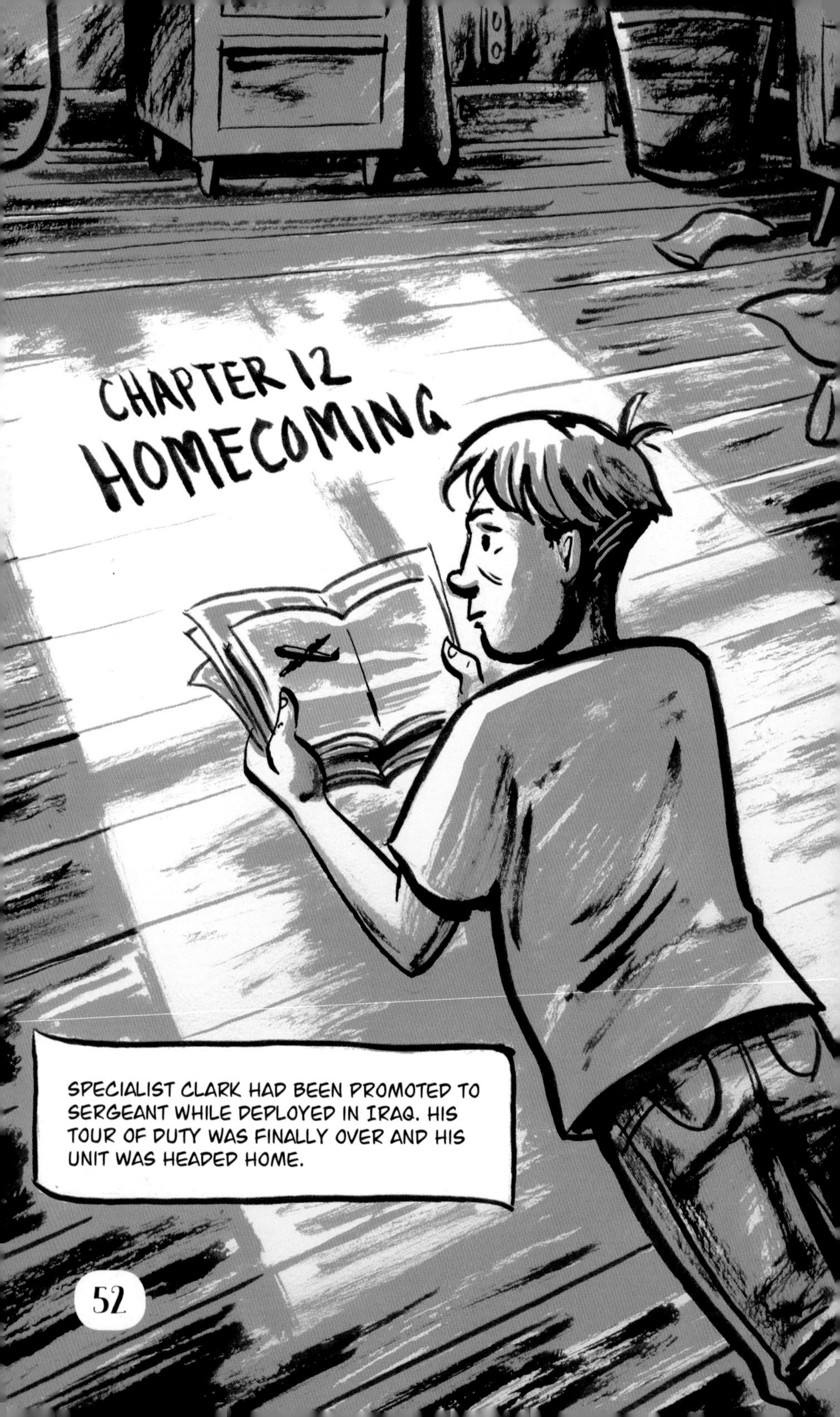
CHAPTER 12
HOMECOMING
SPECIALIST CLARK HAD BEEN PROMOTED TO SERGEANT WHILE DEPLOYED IN IRAQ. HIS TOUR OF DUTY WAS FINALLY OVER AND HIS UNIT WAS HEADED HOME.

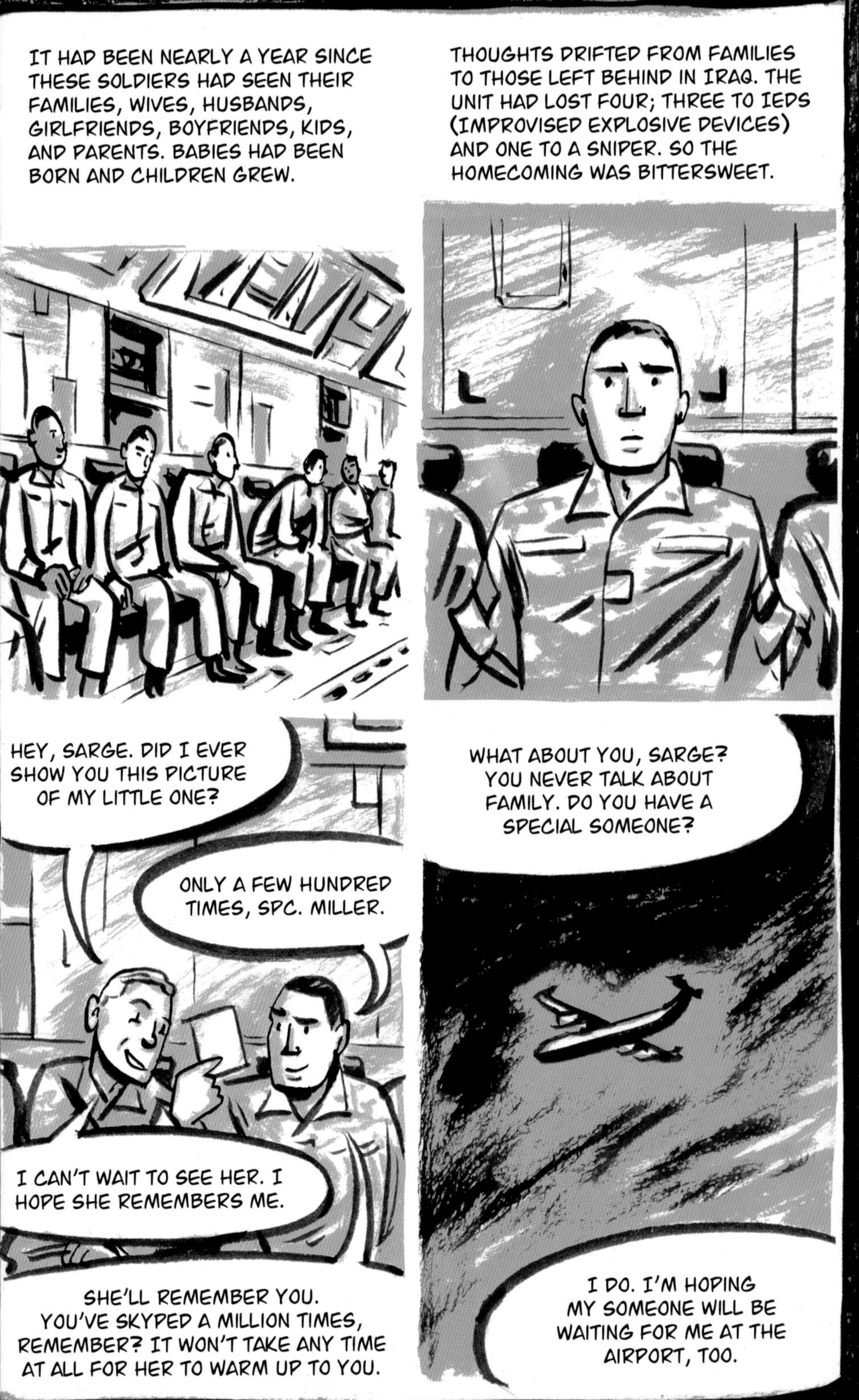
IT HAD BEEN NEARLY A YEAR SINCE THESE SOLDIERS HAD SEEN THEIR FAMILIES, WIVES, HUSBANDS, GIRLFRIENDS, BOYFRIENDS, KIDS, AND PARENTS. BABIES HAD BEEN BORN AND CHILDREN GREW.
THOUGHTS DRIFTED FROM FAMILIES TO THOSE LEFT BEHIND IN IRAQ. THE UNIT HAD LOST FOUR; THREE TO IEDS (IMPROVISED EXPLOSIVE DEVICES) AND ONE TO A SNIPER. SO THE HOMECOMING WAS BITTERSWEET.
HEY, SARGE. DID I EVER SHOW YOU THIS PICTURE OF MY LITTLE ONE?
ONLY A FEW HUNDRED TIMES, SPC. MILLER.
I CAN'T WAIT TO SEE HER. I HOPE SHE REMEMBERS ME.
SHE'LL REMEMBER YOU. YOU'VE SKYPED A MILLION TIMES, REMEMBER? IT WON'T TAKE ANY TIME AT ALL FOR HER TO WARM UP TO YOU.
WHAT ABOUT YOU, SARGE? YOU NEVER TALK ABOUT FAMILY. DO YOU HAVE A SPECIAL SOMEONE?
I DO. I'M HOPING MY SOMEONE WILL BE WAITING FOR ME AT THE AIRPORT, TOO.

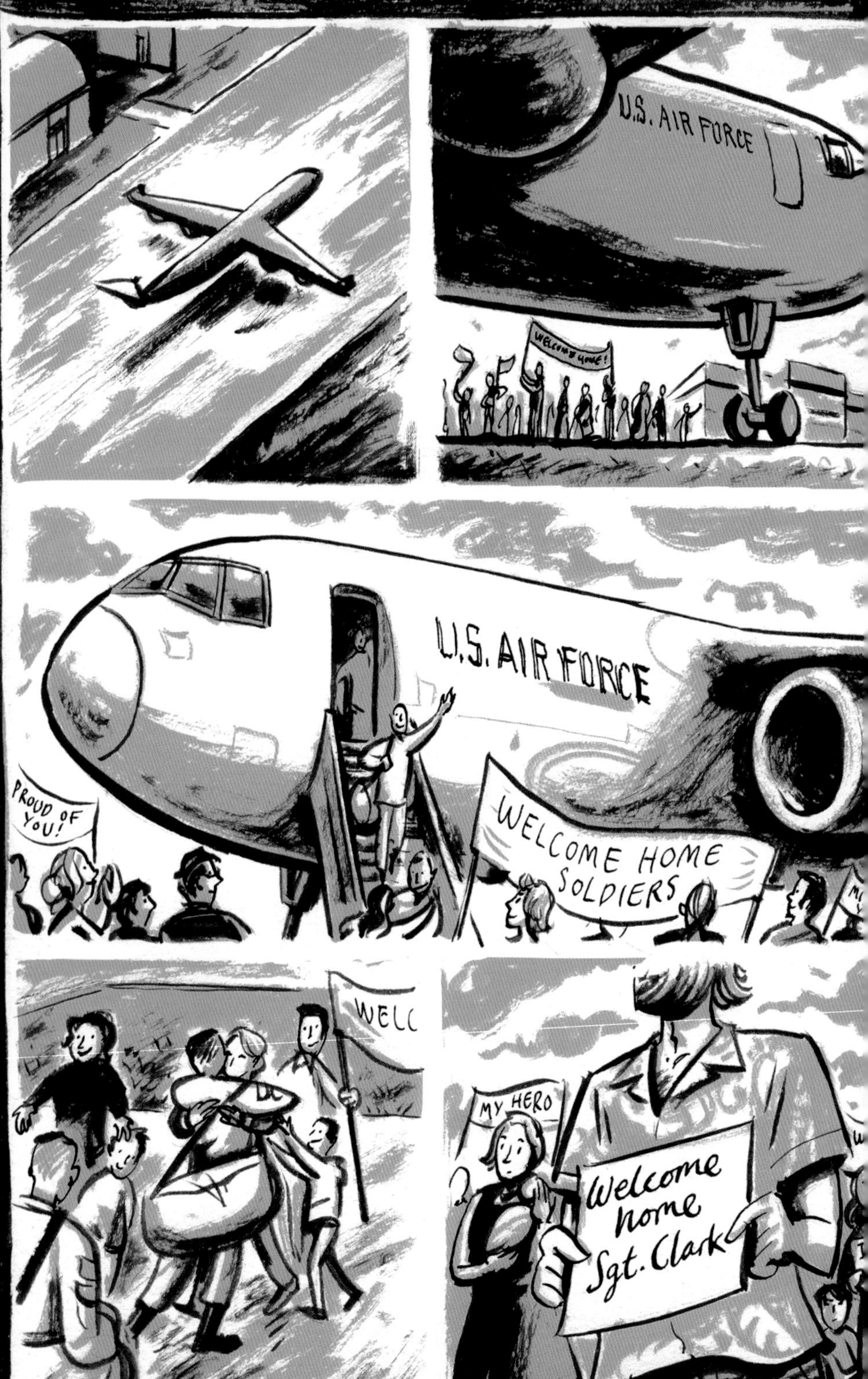
U.S. AIR FORCE
WELCOME HOME!
U.S. AIR FORCE
PROUD OF YOU!
WELCOME HOME SOLDIERS
WELC
MY HERO
Welcome home Sgt. Clark

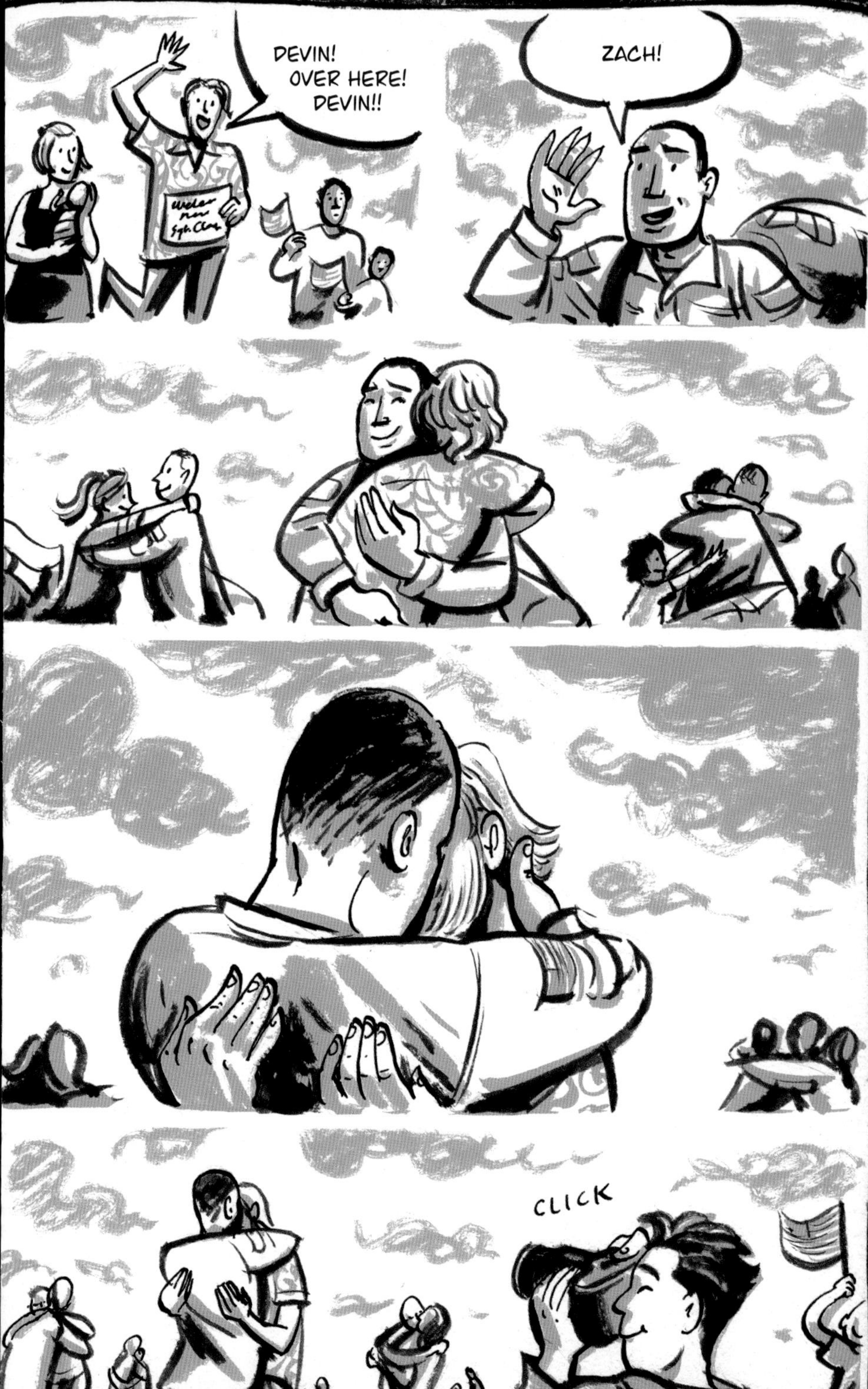
DEVIN! OVER HERE! DEVIN!!
ZACH!
CLICK

MY REPORT IS ON DOMA, THE DEFENSE OF MARRIAGE ACT. DOMA WAS INTRODUCED IN MAY 1996, PASSED BOTH HOUSES OF CONGRESS BY LARGE, VETO-PROOF MAJORITIES AND WAS SIGNED INTO LAW BY PRESIDENT BILL CLINTON IN SEPTEMBER.

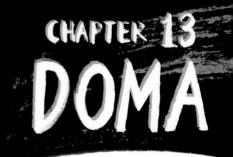

CHAPTER 13
DOMA

THIS IS A FEDERAL LAW THAT ALLOWED STATES TO REFUSE TO RECOGNIZE SAME-SEX MARRIAGES GRANTED UNDER THE LAWS OF OTHER STATES. IT ALSO BARRED SAME-SEX MARRIED COUPLES FROM BEING RECOGNIZED AS SPOUSES FOR PURPOSES OF FEDERAL LAWS, PREVENTING THEM FROM RECEIVING FEDERAL MARRIAGE BENEFITS. OVER A THOUSAND RIGHTS AND BENEFITS WERE AFFECTED BY THIS LAW.

NO! FILING JOINT FEDERAL TAX RETURNS
NO! SOCIAL SECURITY BENEFITS
NO! VETERANS' BENEFITS
NO! HEALTH INSURANCE
NO! HOSPITAL VISITATIONS
NO! ESTATE TAXES
NO! RETIREMENT SAVINGS
NO! PENSIONS
NO! FAMILY MEDICAL LEAVE
NO! IMMIGRATION LAWS
NO! MILITARY BENEFITS
NO! EMPLOYMENT BENEFITS
NO! BANKRUPTCIES
NO! PRISON VISITS
NO! SURVIVOR BENEFITS
NO! REFUSING TO TESTIFY AGAINST A SPOUSE
& 1,000 MORE!!!

WHEW! THAT'S QUITE A LIST.

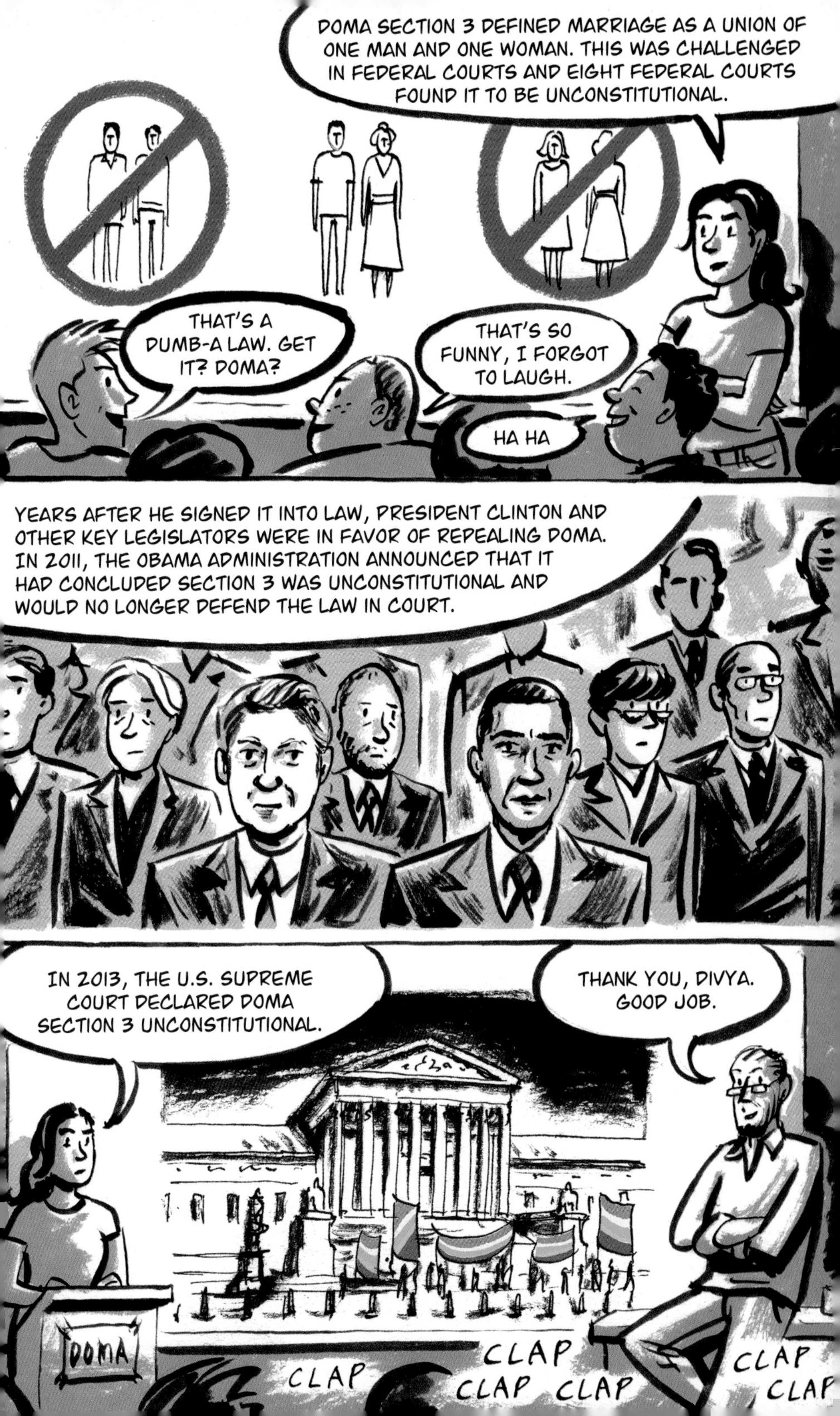
DOMA SECTION 3 DEFINED MARRIAGE AS A UNION OF ONE MAN AND ONE WOMAN. THIS WAS CHALLENGED IN FEDERAL COURTS AND EIGHT FEDERAL COURTS FOUND IT TO BE UNCONSTITUTIONAL.
THAT'S A DUMB-A LAW. GET IT? DOMA?
THAT'S SO FUNNY, I FORGOT TO LAUGH.
HA HA
YEARS AFTER HE SIGNED IT INTO LAW, PRESIDENT CLINTON AND OTHER KEY LEGISLATORS WERE IN FAVOR OF REPEALING DOMA. IN 2011, THE OBAMA ADMINISTRATION ANNOUNCED THAT IT HAD CONCLUDED SECTION 3 WAS UNCONSTITUTIONAL AND WOULD NO LONGER DEFEND THE LAW IN COURT.
IN 2013, THE U.S. SUPREME COURT DECLARED DOMA SECTION 3 UNCONSTITUTIONAL.
THANK YOU, DIVYA. GOOD JOB.
DOMA
CLAP
CLAP
CLAP CLAP
CLAP
CLAP

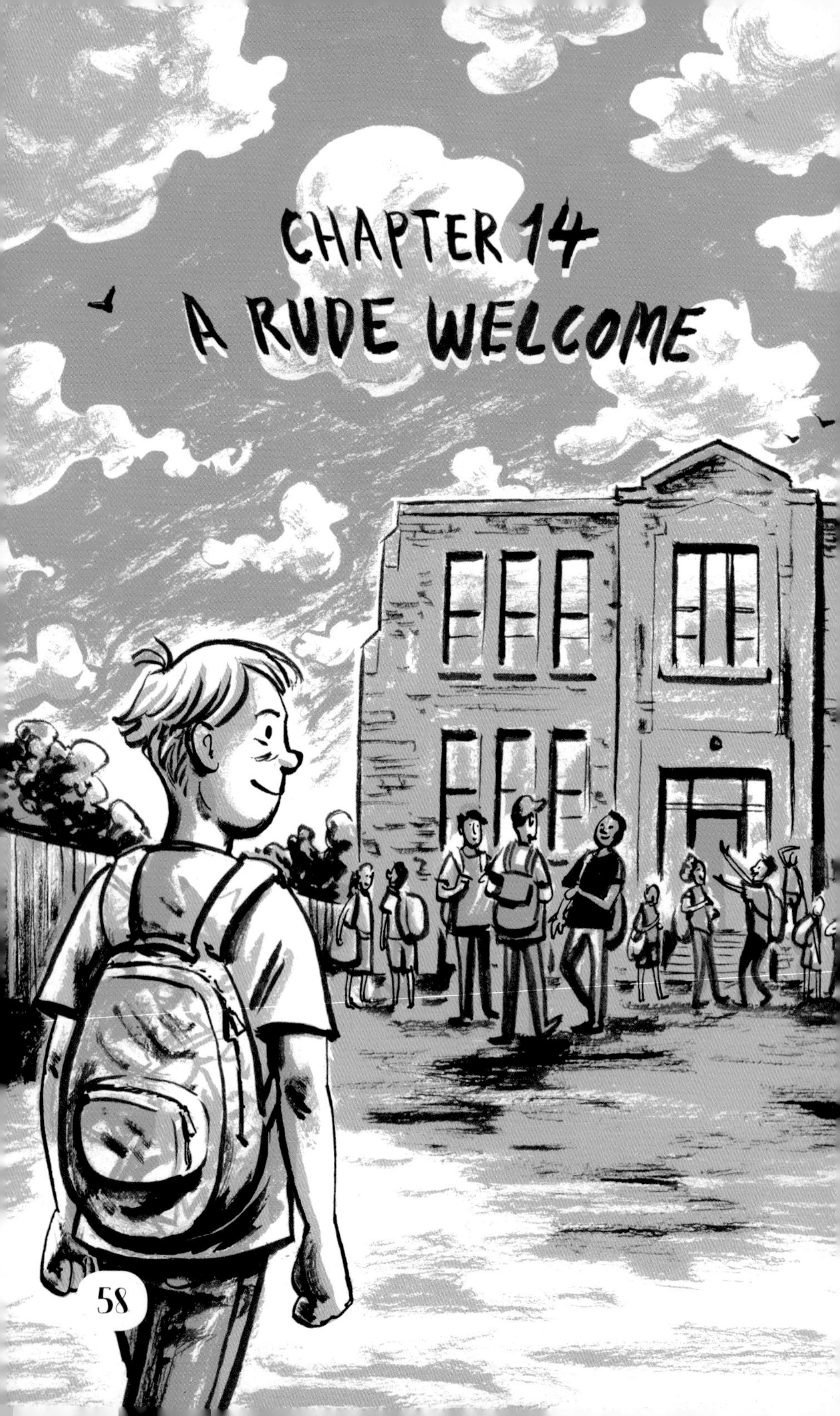
CHAPTER 14
A RUDE WELCOME

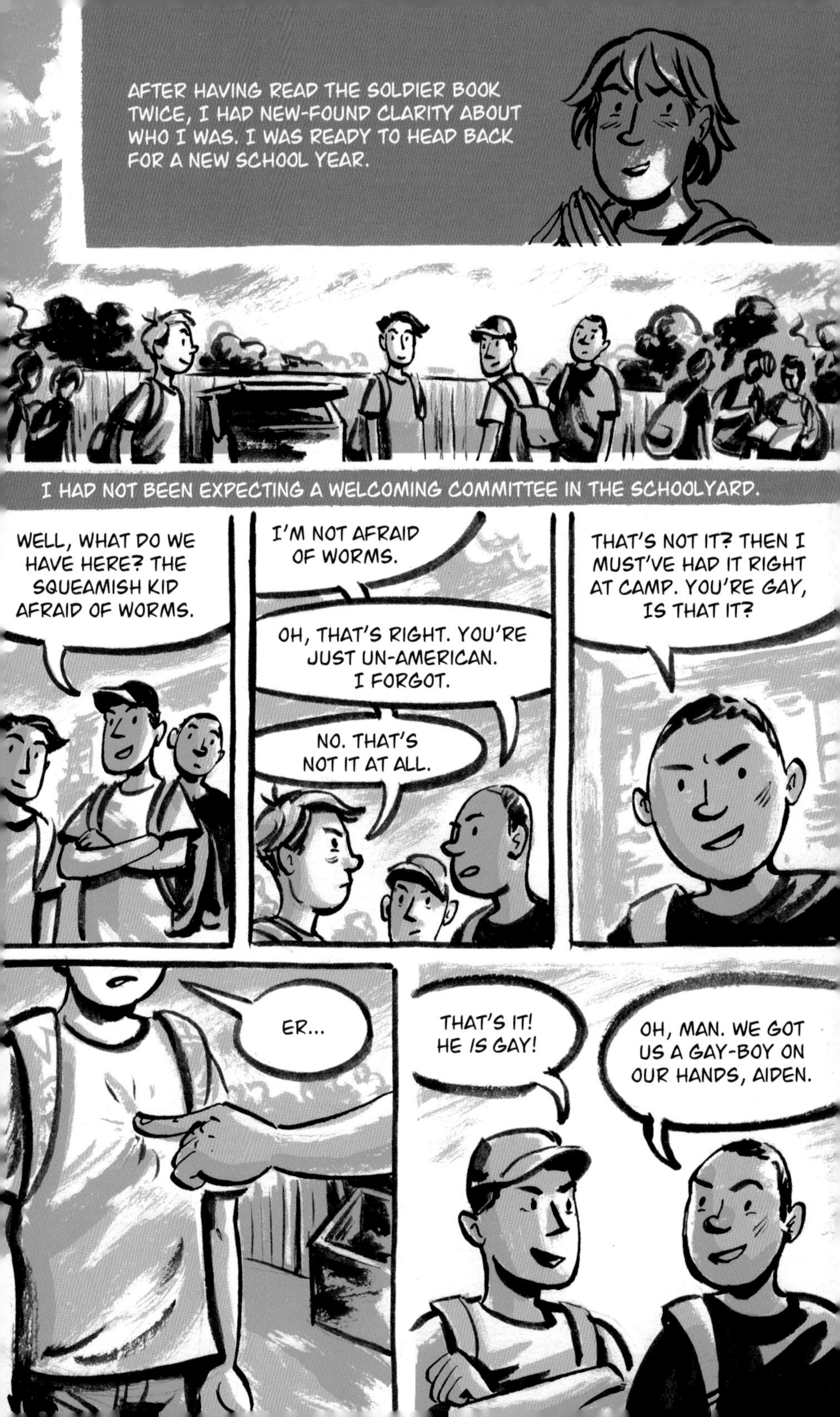
AFTER HAVING READ THE SOLDIER BOOK TWICE, I HAD NEW-FOUND CLARITY ABOUT WHO I WAS. I WAS READY TO HEAD BACK FOR A NEW SCHOOL YEAR.
I HAD NOT BEEN EXPECTING A WELCOMING COMMITTEE IN THE SCHOOLYARD.
WELL, WHAT DO WE HAVE HERE? THE SQUEAMISH KID AFRAID OF WORMS.
I'M NOT AFRAID OF WORMS.
OH, THAT'S RIGHT. YOU'RE JUST UN-AMERICAN. I FORGOT.
NO. THAT'S NOT IT AT ALL.
THAT'S NOT IT? THEN I MUST'VE HAD IT RIGHT AT CAMP. YOU'RE GAY, IS THAT IT?
ER...
THAT'S IT! HE *IS* GAY!
OH, MAN. WE GOT US A GAY-BOY ON OUR HANDS, AIDEN.

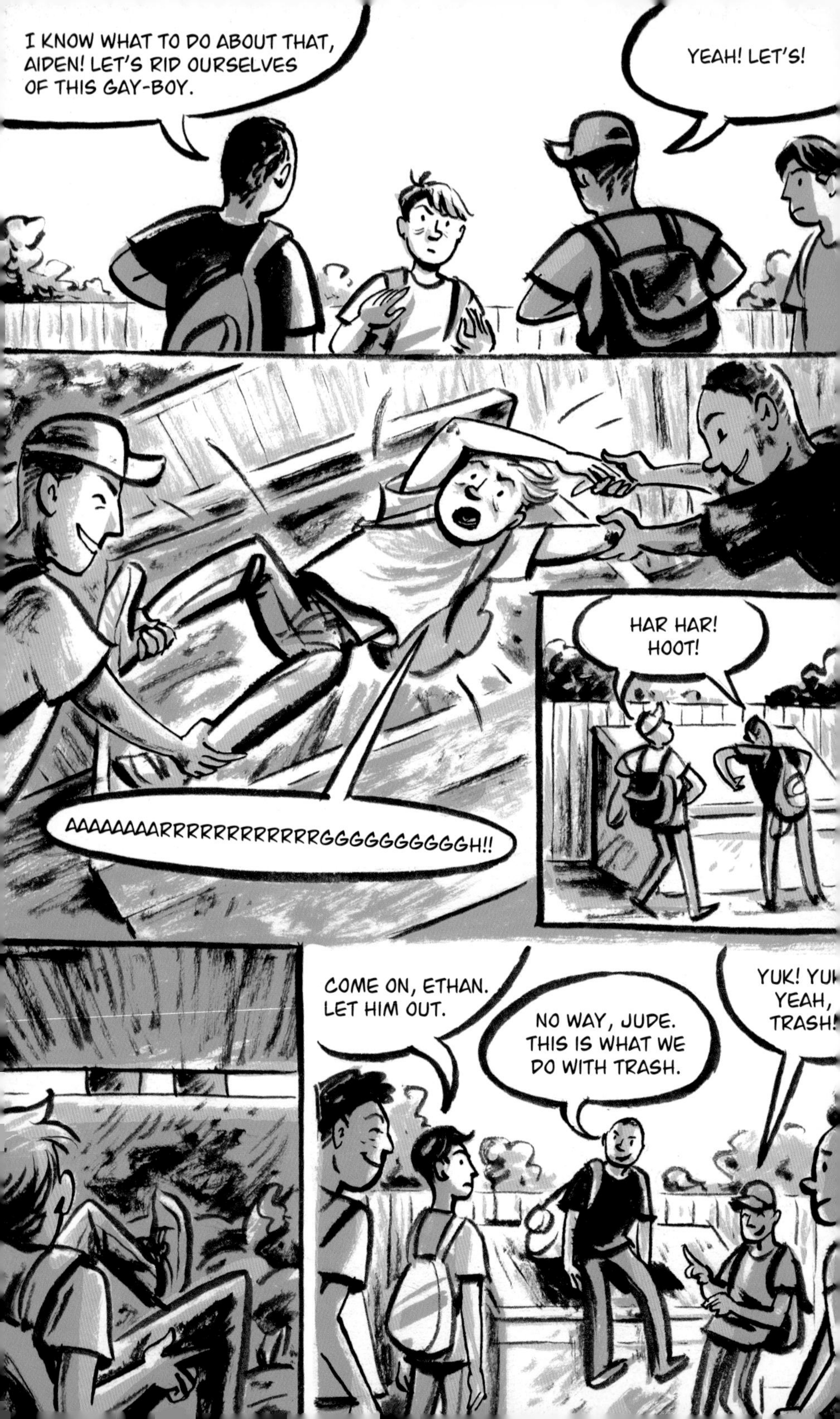
I KNOW WHAT TO DO ABOUT THAT, AIDEN! LET'S RID OURSELVES OF THIS GAY-BOY.
YEAH! LET'S!
AAAAAAAARRRRRRRRRRRGGGGGGGGGGH!!
HAR HAR! HOOT!
COME ON, ETHAN. LET HIM OUT.
NO WAY, JUDE. THIS IS WHAT WE DO WITH TRASH.
YUK! YU
YEAH,
TRASH!

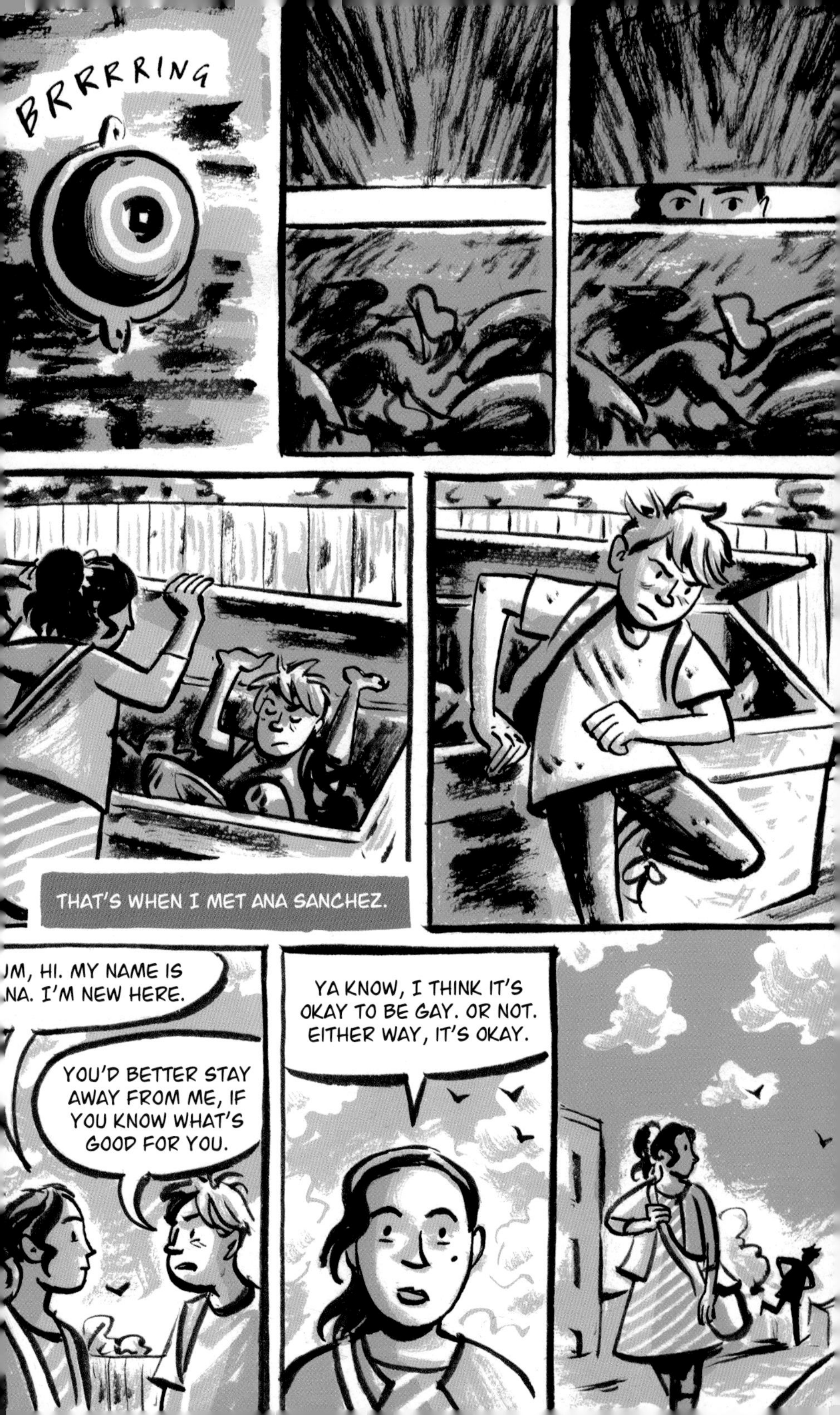
BRRRRING
THAT'S WHEN I MET ANA SANCHEZ.
UM, HI. MY NAME IS ANA. I'M NEW HERE.
YOU'D BETTER STAY AWAY FROM ME, IF YOU KNOW WHAT'S GOOD FOR YOU.
YA KNOW, I THINK IT'S OKAY TO BE GAY. OR NOT. EITHER WAY, IT'S OKAY.

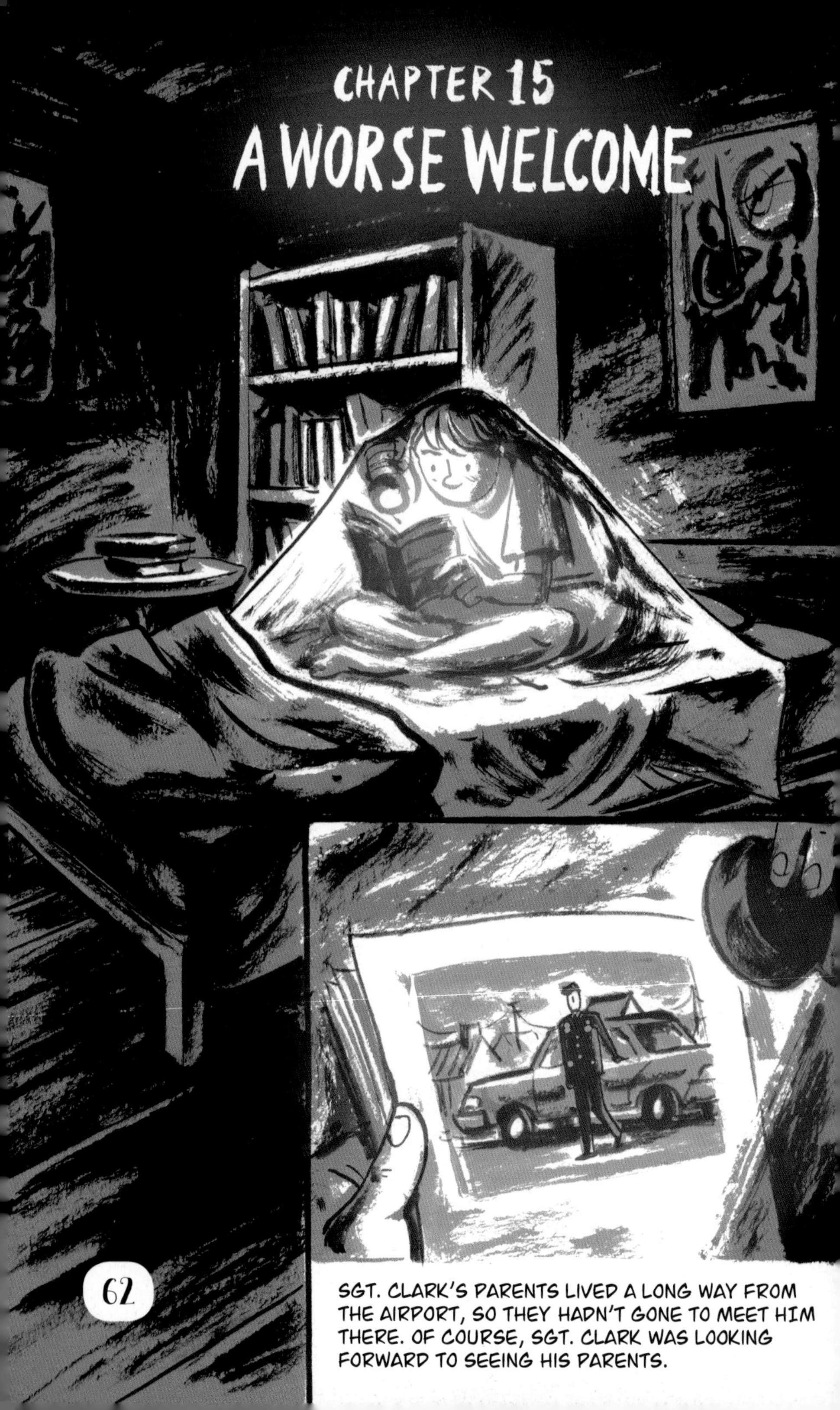
CHAPTER 15
A WORSE WELCOME
SGT. CLARK'S PARENTS LIVED A LONG WAY FROM THE AIRPORT, SO THEY HADN'T GONE TO MEET HIM THERE. OF COURSE, SGT. CLARK WAS LOOKING FORWARD TO SEEING HIS PARENTS.

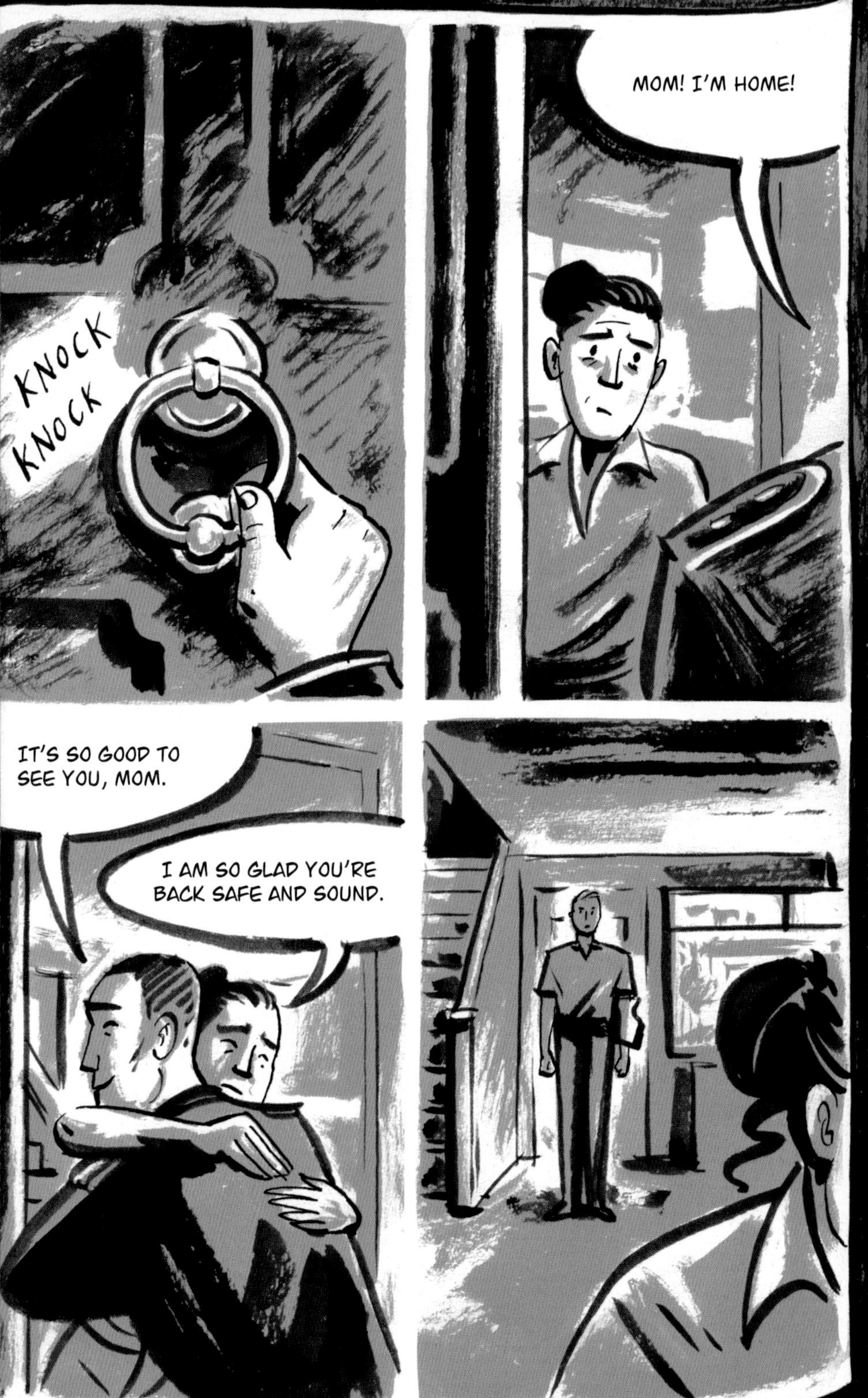
KNOCK
KNOCK
MOM! I'M HOME!
IT'S SO GOOD TO SEE YOU, MOM.
I AM SO GLAD YOU'RE BACK SAFE AND SOUND.

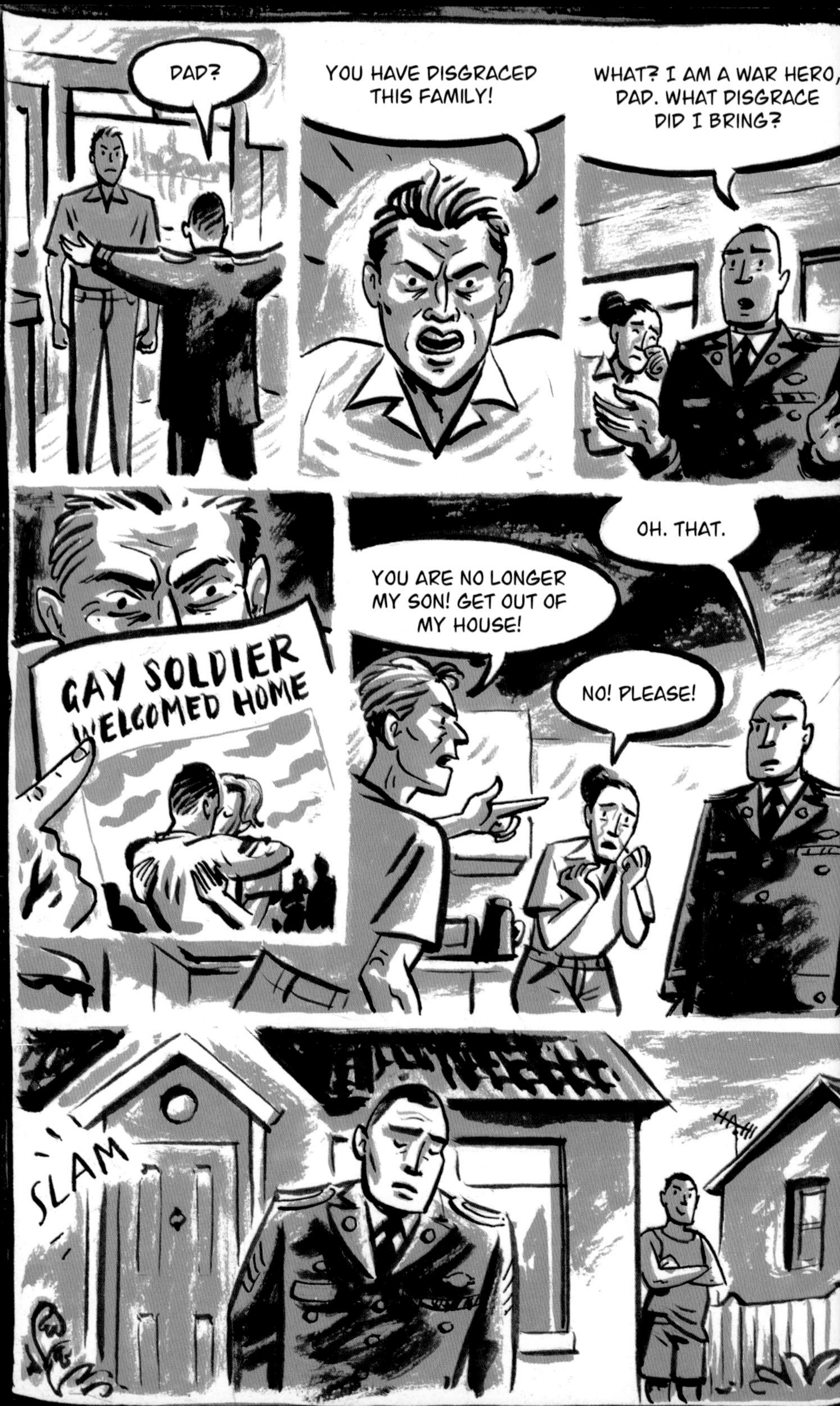
DAD?
YOU HAVE DISGRACED THIS FAMILY!
WHAT? I AM A WAR HERO, DAD. WHAT DISGRACE DID I BRING?
GAY SOLDIER WELCOMED HOME
OH. THAT.
YOU ARE NO LONGER MY SON! GET OUT OF MY HOUSE!
NO! PLEASE!
SLAM
HA

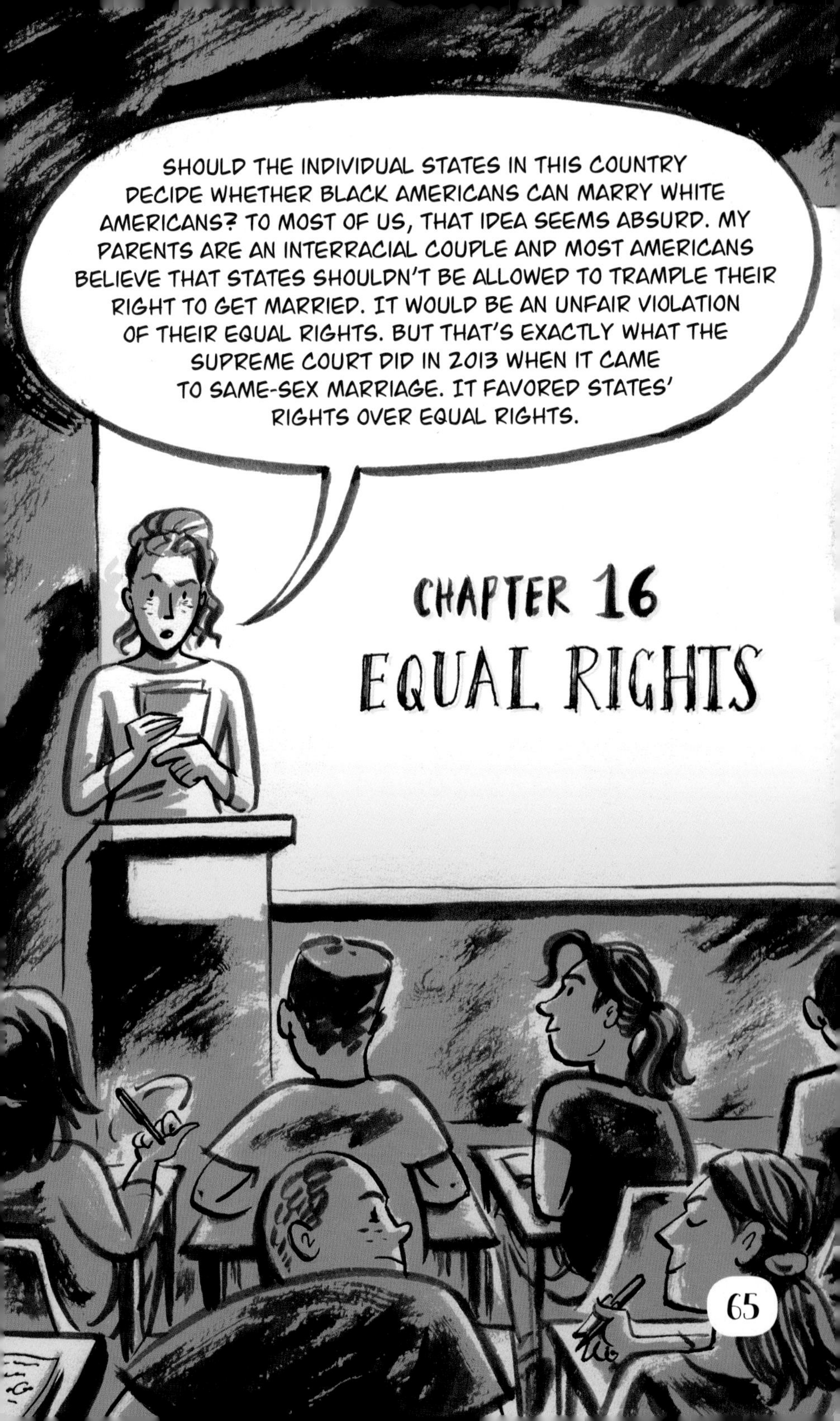
SHOULD THE INDIVIDUAL STATES IN THIS COUNTRY DECIDE WHETHER BLACK AMERICANS CAN MARRY WHITE AMERICANS? TO MOST OF US, THAT IDEA SEEMS ABSURD. MY PARENTS ARE AN INTERRACIAL COUPLE AND MOST AMERICANS BELIEVE THAT STATES SHOULDN'T BE ALLOWED TO TRAMPLE THEIR RIGHT TO GET MARRIED. IT WOULD BE AN UNFAIR VIOLATION OF THEIR EQUAL RIGHTS. BUT THAT'S EXACTLY WHAT THE SUPREME COURT DID IN 2013 WHEN IT CAME TO SAME-SEX MARRIAGE. IT FAVORED STATES' RIGHTS OVER EQUAL RIGHTS.
CHAPTER 16
EQUAL RIGHTS

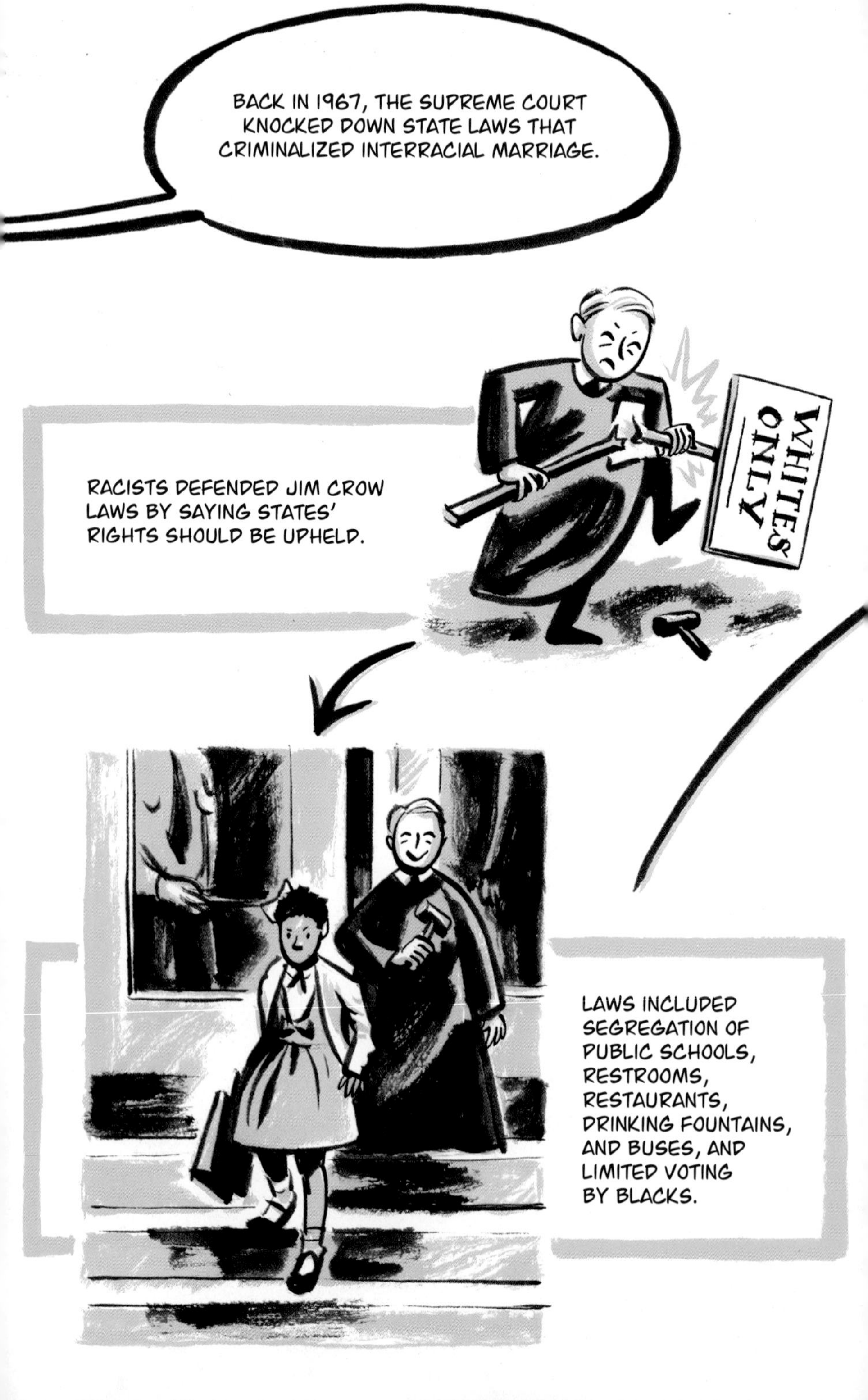
BACK IN 1967, THE SUPREME COURT KNOCKED DOWN STATE LAWS THAT CRIMINALIZED INTERRACIAL MARRIAGE.
RACISTS DEFENDED JIM CROW LAWS BY SAYING STATES' RIGHTS SHOULD BE UPHELD.
WHITES ONLY
LAWS INCLUDED SEGREGATION OF PUBLIC SCHOOLS, RESTROOMS, RESTAURANTS, DRINKING FOUNTAINS, AND BUSES, AND LIMITED VOTING BY BLACKS.

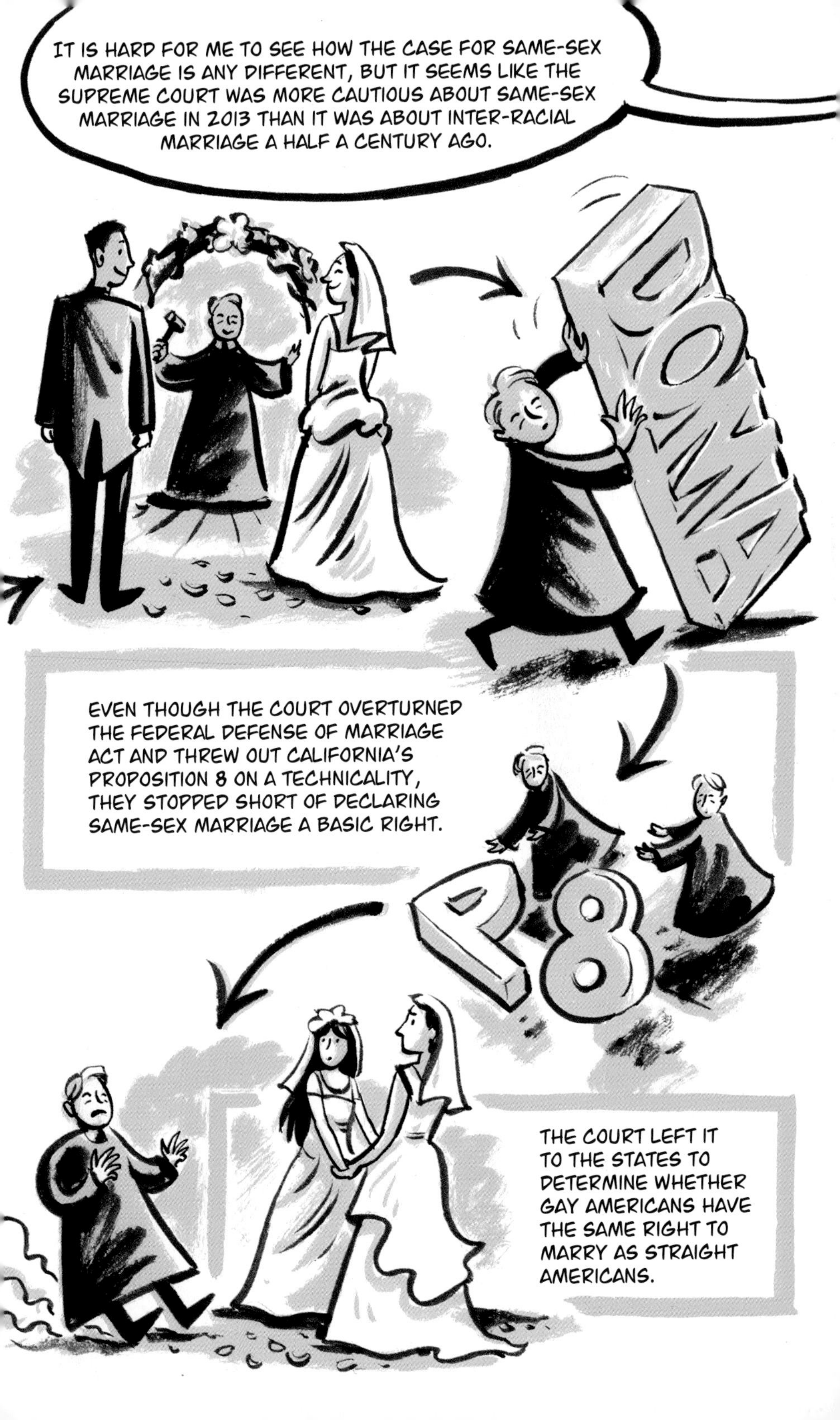
IT IS HARD FOR ME TO SEE HOW THE CASE FOR SAME-SEX MARRIAGE IS ANY DIFFERENT, BUT IT SEEMS LIKE THE SUPREME COURT WAS MORE CAUTIOUS ABOUT SAME-SEX MARRIAGE IN 2013 THAN IT WAS ABOUT INTER-RACIAL MARRIAGE A HALF A CENTURY AGO.
DOMA
EVEN THOUGH THE COURT OVERTURNED THE FEDERAL DEFENSE OF MARRIAGE ACT AND THREW OUT CALIFORNIA'S PROPOSITION 8 ON A TECHNICALITY, THEY STOPPED SHORT OF DECLARING SAME-SEX MARRIAGE A BASIC RIGHT.
P8
THE COURT LEFT IT TO THE STATES TO DETERMINE WHETHER GAY AMERICANS HAVE THE SAME RIGHT TO MARRY AS STRAIGHT AMERICANS.

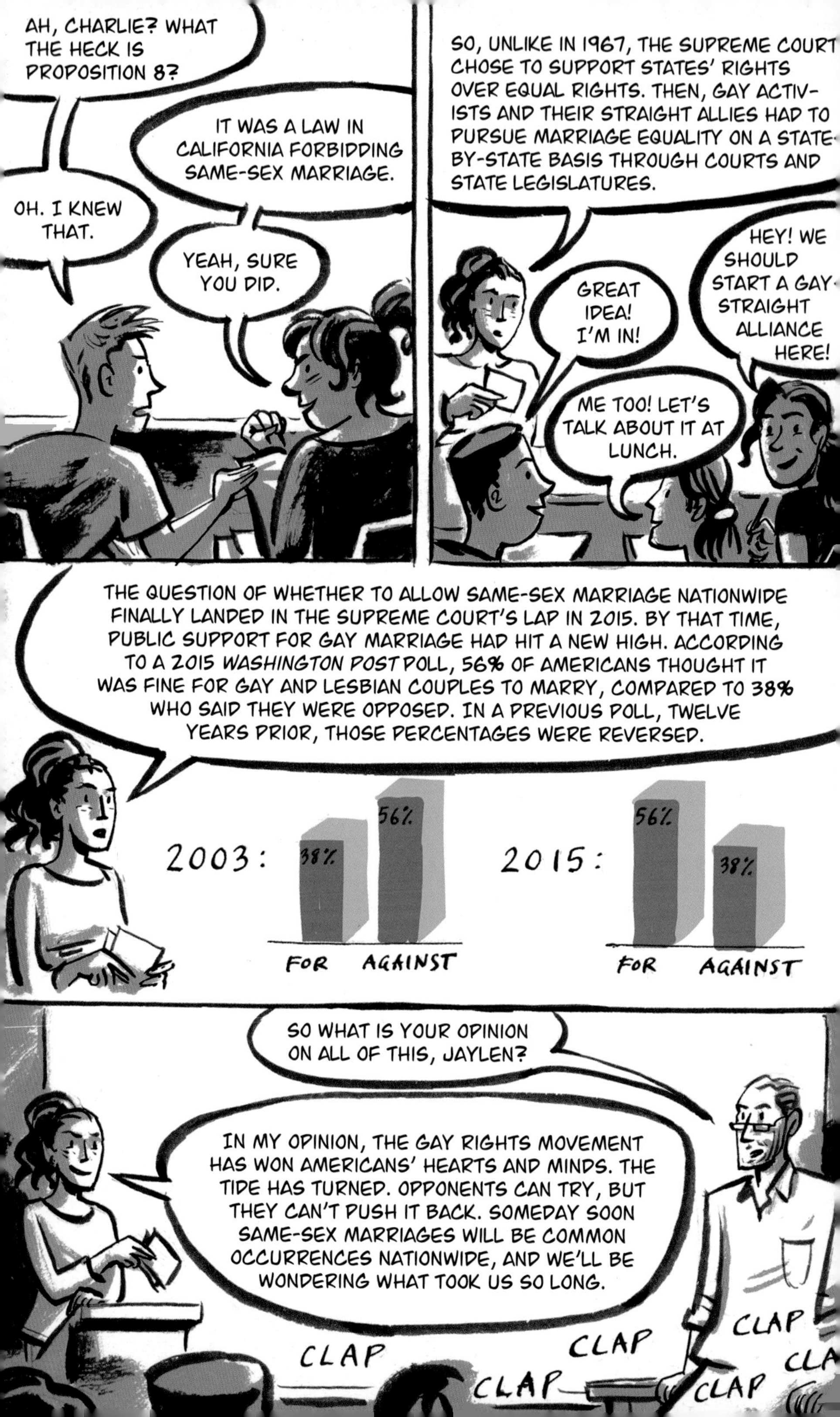
AH, CHARLIE? WHAT THE HECK IS PROPOSITION 8?
IT WAS A LAW IN CALIFORNIA FORBIDDING SAME-SEX MARRIAGE.
OH. I KNEW THAT.
YEAH, SURE YOU DID.
SO, UNLIKE IN 1967, THE SUPREME COURT CHOSE TO SUPPORT STATES' RIGHTS OVER EQUAL RIGHTS. THEN, GAY ACTIVISTS AND THEIR STRAIGHT ALLIES HAD TO PURSUE MARRIAGE EQUALITY ON A STATE-BY-STATE BASIS THROUGH COURTS AND STATE LEGISLATURES.
HEY! WE SHOULD START A GAY-STRAIGHT ALLIANCE HERE!
GREAT IDEA! I'M IN!
ME TOO! LET'S TALK ABOUT IT AT LUNCH.
THE QUESTION OF WHETHER TO ALLOW SAME-SEX MARRIAGE NATIONWIDE FINALLY LANDED IN THE SUPREME COURT'S LAP IN 2015. BY THAT TIME, PUBLIC SUPPORT FOR GAY MARRIAGE HAD HIT A NEW HIGH. ACCORDING TO A 2015 *WASHINGTON POST* POLL, 56% OF AMERICANS THOUGHT IT WAS FINE FOR GAY AND LESBIAN COUPLES TO MARRY, COMPARED TO 38% WHO SAID THEY WERE OPPOSED. IN A PREVIOUS POLL, TWELVE YEARS PRIOR, THOSE PERCENTAGES WERE REVERSED.
2003:
38%
56%
FOR
AGAINST
2015:
56%
38%
FOR
AGAINST
SO WHAT IS YOUR OPINION ON ALL OF THIS, JAYLEN?
IN MY OPINION, THE GAY RIGHTS MOVEMENT HAS WON AMERICANS' HEARTS AND MINDS. THE TIDE HAS TURNED. OPPONENTS CAN TRY, BUT THEY CAN'T PUSH IT BACK. SOMEDAY SOON SAME-SEX MARRIAGES WILL BE COMMON OCCURRENCES NATIONWIDE, AND WE'LL BE WONDERING WHAT TOOK US SO LONG.
CLAP
CLAP
CLAP
CLAP
CLAP
CLA

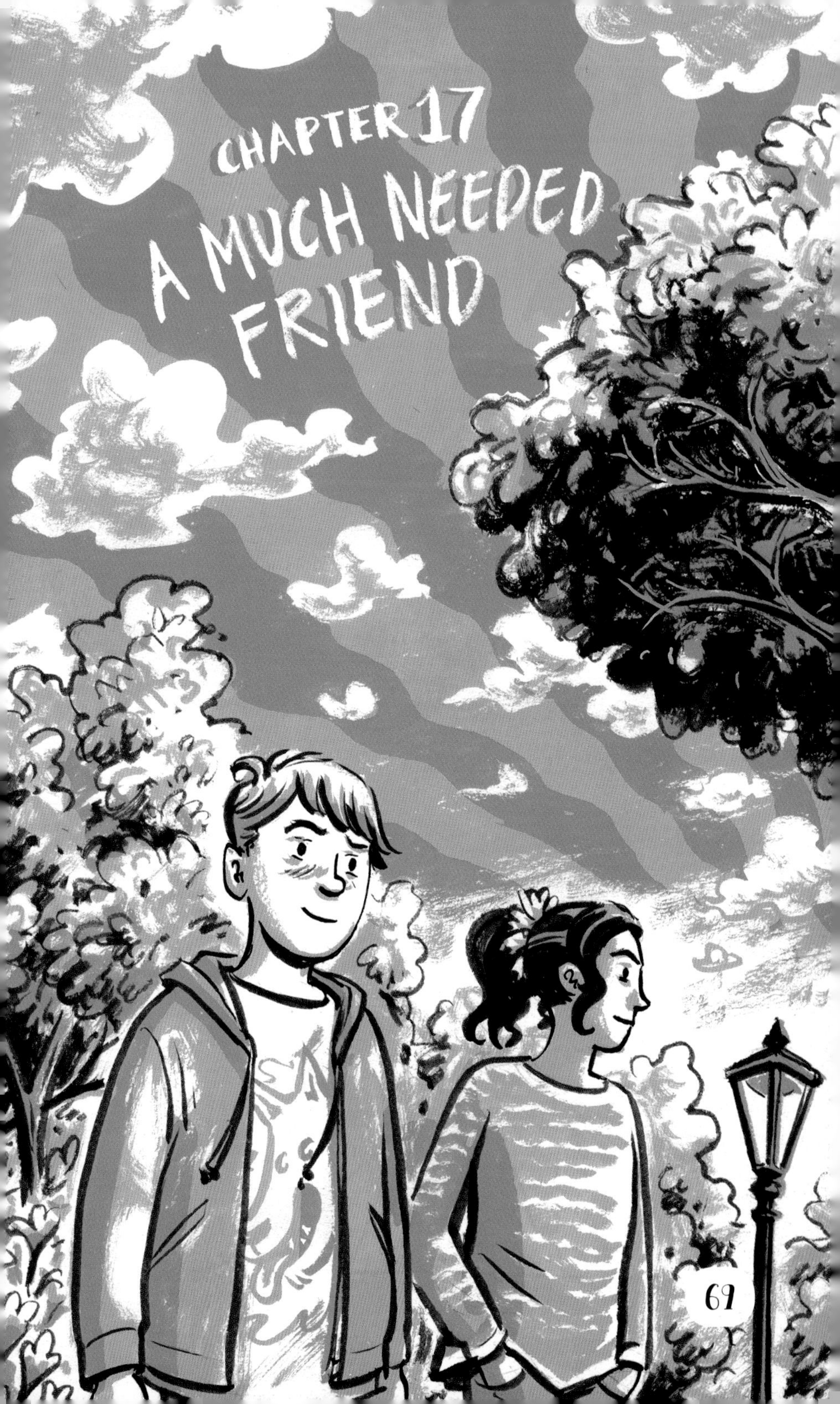
CHAPTER 17
A MUCH NEEDED
FRIEND

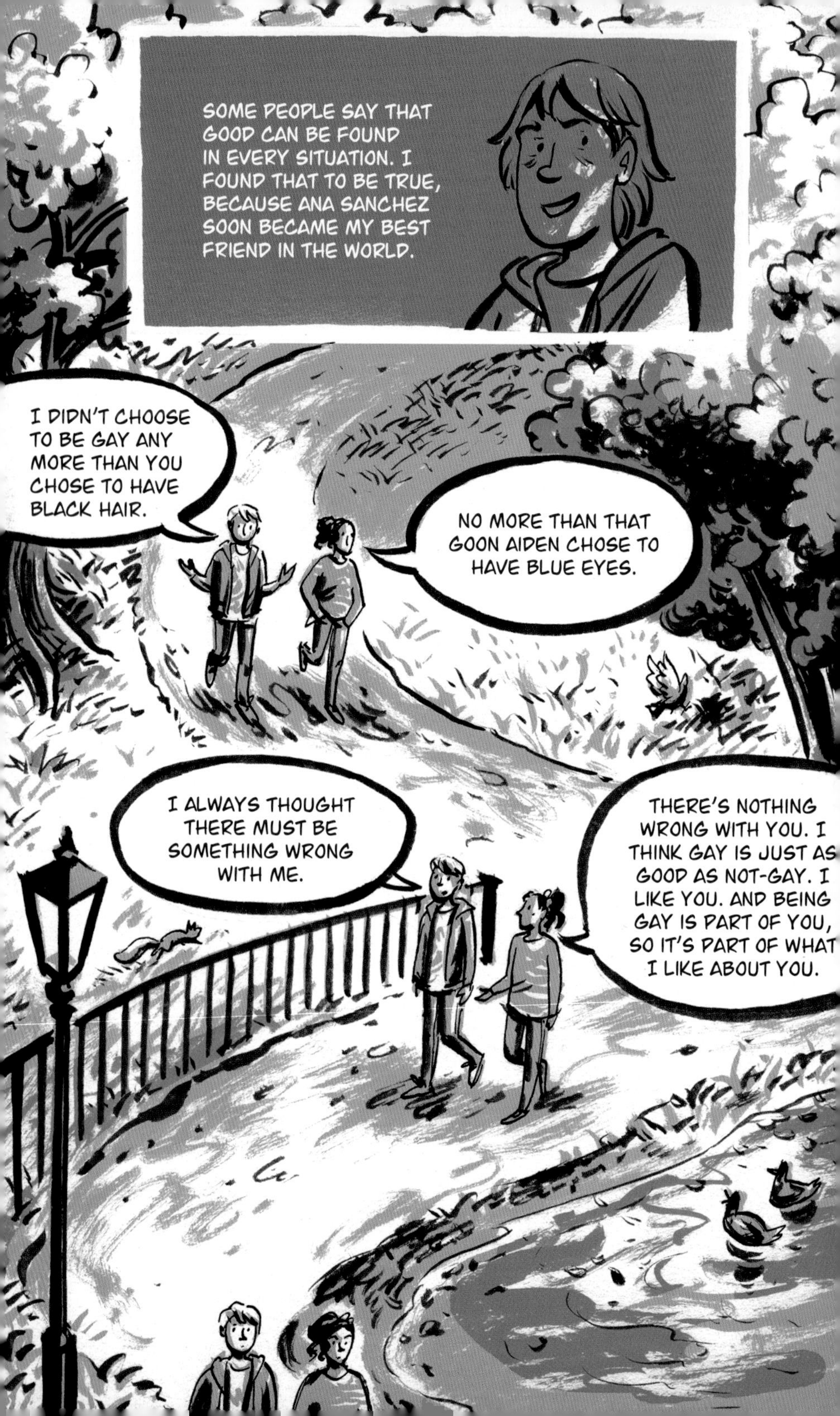
SOME PEOPLE SAY THAT GOOD CAN BE FOUND IN EVERY SITUATION. I FOUND THAT TO BE TRUE, BECAUSE ANA SANCHEZ SOON BECAME MY BEST FRIEND IN THE WORLD.
I DIDN'T CHOOSE TO BE GAY ANY MORE THAN YOU CHOSE TO HAVE BLACK HAIR.
NO MORE THAN THAT GOON AIDEN CHOSE TO HAVE BLUE EYES.
I ALWAYS THOUGHT THERE MUST BE SOMETHING WRONG WITH ME.
THERE'S NOTHING WRONG WITH YOU. I THINK GAY IS JUST AS GOOD AS NOT-GAY. I LIKE YOU. AND BEING GAY IS PART OF YOU, SO IT'S PART OF WHAT I LIKE ABOUT YOU.

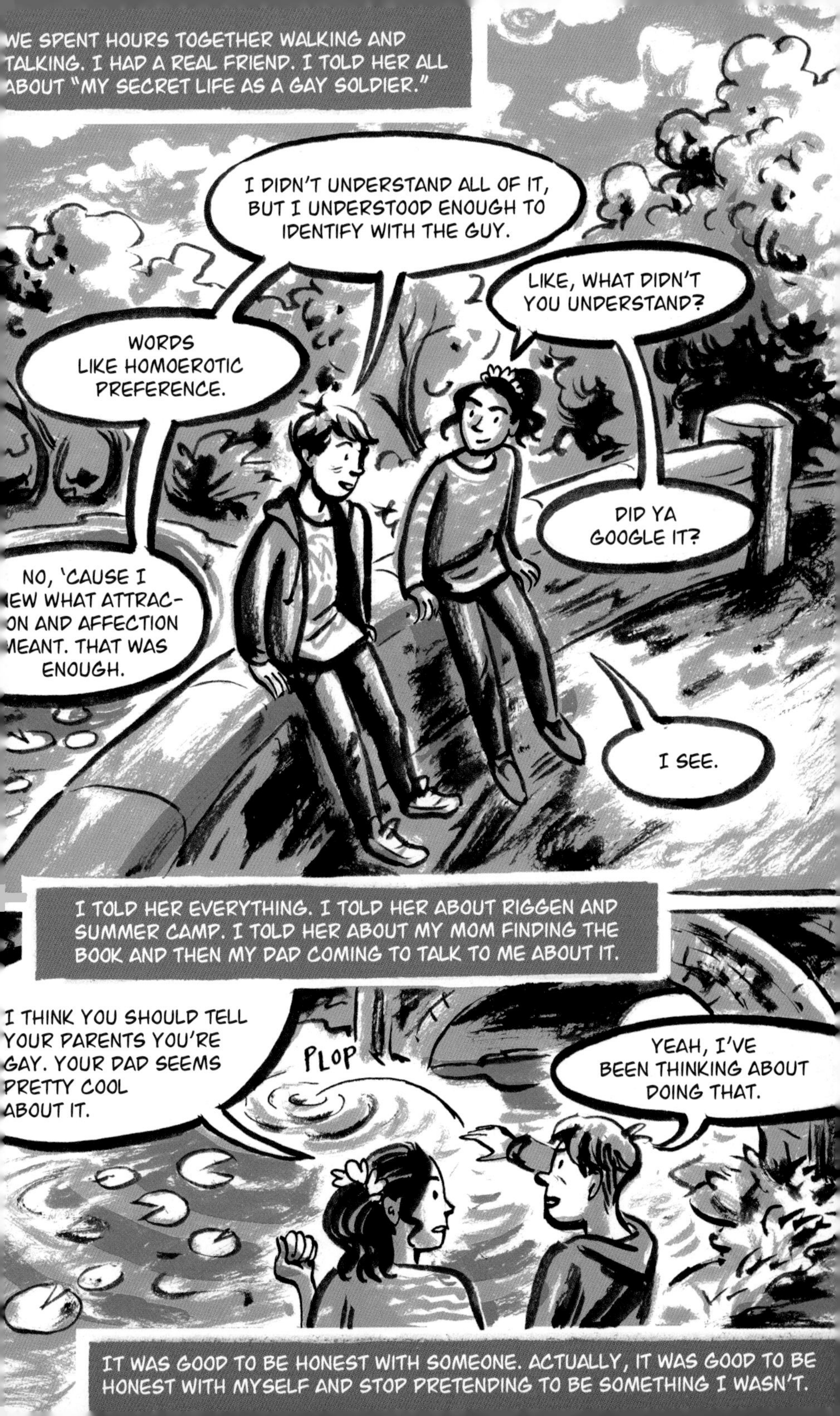
WE SPENT HOURS TOGETHER WALKING AND TALKING. I HAD A REAL FRIEND. I TOLD HER ALL ABOUT "MY SECRET LIFE AS A GAY SOLDIER."
I DIDN'T UNDERSTAND ALL OF IT, BUT I UNDERSTOOD ENOUGH TO IDENTIFY WITH THE GUY.
LIKE, WHAT DIDN'T YOU UNDERSTAND?
WORDS LIKE HOMOEROTIC PREFERENCE.
DID YA GOOGLE IT?
NO, 'CAUSE I IEW WHAT ATTRAC-ON AND AFFECTION IEANT. THAT WAS ENOUGH.
I SEE.
I TOLD HER EVERYTHING. I TOLD HER ABOUT RIGGEN AND SUMMER CAMP. I TOLD HER ABOUT MY MOM FINDING THE BOOK AND THEN MY DAD COMING TO TALK TO ME ABOUT IT.
I THINK YOU SHOULD TELL YOUR PARENTS YOU'RE GAY. YOUR DAD SEEMS PRETTY COOL ABOUT IT.
PLOP
YEAH, I'VE BEEN THINKING ABOUT DOING THAT.
IT WAS GOOD TO BE HONEST WITH SOMEONE. ACTUALLY, IT WAS GOOD TO BE HONEST WITH MYSELF AND STOP PRETENDING TO BE SOMETHING I WASN'T.

CHAPTER 18
APOLOGIZE TO NO ONE

THE KISS ON THE TARMAC CHANGED DEVIN'S LIFE. HE NO LONGER LIVED A SECRET. HE MADE A MOVE FROM DECEPTION TO HONESTY.

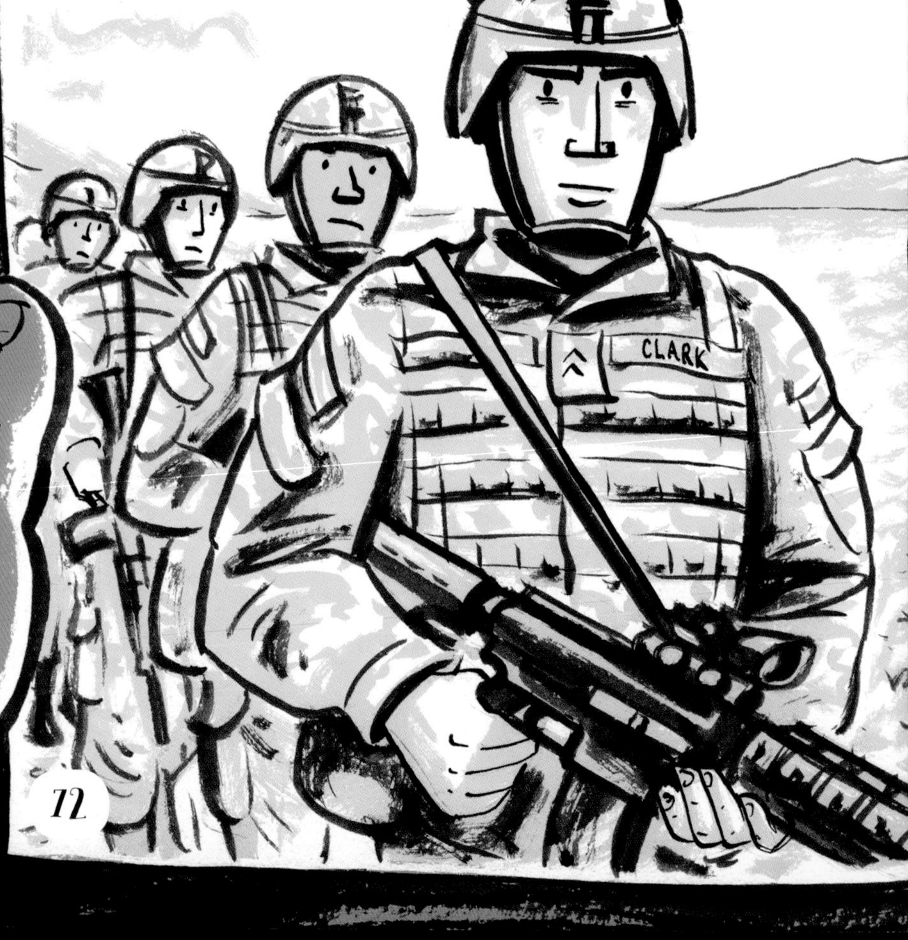
CLARK

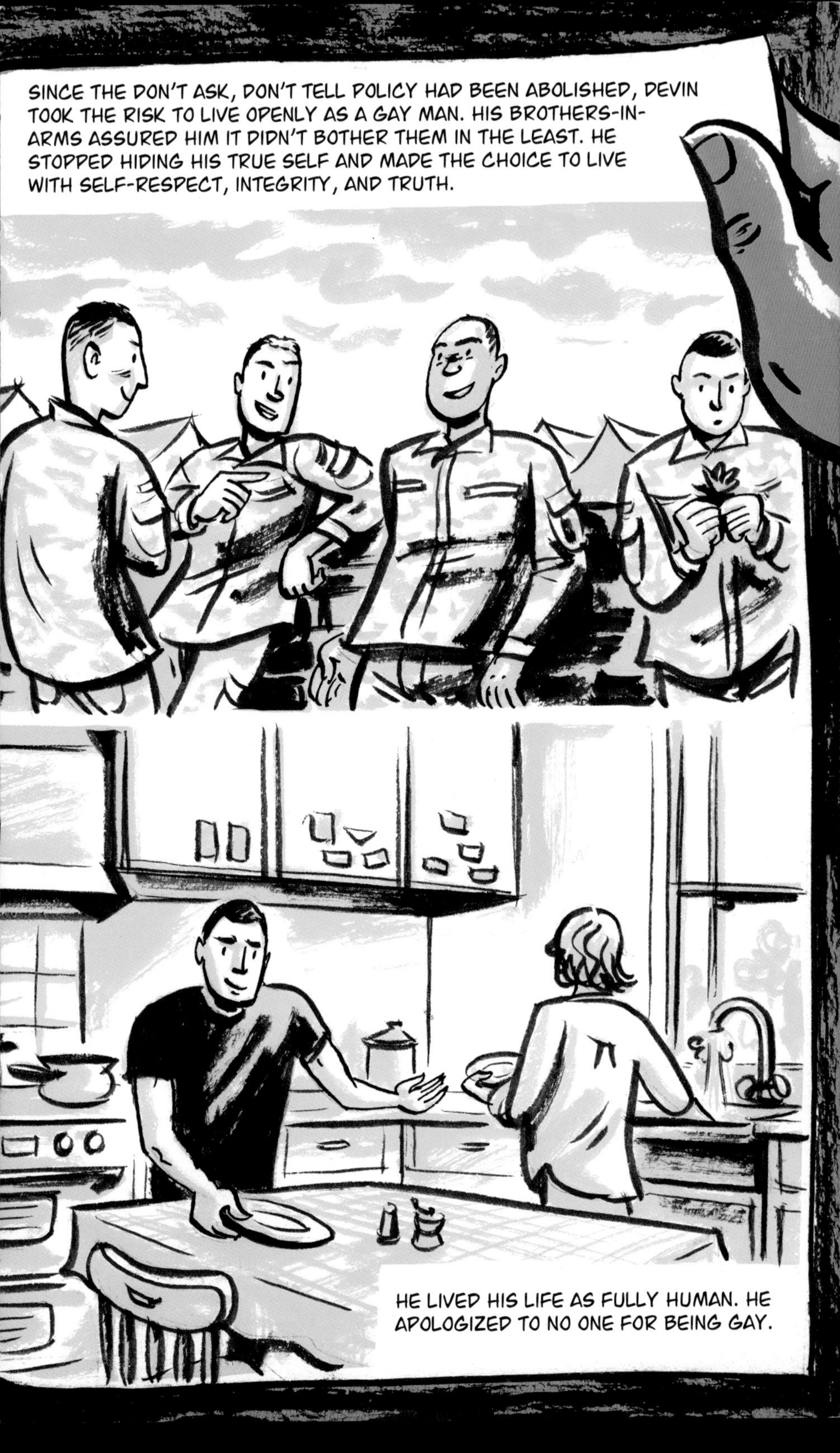
SINCE THE DON'T ASK, DON'T TELL POLICY HAD BEEN ABOLISHED, DEVIN TOOK THE RISK TO LIVE OPENLY AS A GAY MAN. HIS BROTHERS-IN-ARMS ASSURED HIM IT DIDN'T BOTHER THEM IN THE LEAST. HE STOPPED HIDING HIS TRUE SELF AND MADE THE CHOICE TO LIVE WITH SELF-RESPECT, INTEGRITY, AND TRUTH.
HE LIVED HIS LIFE AS FULLY HUMAN. HE APOLOGIZED TO NO ONE FOR BEING GAY.

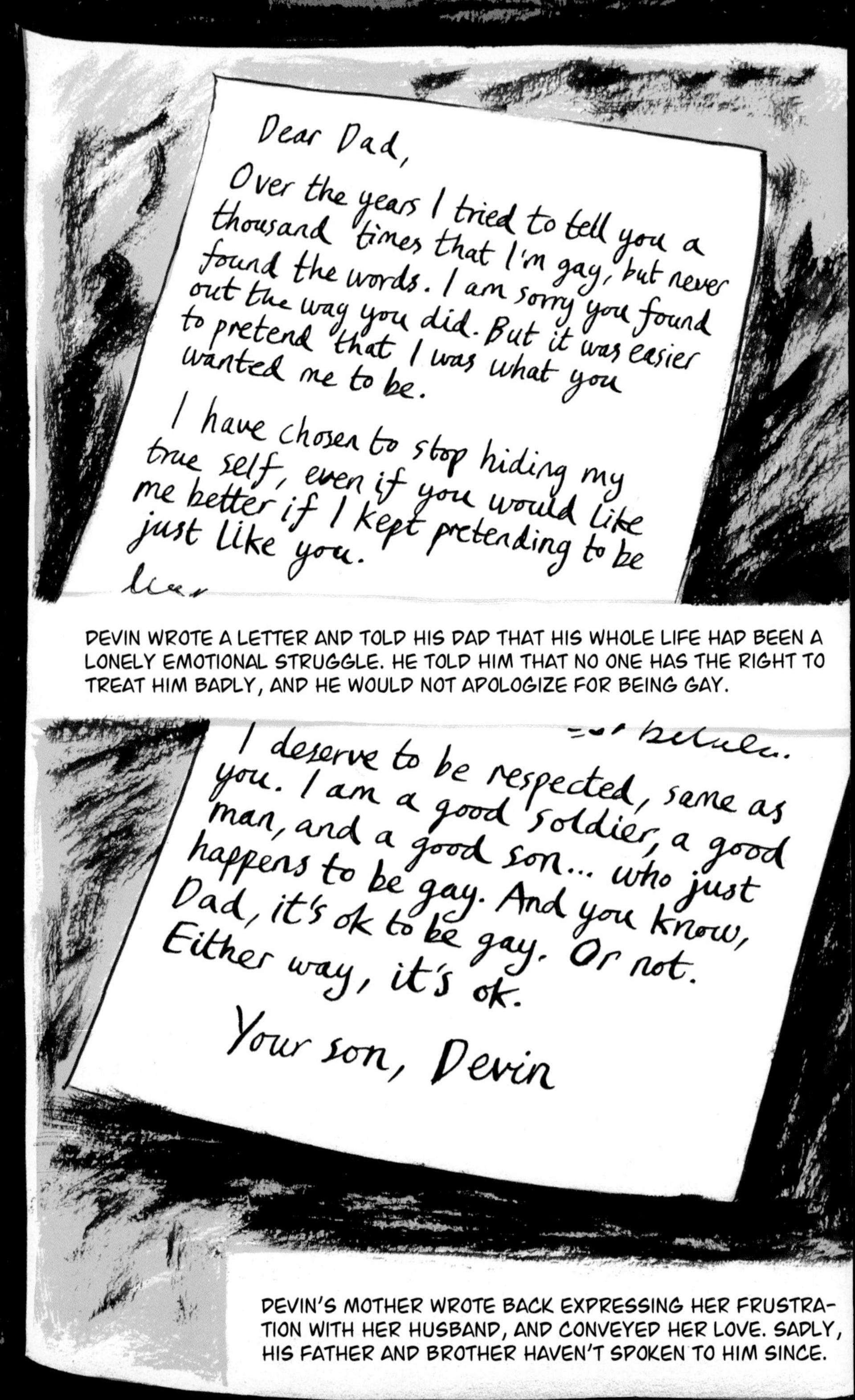
Dear Dad,
Over the years I tried to tell you a thousand times that I'm gay, but never found the words. I am sorry you found out the way you did. But it was easier to pretend that I was what you wanted me to be.
I have chosen to stop hiding my true self, even if you would like me better if I kept pretending to be just like you.
DEVIN WROTE A LETTER AND TOLD HIS DAD THAT HIS WHOLE LIFE HAD BEEN A LONELY EMOTIONAL STRUGGLE. HE TOLD HIM THAT NO ONE HAS THE RIGHT TO TREAT HIM BADLY, AND HE WOULD NOT APOLOGIZE FOR BEING GAY.
I deserve to be respected, same as you. I am a good soldier, a good man, and a good son... who just happens to be gay. And you know, Dad, it's ok to be gay. Or not. Either way, it's ok.
Your son, Devin
DEVIN'S MOTHER WROTE BACK EXPRESSING HER FRUSTRATION WITH HER HUSBAND, AND CONVEYED HER LOVE. SADLY, HIS FATHER AND BROTHER HAVEN'T SPOKEN TO HIM SINCE.

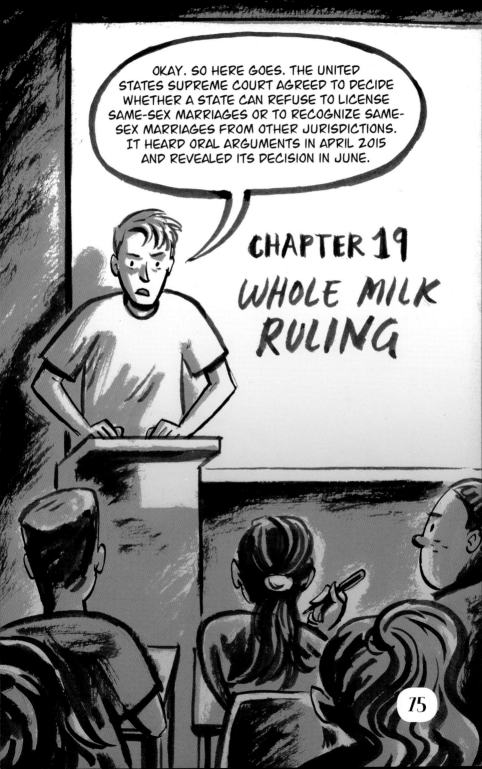

OKAY. SO HERE GOES. THE UNITED STATES SUPREME COURT AGREED TO DECIDE WHETHER A STATE CAN REFUSE TO LICENSE SAME-SEX MARRIAGES OR TO RECOGNIZE SAME-SEX MARRIAGES FROM OTHER JURISDICTIONS. IT HEARD ORAL ARGUMENTS IN APRIL 2015 AND REVEALED ITS DECISION IN JUNE.

CHAPTER 19

WHOLE MILK RULING

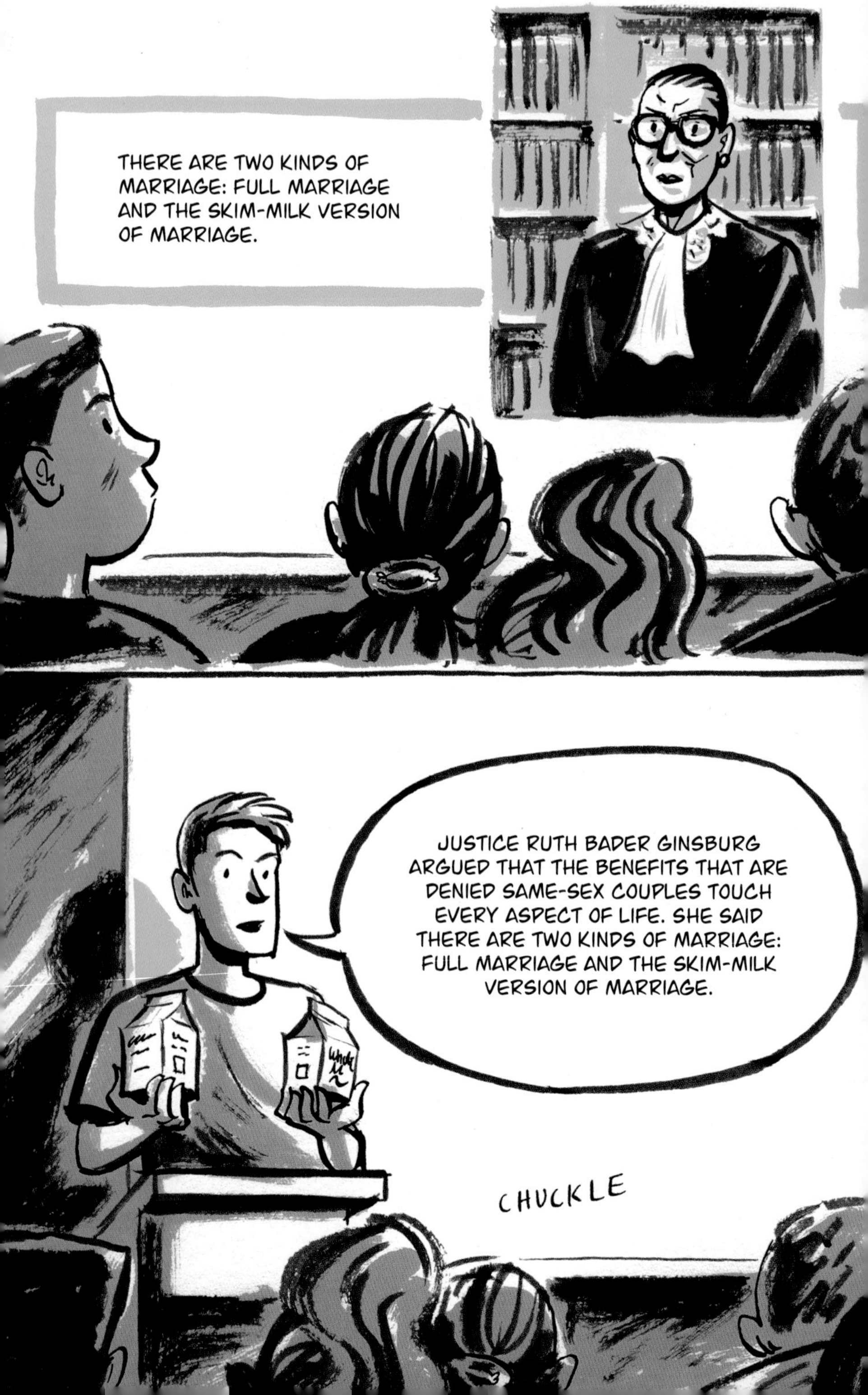
THERE ARE TWO KINDS OF MARRIAGE: FULL MARRIAGE AND THE SKIM-MILK VERSION OF MARRIAGE.
JUSTICE RUTH BADER GINSBURG ARGUED THAT THE BENEFITS THAT ARE DENIED SAME-SEX COUPLES TOUCH EVERY ASPECT OF LIFE. SHE SAID THERE ARE TWO KINDS OF MARRIAGE: FULL MARRIAGE AND THE SKIM-MILK VERSION OF MARRIAGE.
CHUCKLE

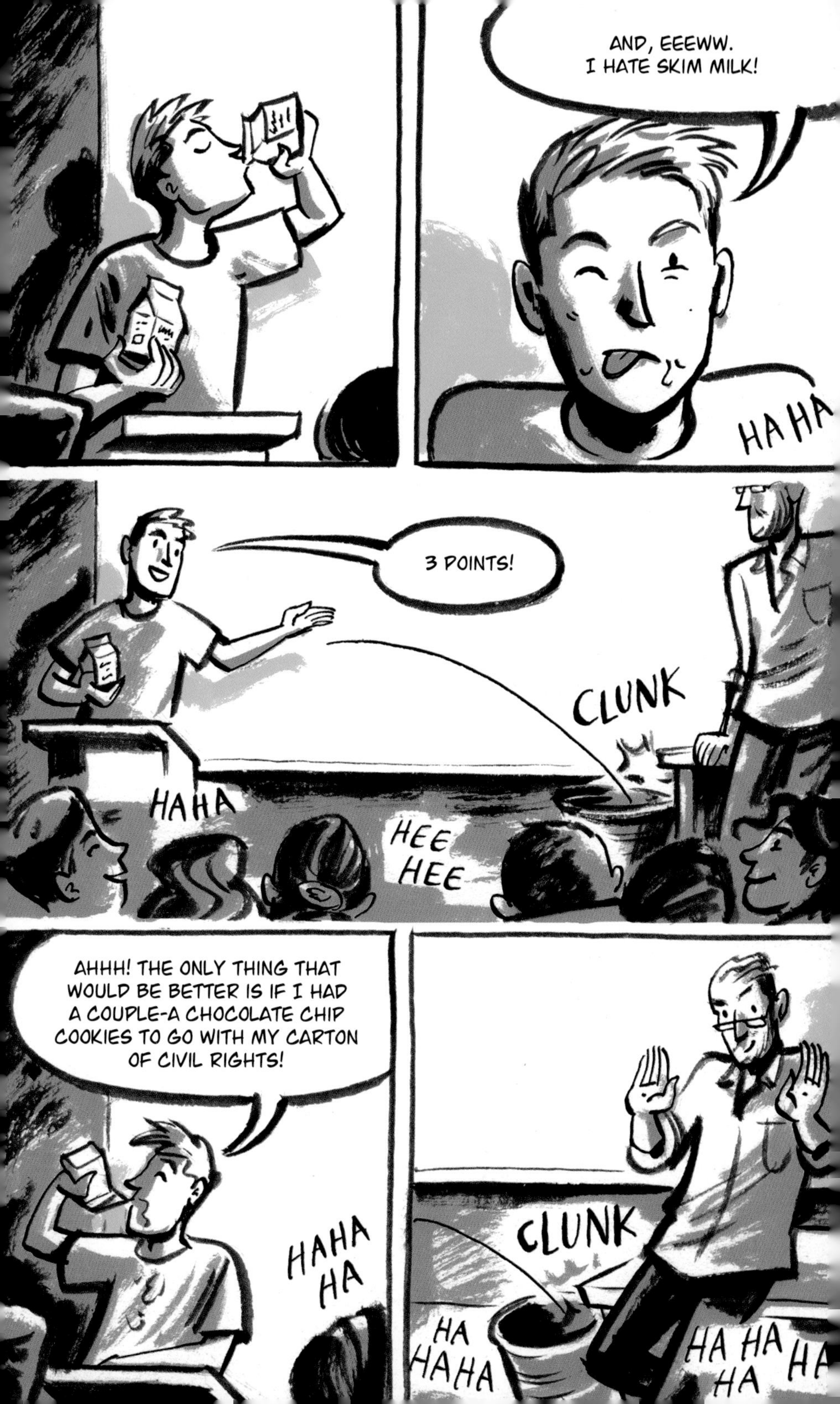
AND, EEEWW.
I HATE SKIM MILK!
HA HA
3 POINTS!
CLUNK
HAHA
HEE HEE
AHHH! THE ONLY THING THAT WOULD BE BETTER IS IF I HAD A COUPLE-A CHOCOLATE CHIP COOKIES TO GO WITH MY CARTON OF CIVIL RIGHTS!
HAHA HA
CLUNK
HA HAHA
HA HA HA
HA

SO IN JUNE THE LONG-AWAITED LANDMARK RULING FINALLY CAME. THE SUPREME COURT OVERTURNED MARRIAGE RESTRICTIONS IN CERTAIN STATES THAT WERE HOLDING OUT AND ENSURED MARRIAGE EQUALITY FOR GAY COUPLES NATIONWIDE.
THEIR HOPE IS NOT TO BE CONDEMNED TO LIVE IN LONELINESS, EXCLUDED FROM ONE OF CIVILIZATION'S OLDEST INSTITUTIONS. THEY ASK FOR EQUAL DIGNITY IN THE EYES OF THE LAW. THE CONSTITUTION GRANTS THEM THAT RIGHT.
JUSTICE ANTHONY KENNEDY WROTE THE MAJORITY OPINION, AND IT WAS AMAZING. HE SAID THAT MARRIAGE RESTRICTIONS IMPOSED BY STATES HAD THE EFFECT OF TEACHING THAT GAYS AND LESBIANS ARE UNEQUAL IN IMPORTANT RESPECTS.

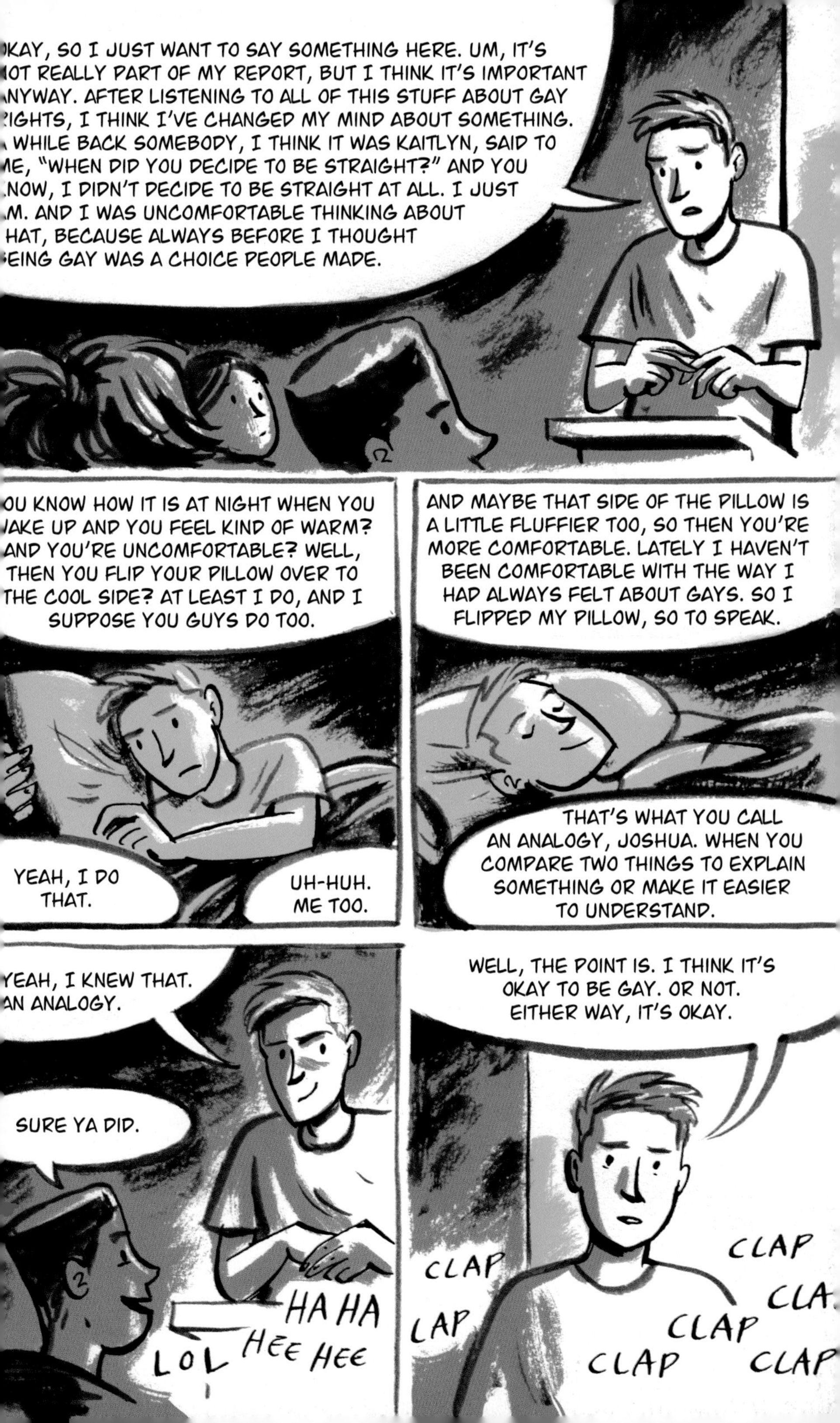
KAY, SO I JUST WANT TO SAY SOMETHING HERE. UM, IT'S OT REALLY PART OF MY REPORT, BUT I THINK IT'S IMPORTANT NYWAY. AFTER LISTENING TO ALL OF THIS STUFF ABOUT GAY IGHTS, I THINK I'VE CHANGED MY MIND ABOUT SOMETHING. WHILE BACK SOMEBODY, I THINK IT WAS KAITLYN, SAID TO E, "WHEN DID YOU DECIDE TO BE STRAIGHT?" AND YOU NOW, I DIDN'T DECIDE TO BE STRAIGHT AT ALL. I JUST M. AND I WAS UNCOMFORTABLE THINKING ABOUT HAT, BECAUSE ALWAYS BEFORE I THOUGHT EING GAY WAS A CHOICE PEOPLE MADE.
OU KNOW HOW IT IS AT NIGHT WHEN YOU AKE UP AND YOU FEEL KIND OF WARM? AND YOU'RE UNCOMFORTABLE? WELL, THEN YOU FLIP YOUR PILLOW OVER TO THE COOL SIDE? AT LEAST I DO, AND I SUPPOSE YOU GUYS DO TOO.
YEAH, I DO THAT.
UH-HUH. ME TOO.
AND MAYBE THAT SIDE OF THE PILLOW IS A LITTLE FLUFFIER TOO, SO THEN YOU'RE MORE COMFORTABLE. LATELY I HAVEN'T BEEN COMFORTABLE WITH THE WAY I HAD ALWAYS FELT ABOUT GAYS. SO I FLIPPED MY PILLOW, SO TO SPEAK.
THAT'S WHAT YOU CALL AN ANALOGY, JOSHUA. WHEN YOU COMPARE TWO THINGS TO EXPLAIN SOMETHING OR MAKE IT EASIER TO UNDERSTAND.
YEAH, I KNEW THAT. AN ANALOGY.
SURE YA DID.
HA HA
LOL
HEE HEE
WELL, THE POINT IS. I THINK IT'S OKAY TO BE GAY. OR NOT. EITHER WAY, IT'S OKAY.
CLAP
LAP
CLAP
CLA
CLAP
CLAP
CLAP

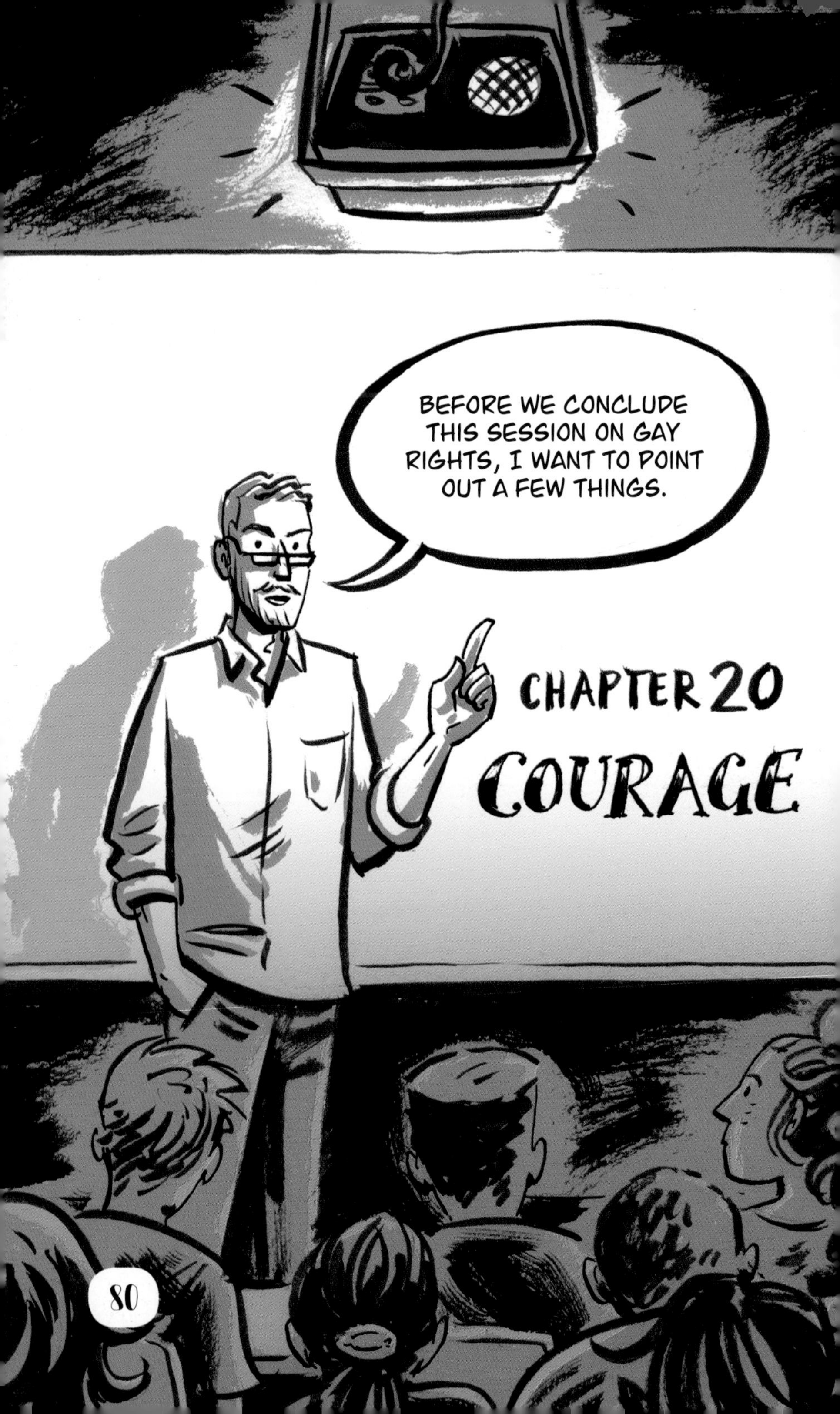
BEFORE WE CONCLUDE THIS SESSION ON GAY RIGHTS, I WANT TO POINT OUT A FEW THINGS.
CHAPTER 20
COURAGE

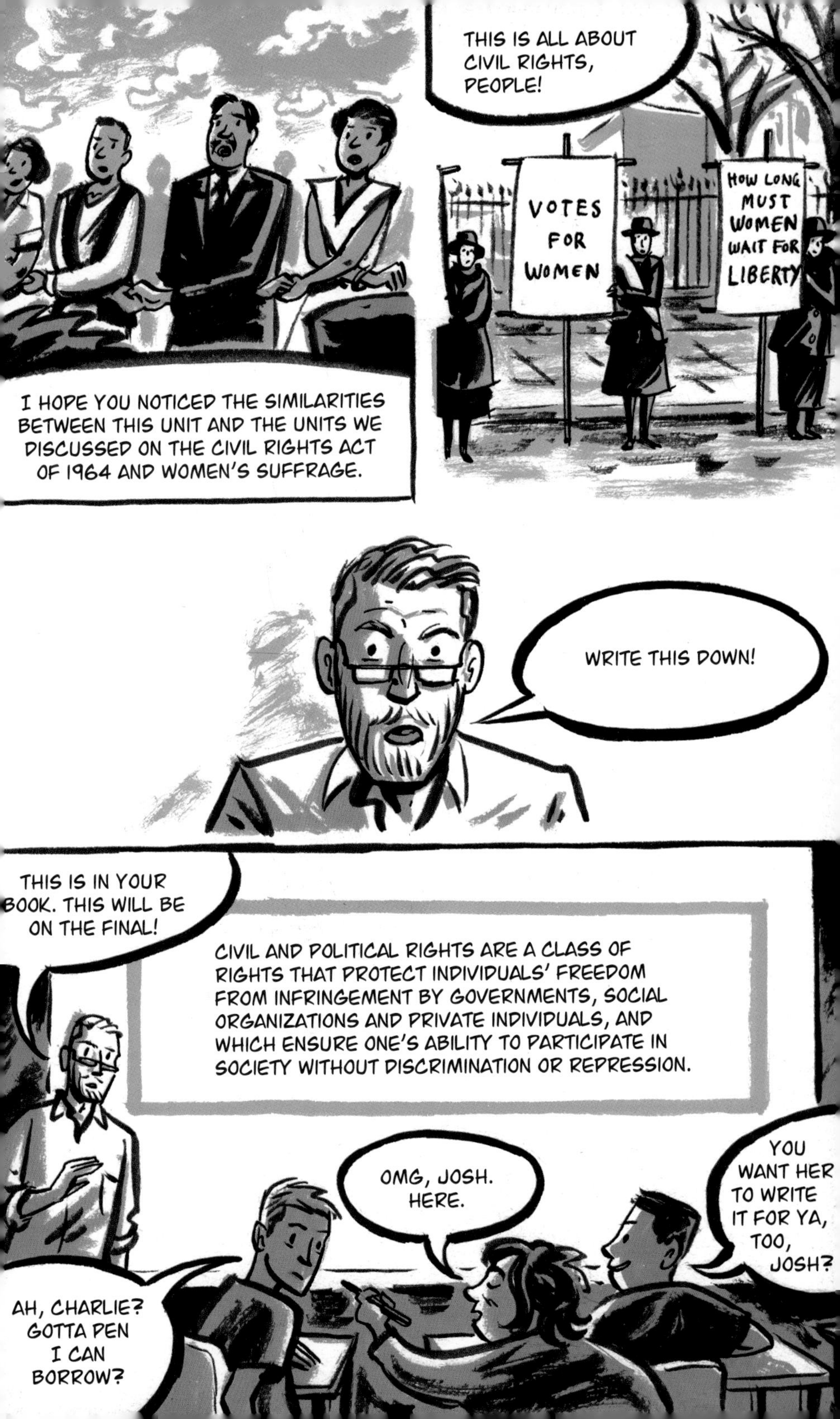
I HOPE YOU NOTICED THE SIMILARITIES BETWEEN THIS UNIT AND THE UNITS WE DISCUSSED ON THE CIVIL RIGHTS ACT OF 1964 AND WOMEN'S SUFFRAGE.
THIS IS ALL ABOUT CIVIL RIGHTS, PEOPLE!
VOTES FOR WOMEN
HOW LONG MUST WOMEN WAIT FOR LIBERTY
WRITE THIS DOWN!
THIS IS IN YOUR BOOK. THIS WILL BE ON THE FINAL!
CIVIL AND POLITICAL RIGHTS ARE A CLASS OF RIGHTS THAT PROTECT INDIVIDUALS' FREEDOM FROM INFRINGEMENT BY GOVERNMENTS, SOCIAL ORGANIZATIONS AND PRIVATE INDIVIDUALS, AND WHICH ENSURE ONE'S ABILITY TO PARTICIPATE IN SOCIETY WITHOUT DISCRIMINATION OR REPRESSION.
AH, CHARLIE? GOTTA PEN I CAN BORROW?
OMG, JOSH. HERE.
YOU WANT HER TO WRITE IT FOR YA, TOO, JOSH?

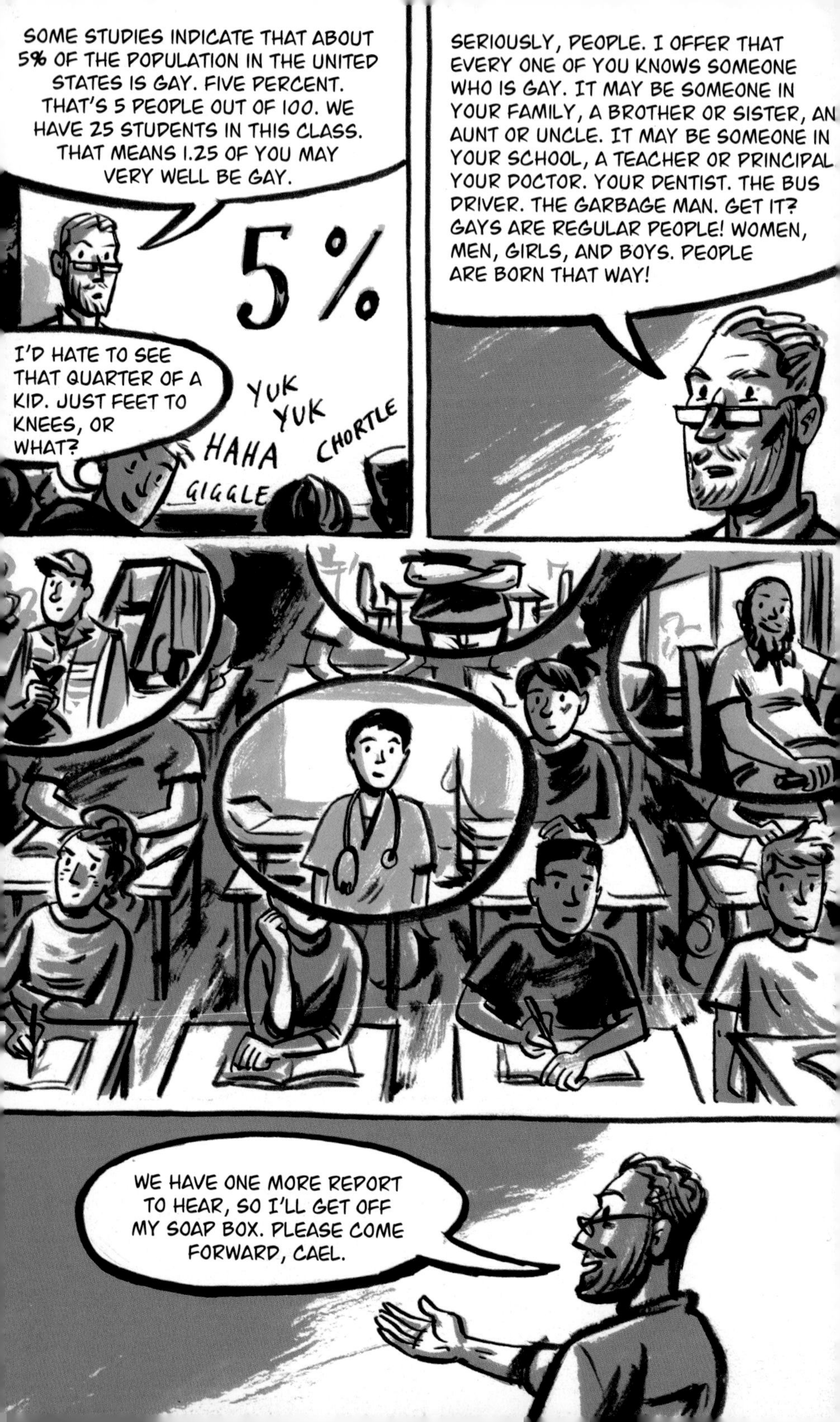
SOME STUDIES INDICATE THAT ABOUT 5% OF THE POPULATION IN THE UNITED STATES IS GAY. FIVE PERCENT. THAT'S 5 PEOPLE OUT OF 100. WE HAVE 25 STUDENTS IN THIS CLASS. THAT MEANS 1.25 OF YOU MAY VERY WELL BE GAY.
5%
I'D HATE TO SEE THAT QUARTER OF A KID. JUST FEET TO KNEES, OR WHAT?
YUK YUK
HAHA
CHORTLE
GIGGLE
SERIOUSLY, PEOPLE. I OFFER THAT EVERY ONE OF YOU KNOWS SOMEONE WHO IS GAY. IT MAY BE SOMEONE IN YOUR FAMILY, A BROTHER OR SISTER, AN AUNT OR UNCLE. IT MAY BE SOMEONE IN YOUR SCHOOL, A TEACHER OR PRINCIPAL YOUR DOCTOR. YOUR DENTIST. THE BUS DRIVER. THE GARBAGE MAN. GET IT? GAYS ARE REGULAR PEOPLE! WOMEN, MEN, GIRLS, AND BOYS. PEOPLE ARE BORN THAT WAY!
WE HAVE ONE MORE REPORT TO HEAR, SO I'LL GET OFF MY SOAP BOX. PLEASE COME FORWARD, CAEL.

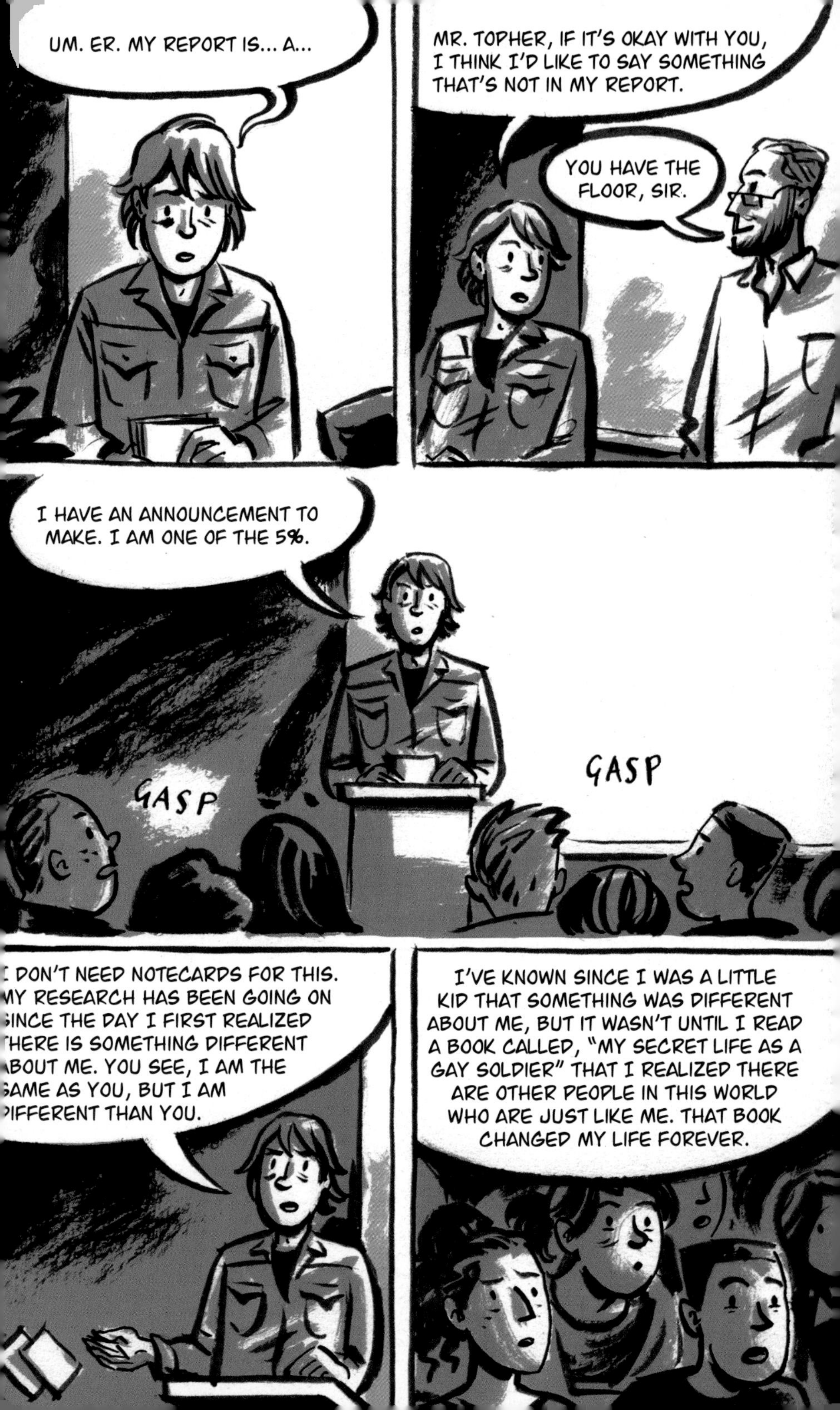
UM. ER. MY REPORT IS... A...
MR. TOPHER, IF IT'S OKAY WITH YOU, I THINK I'D LIKE TO SAY SOMETHING THAT'S NOT IN MY REPORT.
YOU HAVE THE FLOOR, SIR.
I HAVE AN ANNOUNCEMENT TO MAKE. I AM ONE OF THE 5%.
GASP
GASP
I DON'T NEED NOTECARDS FOR THIS. MY RESEARCH HAS BEEN GOING ON SINCE THE DAY I FIRST REALIZED THERE IS SOMETHING DIFFERENT ABOUT ME. YOU SEE, I AM THE SAME AS YOU, BUT I AM DIFFERENT THAN YOU.
I'VE KNOWN SINCE I WAS A LITTLE KID THAT SOMETHING WAS DIFFERENT ABOUT ME, BUT IT WASN'T UNTIL I READ A BOOK CALLED, "MY SECRET LIFE AS A GAY SOLDIER" THAT I REALIZED THERE ARE OTHER PEOPLE IN THIS WORLD WHO ARE JUST LIKE ME. THAT BOOK CHANGED MY LIFE FOREVER.

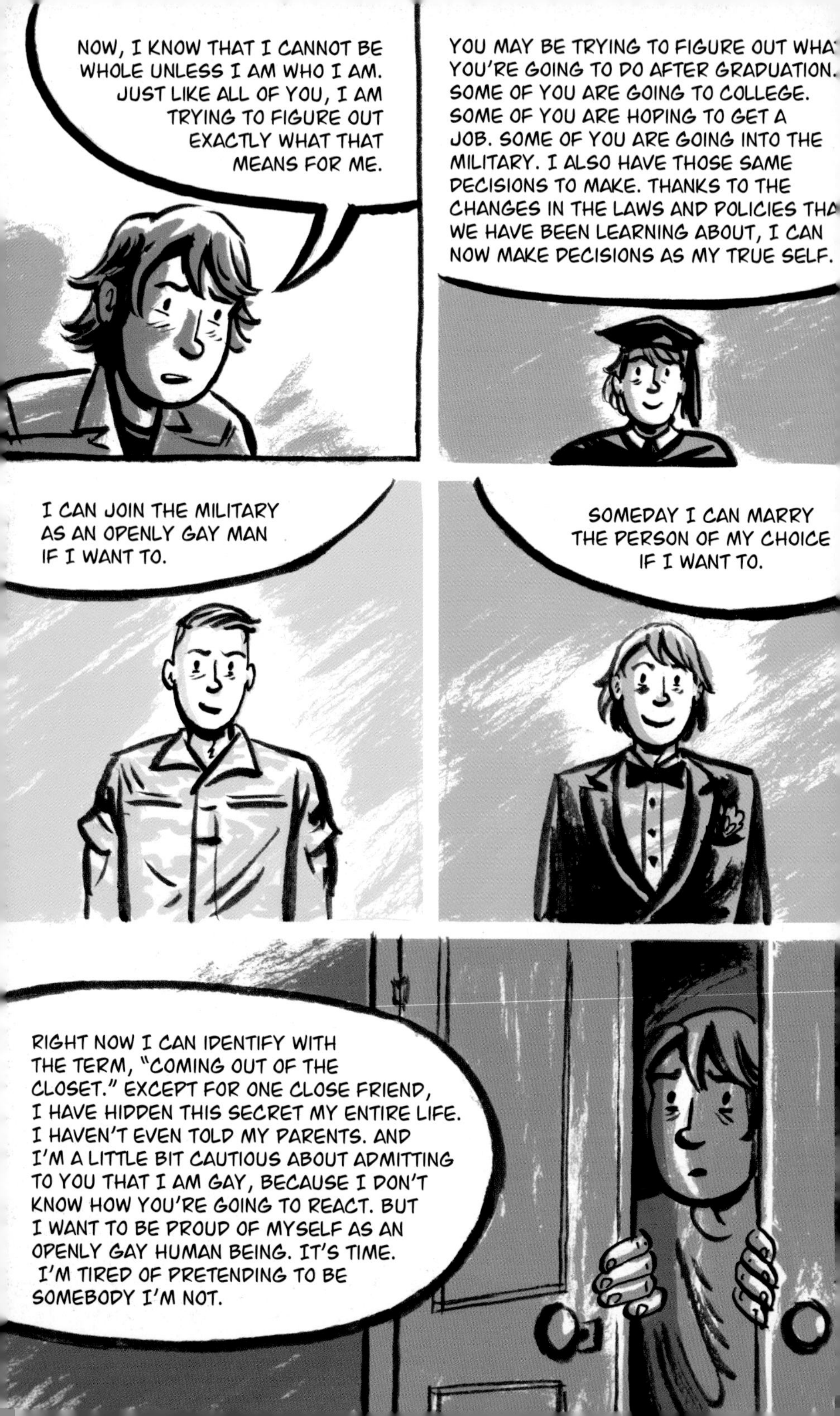
NOW, I KNOW THAT I CANNOT BE WHOLE UNLESS I AM WHO I AM. JUST LIKE ALL OF YOU, I AM TRYING TO FIGURE OUT EXACTLY WHAT THAT MEANS FOR ME.
YOU MAY BE TRYING TO FIGURE OUT WHAT YOU'RE GOING TO DO AFTER GRADUATION. SOME OF YOU ARE GOING TO COLLEGE. SOME OF YOU ARE HOPING TO GET A JOB. SOME OF YOU ARE GOING INTO THE MILITARY. I ALSO HAVE THOSE SAME DECISIONS TO MAKE. THANKS TO THE CHANGES IN THE LAWS AND POLICIES THAT WE HAVE BEEN LEARNING ABOUT, I CAN NOW MAKE DECISIONS AS MY TRUE SELF.
I CAN JOIN THE MILITARY AS AN OPENLY GAY MAN IF I WANT TO.
SOMEDAY I CAN MARRY THE PERSON OF MY CHOICE IF I WANT TO.
RIGHT NOW I CAN IDENTIFY WITH THE TERM, "COMING OUT OF THE CLOSET." EXCEPT FOR ONE CLOSE FRIEND, I HAVE HIDDEN THIS SECRET MY ENTIRE LIFE. I HAVEN'T EVEN TOLD MY PARENTS. AND I'M A LITTLE BIT CAUTIOUS ABOUT ADMITTING TO YOU THAT I AM GAY, BECAUSE I DON'T KNOW HOW YOU'RE GOING TO REACT. BUT I WANT TO BE PROUD OF MYSELF AS AN OPENLY GAY HUMAN BEING. IT'S TIME. I'M TIRED OF PRETENDING TO BE SOMEBODY I'M NOT.

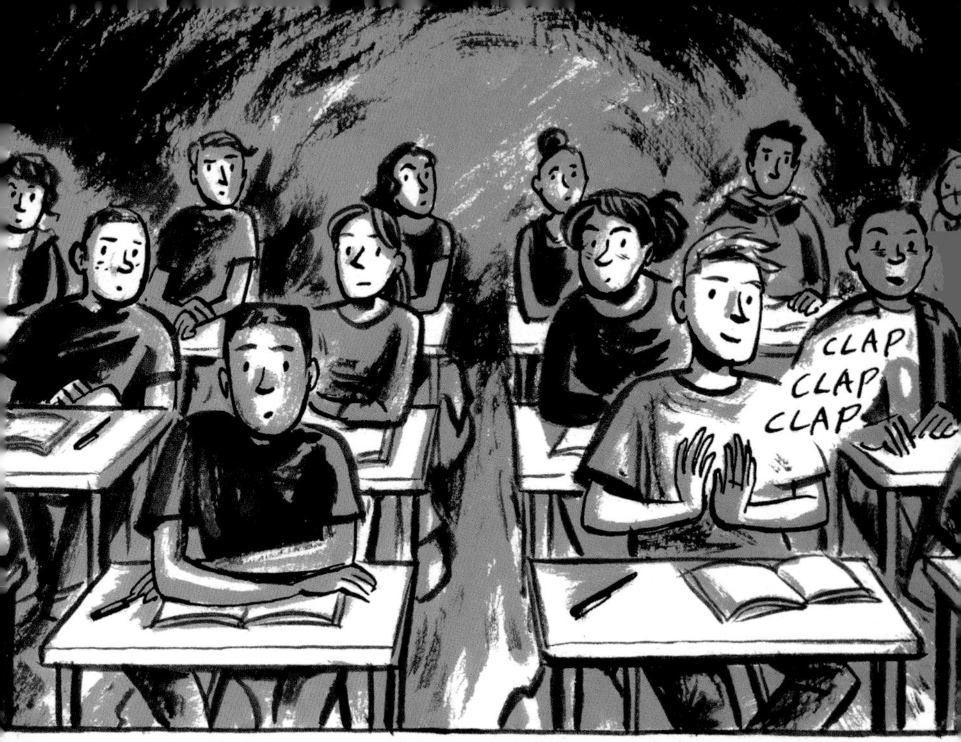
CLAP
CLAP
CLAP

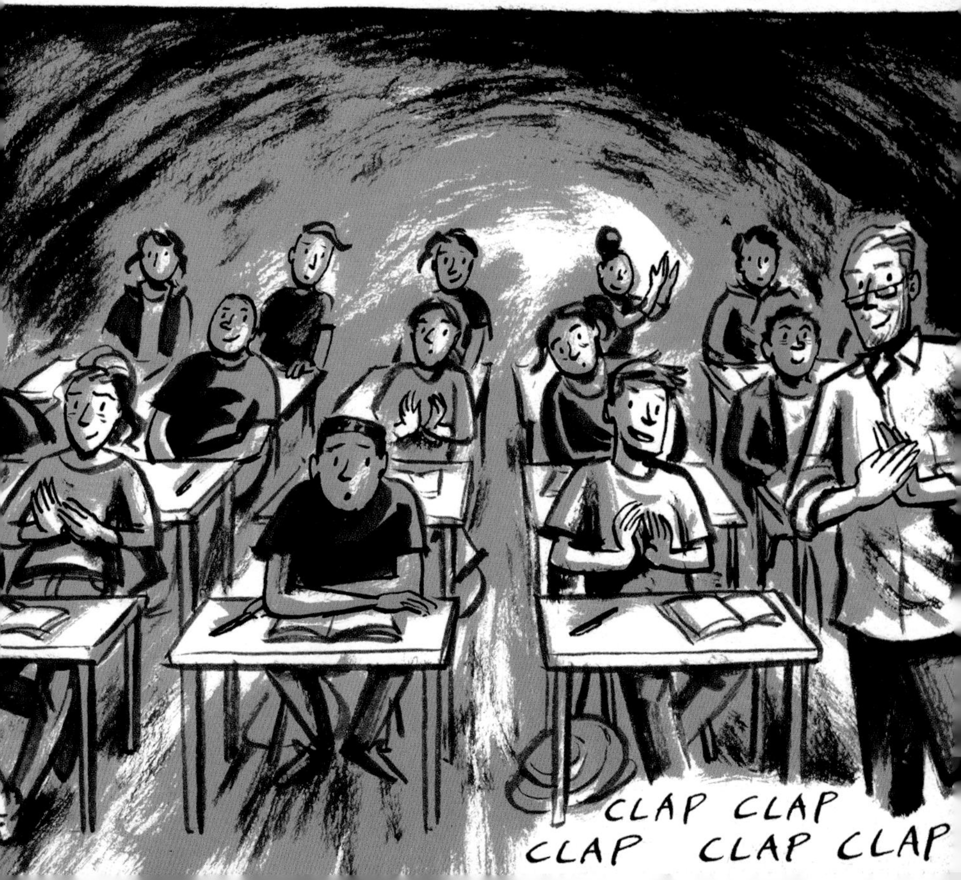
CLAP CLAP
CLAP CLAP CLAP

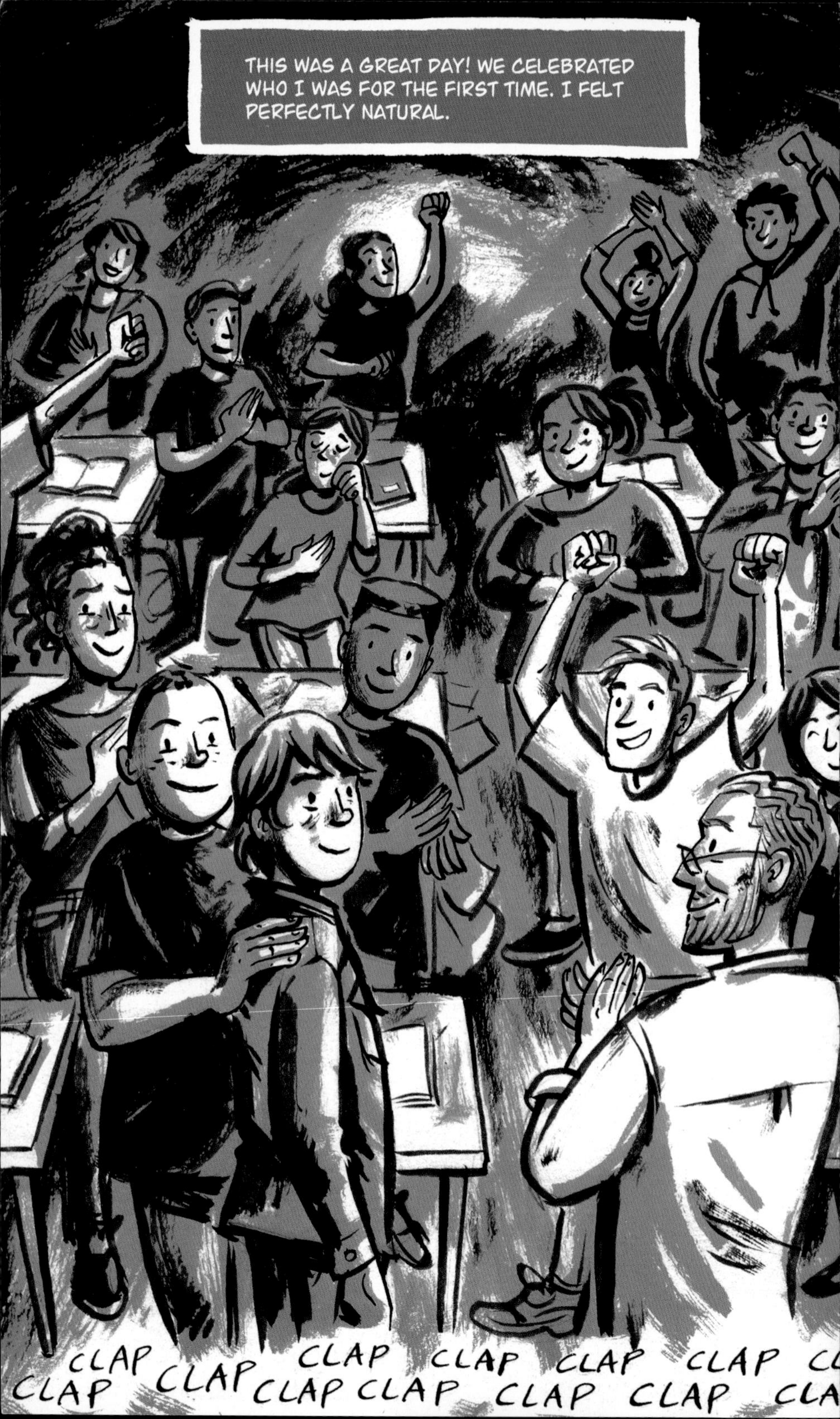
THIS WAS A GREAT DAY! WE CELEBRATED WHO I WAS FOR THE FIRST TIME. I FELT PERFECTLY NATURAL.
CLAP CLAP CLAP CLAP CLAP CLAP CLAP CLAP CLAP CLAP CLAP

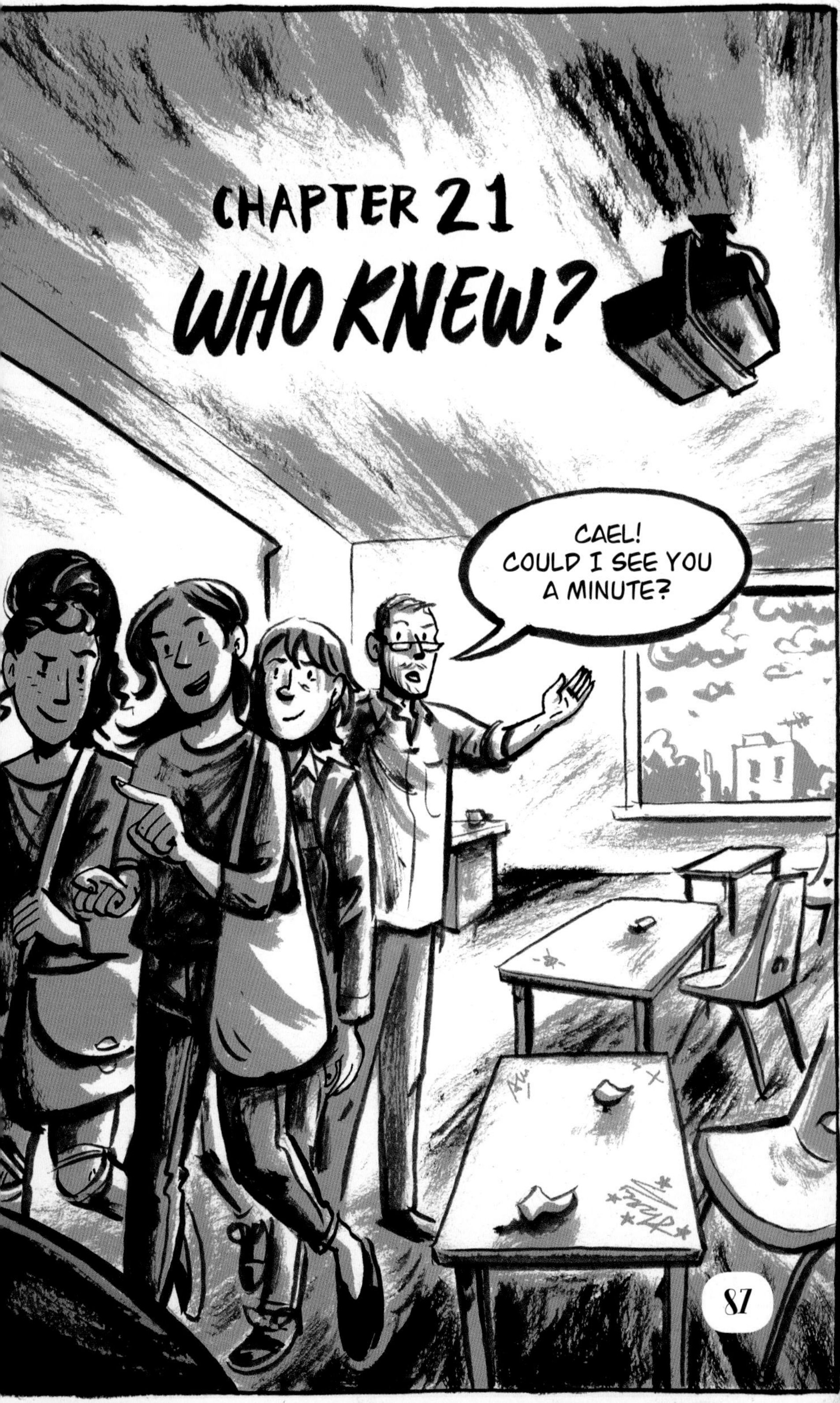
CHAPTER 21
WHO KNEW?
CAEL!
COULD I SEE YOU
A MINUTE?

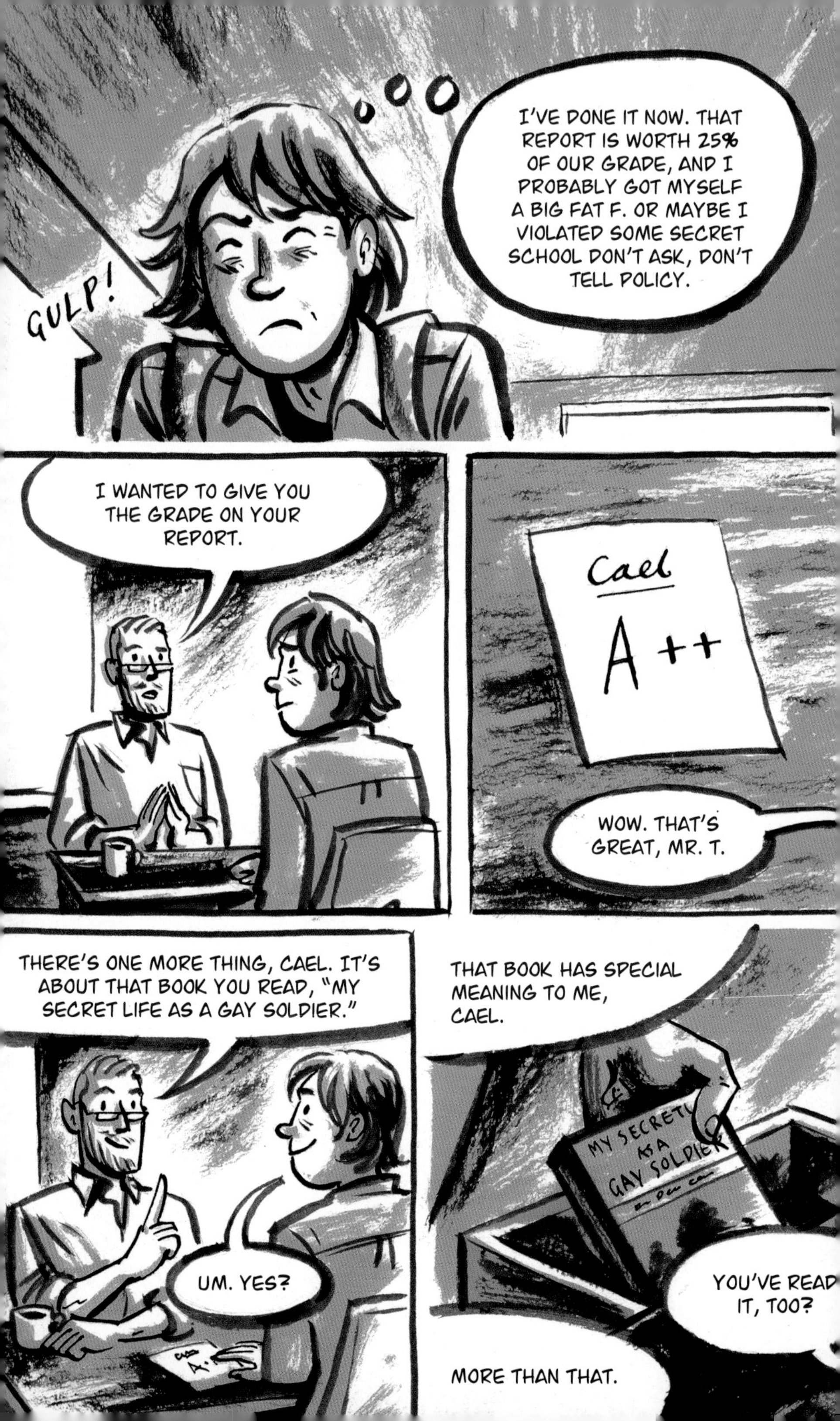
GULP!
I'VE DONE IT NOW. THAT REPORT IS WORTH 25% OF OUR GRADE, AND I PROBABLY GOT MYSELF A BIG FAT F. OR MAYBE I VIOLATED SOME SECRET SCHOOL DON'T ASK, DON'T TELL POLICY.
I WANTED TO GIVE YOU THE GRADE ON YOUR REPORT.
Cael
A++
WOW. THAT'S GREAT, MR. T.
THERE'S ONE MORE THING, CAEL. IT'S ABOUT THAT BOOK YOU READ, "MY SECRET LIFE AS A GAY SOLDIER."
UM. YES?
THAT BOOK HAS SPECIAL MEANING TO ME, CAEL.
YOU'VE READ IT, TOO?
MORE THAN THAT.

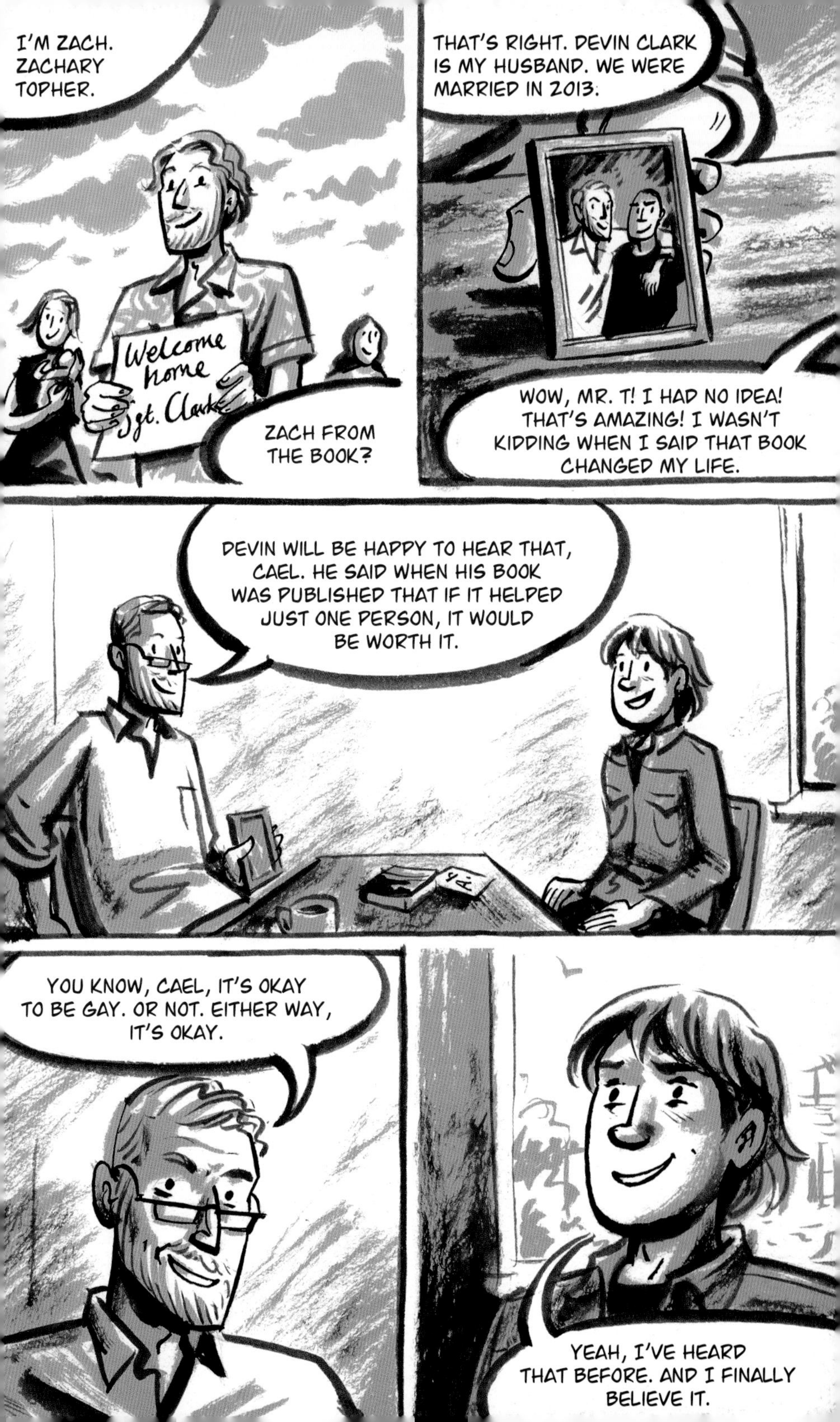

I'M ZACH. ZACHARY TOPHER.
Welcome home Sgt. Clark
ZACH FROM THE BOOK?
THAT'S RIGHT. DEVIN CLARK IS MY HUSBAND. WE WERE MARRIED IN 2013.
WOW, MR. T! I HAD NO IDEA! THAT'S AMAZING! I WASN'T KIDDING WHEN I SAID THAT BOOK CHANGED MY LIFE.
DEVIN WILL BE HAPPY TO HEAR THAT, CAEL. HE SAID WHEN HIS BOOK WAS PUBLISHED THAT IF IT HELPED JUST ONE PERSON, IT WOULD BE WORTH IT.
YOU KNOW, CAEL, IT'S OKAY TO BE GAY. OR NOT. EITHER WAY, IT'S OKAY.
YEAH, I'VE HEARD THAT BEFORE. AND I FINALLY BELIEVE IT.

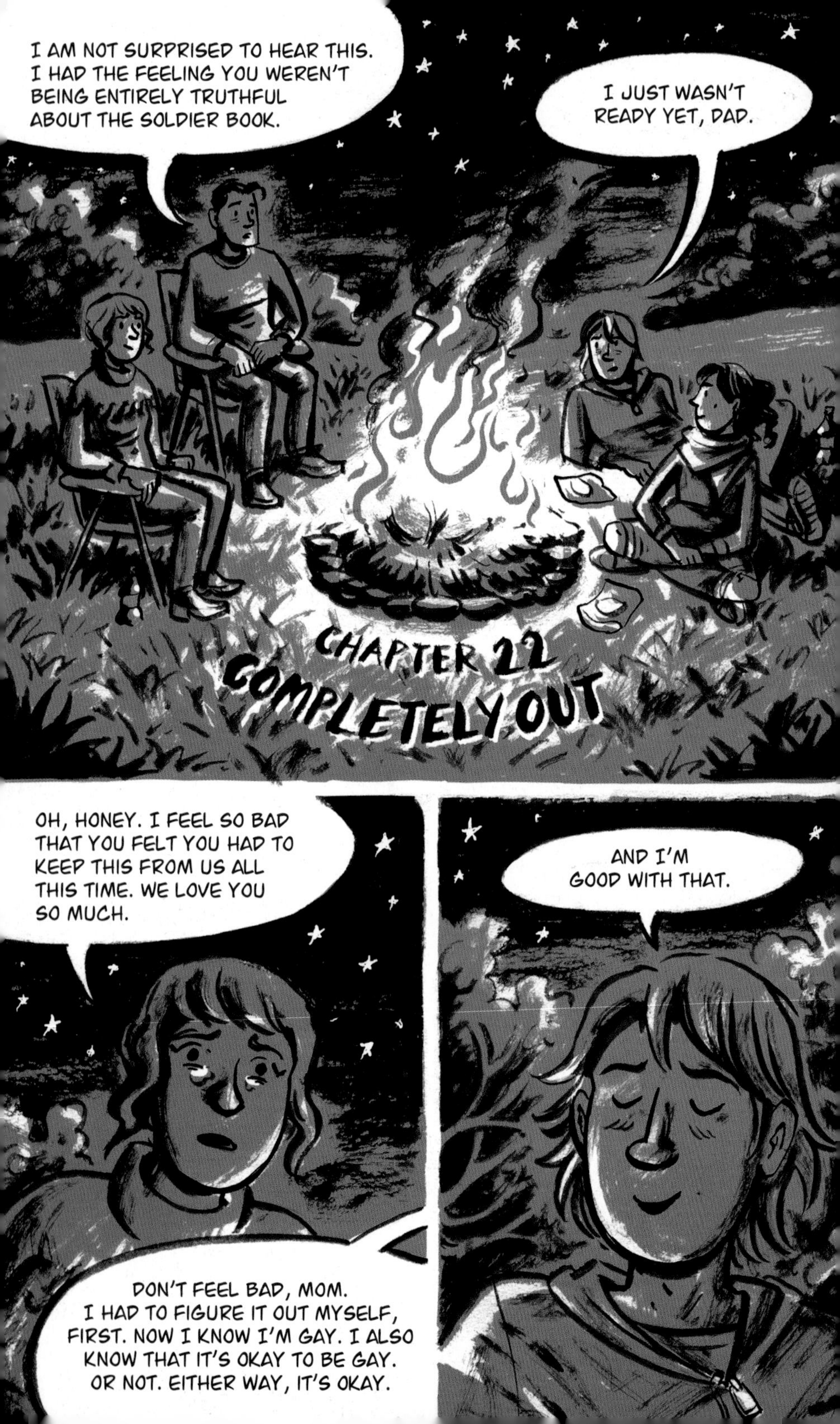
I AM NOT SURPRISED TO HEAR THIS. I HAD THE FEELING YOU WEREN'T BEING ENTIRELY TRUTHFUL ABOUT THE SOLDIER BOOK.
I JUST WASN'T READY YET, DAD.
CHAPTER 22
COMPLETELY OUT
OH, HONEY. I FEEL SO BAD THAT YOU FELT YOU HAD TO KEEP THIS FROM US ALL THIS TIME. WE LOVE YOU SO MUCH.
DON'T FEEL BAD, MOM. I HAD TO FIGURE IT OUT MYSELF, FIRST. NOW I KNOW I'M GAY. I ALSO KNOW THAT IT'S OKAY TO BE GAY. OR NOT. EITHER WAY, IT'S OKAY.
AND I'M GOOD WITH THAT.

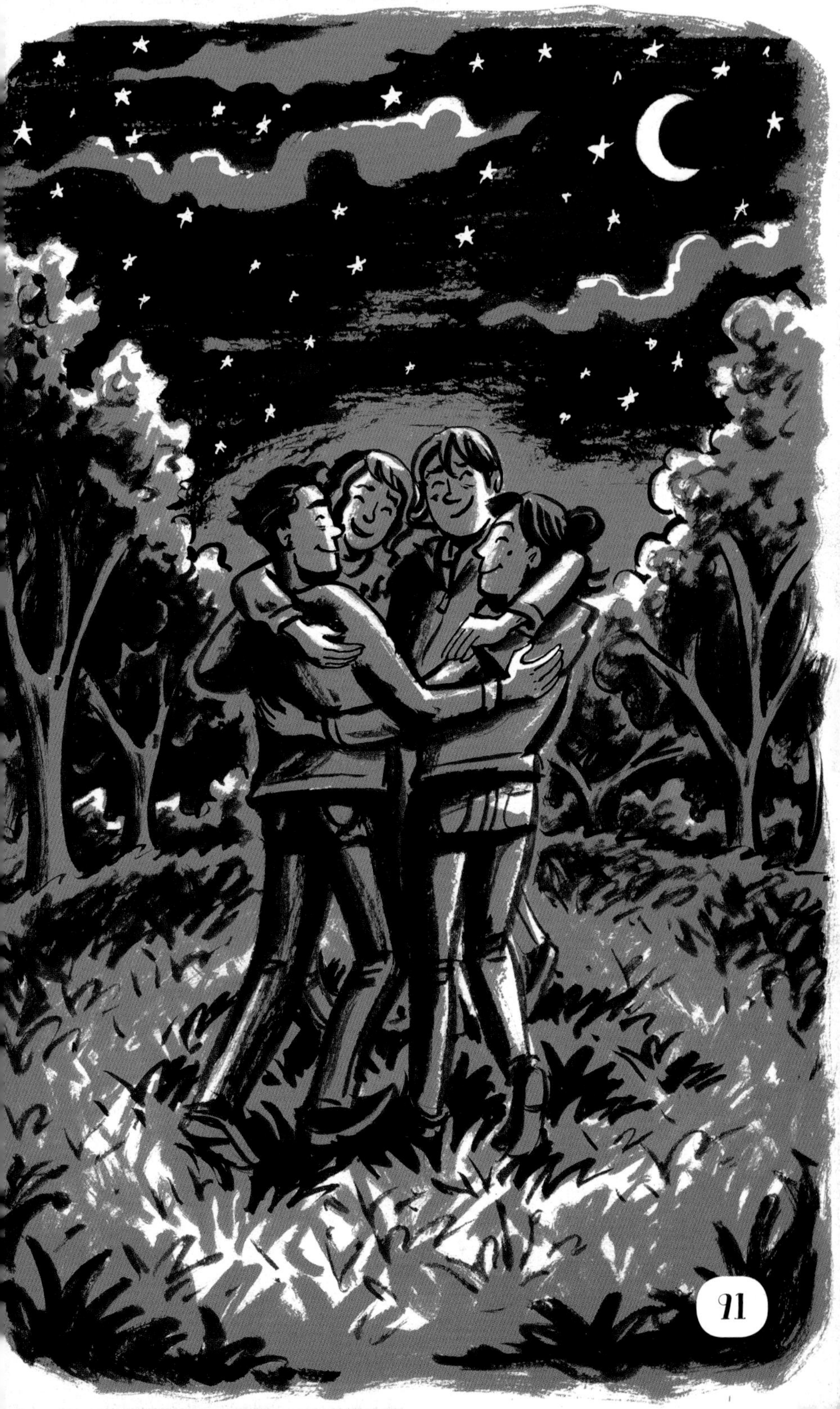

RESOURCES

ORGANIZATIONS

About.com: GLBT Teens
www.gayteens.about.com
Here you will find discussions on important LGBT issues including coming out; getting involved in your community and gay-straight alliances; and personal stories and advice about relationships, sex, and dealing with homophobia. (See also About.com: Gay Life and About.com: Lesbian Life.)

Advocates for Youth
www.advocatesforyouth.org
Find LGBT-friendly sexual health information for youths, including accessible and affordable sexual health services and resources.

Center Link
www.lgbtcenters.org
This organization develops strong, sustainable LGBT community centers, creating thriving and vibrant LGBT communities nationwide.

Gay, Lesbian, and Straight Education Network
www.glsen.org
Help GLSEN in their mission to ensure that LGBT students are able to learn and grow in a school environment free from bullying and harassment. Find information on how to start a gay-straight alliance at your school and how to join the Day of Silence Movement.

Gender Spectrum
www.genderspectrum.org
This online community for transgender, non-gender-conforming youth, and their friends and family aims to create a gender sensitive and inclusive environment for all children and teens.

GLBT National Help Center
www.glbthotline.org
Find free and confidential peer-support for GLBTQ people.
Call 1-800-246-PRIDE for their youth hotline.

GSA Network
www.gsanetwork.org
GSA Network is a next-generation LGBTQ racial and gender justice organization that empowers and trains queer, trans, and allied youth leaders to advocate, organize, and mobilize an intersectional movement for safer schools and healthier communities.

Human Rights Campaign—Coming Out
www.hrc.org/explore/topic/coming-out
Provides guidelines and support for coming out and living openly at home and in your community.

It Gets Better Project
www.itgetsbetter.org
A worldwide movement dedicated to creating and inspiring the changes needed to make the world better for LGBT youth around the world.

Just Left the Closet
www.justleftthecloset.com
A social network where LGBT youth and their friends (ages 13 and up) can chat, offer support, and share their stories.

PFLAG: Parents, Families, and Friends of Lesbians and Gays
www.PFLAG.org
Provides support, resources, and information for friends and families of people who are LGBTQ.

The Trevor Project
www.thetrevorproject.org
This organization offers accredited life-saving, life-affirming programs and services to LGBTQ youth, including their 24-hour suicide helpline (1-866-4-U-Trevor).

QUEER RELIGIOUS WEBSITES

Gaychurch
www.gaychurch.org
The largest welcoming and affirming church directory in the world, gaychurch.org also has online discussions and interpretations of Bible passages concerning homosexuality.

The Gay and Lesbian Vaishnava Association, Inc.
www.galva108.org
A nonprofit religious organization offering positive information and support to LGBTI Vaishnavas and Hindus, their friends, and any interested in all-inclusiveness.

Human Rights Campaign—Faith Positions
www.hrc.org/resources/faith-positions
Includes overviews of dozens of faith traditions and their positions on LGBTQ people and the issues that affect them.

Whosoever
www.whosoever.org
An online magazine for LGBT Christians with online discussion groups and a podcast.

World Congress of GLBT Jews
www.worldcongressglbtjews.net
This organization is a networking resource for LGBTQ Jews to connect, engage, and support all around the world.

BOOKS

Becoming Nicole: The Transformation of an American Family
by Amy Ellis Nutt

Becoming Visible: A Reader in Gay and Lesbian History for High School and College Students
edited by Kevin Jennings

Come Out and Win: Organizing Yourself, Your Community, and Your World
by Susie Hyde

Coming Out, Coming In: Nurturing the Well-Being and Inclusion of Gay Youth in Mainstream Society
by Linda Goldman

Completely Queer: The Gay and Lesbian Encyclopedia
by Steve Hogan

Family Pride: What LGBT Families Should Know About Navigating Home, School, and Safety in Their Neighborhoods
by Michael Shelton

Free Your Mind: The Book for Gay, Lesbian, and Bisexual Youth— and Their Allies
by Ellen Bass and Kate Kaufman

Gay America: Struggle for Equality
by Linas Alsenas

Gay-Straight Alliance: A Handbook for Students, Educators, and Parents
by Ian K. Macgillivray

GLBTQ: The Survival Guide for Queer and Questioning Teens
by Kelly Huegel

Growing Up Gay in America: Informative and Practical Advice for Teen Guys
by Jason R. Rich

Intersex
by Catherine Harper

Intersex (For Lack of a Better Word)
by Thea Hillman

Kicked Out
edited by Sassafras Lowrey and Jennifer Clare Burke

The Meaning of Matthew: My Son's Murder in Laramie, and a World Transformed
by Judy Shepard

Odd Girls and Twilight Lovers: A History of Lesbian Life in Twentieth-Century America
by Lillian Faderman

Out Law: What LGBT Youth Should Know About Their Legal Rights
by Lisa Keen

Queer: The Ultimate LGBT Guide for Teens
by Kathy Belge and Marke Bieschke

Stonewall
by Martin B. Duberman

Stonewall: The Riots That Sparked the Gay Revolution
by David Carter

This Day in June
by Gayle Pitman

This Is a Book for Parents of Gay Kids
by Dannielle Owens-Reid, Kristin Russo, and Linda Stone Fish

Transgender 101: A Simple Guide to a Complex Issue
by Nicholas Teich

Transgender Warriors: Making History, from Joan of Arc to Dennis Rodman
by Leslie Feinberg

What If? Answers to Questions About What It Means to be Gay and Lesbian
by Eric Marcus

ABOUT THE AUTHOR

Sandra Levins lives in Burlington, Iowa with her husband, Jim. Their diverse family includes their five sons, their sons' partners, and six adorable grandchildren. She is the author of award-winning books such as *Eli's Lie-O-Meter: A Story About Telling the Truth; Bumblebee Bike; Was It the Chocolate Pudding? A Story For Little Kids About Divorce;* and *Do You Sing Twinkle? A Story About Remarriage and New Family,* also published by Magination Press.

ABOUT THE ILLUSTRATOR

Euan Cook is an illustrator living and working in London, where he enjoys watching scruffy foxes and a variety of birds that frequent his garden. Although he has drawn for books and magazines published around the world, this is his first full-length graphic novel.

ABOUT MAGINATION PRESS

Magination Press is an imprint of the American Psychological Association, the largest scientific and professional organization representing psychologists in the United States and the largest association of psychologists worldwide.